TALL WOMAN

The Story of Virginia Dare

Harry Scott Gibbons

A Bleecker Street Associates, Inc. Book

BANTAM BOOKS

TORONTO • NEW YORK • LONDON • SYDNEY • AUCKLAND

TALL WOMAN:
THE STORY OF VIRGINIA DARE
A Bantam Book / January 1985

For information address: Bantam Books, Inc.

ISBN 0-553-24701-8

Published simultaneously in the United States and Canada

Bantam Books are published by Bantam Books, Inc. Its trademark, consisting of the words "Bantam Books" and the portrayal of a rooster, is Registered in U.S. Patent and Trademark Office and in other countries. Marca Registrada. Bantam Books, Inc., 666 Fifth Avenue, New York, New York 10103.

PRINTED IN THE UNITED STATES OF AMERICA

H 0 9 8 7 6 5 4 3 2 1

Abandoned in a primeval land . . .
Virginia Dare's mysterious disappearance
was just the beginning
of one courageous woman's survival
and triumph against all odds.

TALL WOMAN—Virginia Dare's clouded origins faded into a dim memory as she became a legendary warrior among an ancient Indian tribe . . . until a terrifying tragedy sent her searching alone for a special destiny, for a timeless love.

BADGER—Powerful leader of a vanishing tribe, his heart was captured by a little gray-eyed girl's spirit and beauty, and he alone could save her from a pitiless captivity and savage bondage.

SHE SMILES—A gentle, sensual Indian maiden, her sweetness taught Tall Woman the depth of devotion and love, her fate would show her a horrifying reality.

KING OPEKANKANO—Great ruler of a vast Indian empire, he plotted to defeat the English with treachery and blood, even if he led Tall Woman into a heartbreaking betrayal.

JOHN TREVELYAN—Handsome son of an English Lord, his eyes were the color of the summer sky, his fierce courage was the equal of an Indian brave's, and his passion was the irresistible force that moved Tall Woman to risk her future and her life.

TALL WOMAN

1

The scream rang through the forest, terrified and terrifying, and the seven-year-old girl froze, petrified with fear.

She instantly forgot everything her parents had told her to do if the heathen found them—and she knew instinctively that this had happened, just as her child's instinct told her that the blood-curdling scream, piercing, outraged, had come from her mother.

She had been carefully coached for this moment, the moment the savages might discover them before the great ships with the white sails had returned from the magic land of England to rescue them from this accursed country.

Her parents had drilled into her, ever since she could understand, ever since they had escaped the island prison of Roanoke, that if they were ever spotted, ever surprised, out in the open, she was to make her way as quickly and silently as possible to the place they called "home," the cave hollowed out in the grassy bank under the mighty trees.

There had been many such homes, dark and dank, in her short life. It was because of the savage Indians, her father told her, that they had to live underground like animals, to skulk around by day gathering fruit and berries, only able to light a cooking fire at night, when the heathen were asleep in their idolatrous and immoral villages.

They had showed her how to crawl through the undergrowth to the entrance, which was camouflaged with leaves woven into a lacework of vines to make a door, and to slip inside and close it behind her. To wait there until her parents joined her.

And if, instead, she was joined by the devil Indians, then she knew to take the sharp little dagger she carried at all times, hold its point to her breast, and throw herself face down on the floor. For capture by the heathen savages would mean a life that would be an abomination in the eyes of the Christian God.

The girl knew exactly what she had to do. But when she heard that scream, the first time she had ever heard her mother's voice raised louder than a gentle call admonishing her not to stray too far from the dugout, she forgot the instructions that had been a part of her daily life since she could remember.

The little body went cold with shock. The pitifully thin arms shook with terror. The dagger, which she had been using to slice off short branches of pussy willows that her parents would spread thickly on the floor of their burrow, slipped from her nerveless fingers.

When the awful cries of the savages followed that single, shuddering scream, hideous screeches that must surely have come out of the very bowels of Hell itself, the strength left her limbs and she collapsed to the moist ground, her body twitching uncontrollably.

Then there came an answering cry, a roar as though from a large wounded animal, the voice her father had used when he attacked the great black bear with his sword.

Her father's cry was cut off suddenly, and there was silence. A silence that struck her with the same suddenness as that first piercing shriek of terror.

The girl lay, moaning softly. Thinking she heard something, she raised her head and looked around, her eyes dull with fear and shock. But there were no heathens, no painted savages to be seen. She raised herself to her hands and knees and began to crawl aimlessly. She began to sob, a very faint wail coming from her pale lips as she repeated the words.

"Mother, Father, where are you? Please, Mother, please Fath—"

A rabbit scuttled across her path, barely a foot in front of her face, and she reared up to her knees in terror, her heart thumping so hard her whole body palpitated. A cry escaped from her mouth and suddenly, as though her voice had been the strings that drew them together like marionettes, the savages were around her.

One stood directly in front of her, where the rabbit had

shot by a moment before, and she could sense, rather than hear, that others were pressed close behind her. They must have been creeping silently through the trees, searching—perhaps the rabbit had been startled by one of them.

Someone behind her suddenly grabbed her by the hair and she was yanked cruelly to her feet. Her legs wobbled under her and the man clasped her left arm and held her steady. She was panting in terror, her mouth had fallen open, and the pressure of those steely fingers in her hair forced her to look at the man in front of her.

Her eyes dilated with fresh shock. It was true—everything her parents had told her was true—the savages were painted and naked! The horror of what she was forced to witness made her whole body shake with disgust.

Why was her Christian God forcing her to behold this evil, this naked evil?

Through fear-glazed eyes she saw the savage's thickly muscled body, copper brown in the bright morning light. The great legs were ringed with blue tattoos and red paint, the arms were painted, too, but it was the grotesquely colored torso that told her she was beholding a spawn of the Devil himself.

The stomach and chest were crisscrossed with vermilion, white and black circles and stripes. The nipples on the hard pectoral muscles were ringed in white and red. Around the neck there hung, incongruously, several chains of large pearls. The face was a monstrosity of painted whorls, and from the coxcomb obscenity that was the creature's hair, brightly colored feathers protruded.

Although the hand grasping her hair was forcing her to stare straight ahead, the little girl tried hard not to look at the savage's midsection. She could see that around his waist he was wearing a hairless animal skin, heavily fringed, which covered his private parts. But she knew from her parents' teaching that Christians covered all of their bodies from the gaze of others.

Then something moved under that short, fringed loincloth, something hanging down behind the savage, something that jerked as though prehensile when the creature changed his position. The girl gasped in horror as she recognized the dangling thing as a tail, an animal's tail, with a tuft of hair at the end. Like a bull's tail. Or a devil's!

The Indian towering above Virginia examined her with black inquisitive eyes. His name was Menatonon, which meant He-Listens-Carefully-To-What-He-Sees. That was the way the Lenapowaki, the True People, described the wolf. And Menatonon, the Wolf, had all the attributes of that fierce, cunning predator.

If Wolf's hearing had not been so acute, if he had not heard that strange low singing, a woman's voice, he would have gone swiftly past this spot. And that might have been the best thing to do, for now the war cries of the young braves had spread through the forest like ripples from a stone cast into a pool. If they were being followed, their pursuers could now home in on them like the fox to a small creature threshing in a trap.

But again, as the leader of the party it was his duty to clear away any danger to the front while Badger, his uncle, guarded their rear and laid false trails. To have avoided the danger would have been to expose the lone Badger to it when he passed through this spot later.

They had been fleeing with the stolen maidens for a whole day and part of the night and Menatonon, the Wolf, was beginning to believe they had outdistanced their pursuers when he had heard that peculiar noise. He stopped and signaled, and the braves behind him grabbed the captives and forced them to the ground.

Wolf motioned to the right, and several of the war party vanished into the underbrush. He slipped an arrow out of the quiver slung across his back and nocked it into his bow. Then came a scream, pulsating with terror. Wolf motioned to the remaining braves guarding the maidens and they, too, strung their arrows.

A moment later the war cries of the young braves split the clear morning air and Wolf clenched his teeth in anger. Then came the inhuman roar, the sound of blows, and finally silence.

Runs-Like-Deer came walking out of the trees to the little clearing where Wolf and the others were crouched. That he came openly and not disguising his approach told that the danger, whatever it was, had been dealt with. He was holding something high in his hand, a scalp with long hair, gray hair like that of an old woman, but with golden streaks in it that glinted in the light. He opened his mouth to shout of the victory but Wolf stopped him with a peremptory wave of his hand. Behind him another brave crashed clumsily through the bushes, holding the bloody stump of another scalp, a dark-haired one, and this time Wolf hissed his anger.

The whole group froze while Wolf moved his head, seeking the direction of the new sound. This one was like someone speaking in a murmur, a repetitive sound, somewhere in the undergrowth.

He located the direction it was coming from and, half rising, moved forward, the string of his bow pulled taut. Runs-Like-Deer dropped his scalp, pulled the stone ax out of his belt, and silently followed. Two other braves crept behind him. So intent were they on watching their leader that they became careless of their own progress and one of them nudged with his knee a rabbit that was crouched in the grass.

The rabbit leaped forward in reflex flight, Wolf turned swiftly and almost shot an arrow through the careless brave—then all of them froze at the cry that came from the thicket into which the rabbit had bolted. In a couple of bounds Wolf was at the spot, and they saw him standing up and looking down at the ground, his bowstring loosened. The others joined him, formed a circle, and stared at the strange sight at their feet.

An odd being was crawling through the grass and underbrush, a faint moaning coming from it. It was dressed from neck to foot in some sort of clothing, a multicolored material unlike any animal skin they had ever seen.

Wolf bent over and looked more closely and saw that the different colors on the covering were in squares and circles.

It was the first time the Indian had ever seen patches on clothing.

He saw the strange thing had long, dark hair that hung untethered down its back and to the ground. He thought it might be a woman creature.

At that moment, the thing in the grass saw him standing there, blocking its way, and stopped moving. Straight-As-Tree stepped behind it, grabbed it by the hair, and yanked it upright.

The creature's eyes went slowly from Wolf's feet to his face, and he found himself looking into the strangest eyes he had ever seen. Not the eyes of a Person, perhaps not even of a human. Gray, like the morning mist, or the smoke from a campfire.

The naked savage was leaning on an enormous bow, an arrow held negligently in his other hand. She could see that he was tall, much taller than her father, who was the largest creature she had ever seen except the black bear standing upright when her father had fought it.

He spoke, and to the girl it was the Devil's own tongue, the clicks and grunts of his speech from the pit of Hell.

"What sort of creature is this?" Wolf asked.

"She is an Oki, a devil," answered someone behind her. "Just like the two devils we killed."

"Did they wear these things, too?" Wolf asked, motioning with the arrow at the girl's clothing.

"One of them was covered like this one, the one with the long hair with the yellow colors. The other, the one that roared like the bear, had also strange things that covered its arms and legs. Yes, this one is a small devil!"

The young warrior holding the girl by the hair released her abruptly and stepped back. There was a shout of laughter.

"Are you afraid of a little devil, Straight-As-Tree?" one of the others called.

"I do not like to touch devils, even little ones," said Straight-As-Tree.

"Then you would have run like a woman from the two devils we slew," said Runs-Like-Deer, who was a very young warrior and sometimes very boastful.

"Ai, you should have seen their faces when we attacked them—savage faces with devil eyes, and the short-haired devil's face covered in hair like the black bear—" He stopped speaking when Menatonon raised his hand.

"Someone is coming," he said. Several of the warriors started to move off to intercept the newcomer, but Wolf waved them still.

"It is Badger," he said. He glared at the braves. "He has heard the noises made by inexperienced warriors and comes quickly to find out what mighty battle they have fought."

His sarcasm was not lost on them, but they marveled, too, at his hearing powers. Even now, when they strained their ears, they could not tell which of the forest sounds was animal or human.

A few minutes later Badger was walking up to them with the long, easy stride of the People. Badger was painted and feathered like the others, but was shorter, and broad and immensely powerful. He stepped up to his nephew and asked what had happened. Wolf told him, not neglecting his sarcasm.

Badger stared at the girl. She turned and looked directly at him and he, like Wolf, was taken aback at the strange color of her eyes.

"Where are the ones you slew?" he asked the young braves. Runs-Like-Deer pointed. "I will find them," said Badger. "You will look at them?" someone asked. "I will look at them," he said.

Badger was one of the most respected warriors of the tribe, and all deferred to him when battle was discussed, even Wolf, although he was the leader of this raiding expedition.

"What will you do with this one?" he asked Wolf.

"It is a devil, and must be killed," one of the braves blurted out, although he had not been spoken to. Wolf and Badger silenced him with glares, and he hung his head in shame.

"If she is a devil, perhaps we should kill her," Wolf said.

Badger sighed and glanced up through the trees in the direction of the sun, signifying he thought time was being wasted.

"Will the noises have been heard by our pursuers?" Wolf asked him.

"I was in a tall tree, watching the trail behind us, but no one followed for a long way, so I do not think they have heard the noises. But they may have heard the silence of the forest that follows the noise."

The others understood what he meant. As a sudden sound spread out through the forest, the creatures of the woods would fall silent, and the silence would also spread like the ripples on a pool. Even when the animals and birds at the source of the sound had resumed their activities with the passing of danger, the silent waves would continue outward, beyond where the sound had vanished into the air, and pursuers who heard no noise might hear the silence and would know something had occurred ahead and would continue the chase.

Badger stared at the girl. He realized they were all waiting for him, as the oldest warrior—he was twice the age of Wolf—to decide what to do with the strange creature.

"If it is a devil, we should kill it. Is it not so?"

"It is so," said Wolf.

"But if it is not a devil, then it is a girl child, and I do not kill children." He glared at the young braves. "I have many scalps taken in battle with warriors. I do not need to make war with children."

"I, too, do not make war with children," said Wolf.

"Then we will take her to our chief, Nahyapuwa, and let him decide. He is wise and will know what to do. Is it good?"

"It is good," said Wolf and, the strange being's fate having been decided, at least for the present, he put out his hand to take her arm and turn her in the direction they were going. But the girl jumped back, turned to Badger, and let loose a torrent of words.

While they had been talking about her in their incomprehensible, savage tongue, the girl's mind had been trying desperately to remember the instructions of her parents. What to do if confronted by the Indians still eluded her, but she remembered something else she had been painfully trained to repeat until word perfect.

It was the speech she was to make if ever she met a man from the great ships with the white sails, an Englishman, and her parents were not there. What they meant by "not there" was "dead," although she did not, could not, comprehend that.

One part of her brain told her that these were not English, that they were the dreaded Indians. But so numb with fear was she that the survival instinct rose uppermost and she attempted to establish, as prisoners often do, a bond with her captors.

"I am Virginia Dare and I am English," the little girl barked at the startled Badger. She spoke so rapidly it sounded like one word. "My father is Ananias Dare and my mother is Elinor, daughter of John White. We were attacked by the savages and made to flee Roanoke and seek refuge in the—the—" She searched for the word "interior" but could not find it, and lapsed into silence, still gazing earnestly at Badger.

The broad-shouldered Indian gazed back in amazement. He understood nothing of what she had said, but knew from the way she spoke and from the intense way she looked at him that she was trying to tell him something. The words meant something.

"Ai," said one of the braves. "She spoke like a devil."

"No," said Badger. "I do not think so. I think the language she spoke is that of another tribe of the People."

"Do you think she is a Person?" Wolf asked.

"Perhaps not a Person," said Badger. "But I think she speaks one of the tongues of the Lenapowaki, the People, so I believe she is a human, even if she is not a Person."

He looked again at the sky.

"It is time to go. I will meet you at the river with the white ash on its banks. If you rest on the other side of the river, I will meet you there."

Without answering him, Wolf, also impatient to be on his way again, sent a young warrior to fetch the rest of the party and the captives from where they had been left.

Badger watched as the others came up, a dozen young men resplendent in their war paint, their smooth-muscled bodies glinting in the dappled light under the tall trees.

As the captured maidens neared them, Wolf took Virginia by the arm and pushed her toward them. The little girl stopped and stared, and Badger watched her carefully.

The girl was staring in horror at the girls' bodies. They were completely naked to the waist! Their pointed breasts jutted out firmly ahead of them and some of them put their hands up on their shoulders, but not crisscrossed, as though in some savage show of modesty. As the first ones went by, she saw that the fringed deerskin around their waists hung in front only, and that their buttocks were naked also. Then she saw that the men were naked from the rear too.

The girl had never seen a naked person before, not even her own body. She opened her mouth to scream at the sight of so much evil, but the voices of her parents suddenly came to her, and she remembered their admonitions always to stay silent in the forest, where Indians might be about.

And that saved her life, for if she had screamed, even Badger would have had to agree that they would have to kill her.

Wolf gave her a push with the end of his bow and spoke to one of the captives. She immediately slowed and pulled Virginia into the middle of the group of girls and they trotted away. The Indian maidens were resigned to their fate, some of them were already starting to giggle at the young braves. The little newcomer, unaware of what was happening to her, stumbled along on her thin legs, her brain mercifully numbed with shock.

She did not see that two of the Indians were carrying the scalps of her parents.

Badger turned to look for the bodies of the two "devils." He found them fifty yards away by a grassy bank. He could see immediately that one appeared to be a man, the other a woman, but creatures as he had never seen before.

The man had short black hair, but most of his face, up to his eyes, was covered in long, dark, crinkly hair with white streaks in it. Badger was astounded at the sight. He had never seen a full-bearded man before, he knew only the wispy hairs on the chins of some of the old men.

The man's upper body, except for his face and hands, was completely covered in a material that Badger—he felt it with his fingers—had also never seen before. Like the girl's clothing, it consisted of squares and circles, some of them of different colors. His legs were bound in badly cured animal skins and his feet were encased in rabbit skins with the fur on the outside.

Badger was puzzled at this, for the Lenapowaki, the True People, went in their bare feet; only in the winter, and then only occasionally, did the women and children cover their legs and feet.

He had a thought and went to where the woman lay. He lifted the ragged, patched dress she wore and saw she, too, wore the rabbit-skin foot coverings with the fur outside. Badger thought deeply. He knew there had to be a reason for wearing untanned skins, for the hair was where the little biting creatures, lice, liked to make their home, unless they were smoked out regularly.

It came to him, and he nodded his head in approval at the cleverness of the devils. The hair or fur side of a skin left almost no tracks on the ground. If they wished to live in the midst of the People without being discovered by them, they would not want to leave any tracks.

Badger thought of the girl again and wondered if she, too, wore the rabbit shoes. Then he remembered her eyes and raised one of the woman's eyelids. It revealed another peculiar sight, an eye as blue as the spring sky. He turned to the man and did the same. This time he nodded in satisfaction. The man's eyes were the same gray as the girl's. This was her father, even though the woman could not be her mother, with different eyes.

Perhaps only the woman was a devil, although, when one looked at the grotesquely hairy face of the man, he looked more like a devil than any creature Badger had ever seen. He shook his head in confusion. He would think more about it when they returned to their tribe and he could discuss it with the chief and the old, wise men. It was time for him to guard the back trail.

As he was striding away, he remembered something and stopped. Something about the woman. He retraced his steps and stood looking down at her for a few moments before he saw what had caught his attention. It was something in the woman's hair, the side of the hair that had not been removed with the scalp. He bent down and pulled it loose. He recognized it as a hair comb but it was made of a substance he had also not seen before. He slipped it into the small satchel at his waist in which he carried his fire-making materials. Perhaps the girl, when she learned to speak like a Person, would tell him about it. If they did not have to kill her.

Before he left the little glade, he gave the two still figures a last examination. The man had never had his hair shaved like a warrior, although from what he had been told the man had charged, roaring like a warrior, to defend the woman. Badger ran his hand over his own head, fingering the shaved sides and stiff cockscomb, the long hair wrapped in knots under the ears, and the feathers on top and at the sides. That was how a man's head should look.

He thought of the girl and wondered why he had decided to spare her, at least until the werowance, the chief of the tribe, could see her and give his opinion.

He thought again of her strange eyes and decided that it was something in them that had appealed to him. She had turned to him, and none of the others, to speak and try to tell him something, something that must have been important to her, for he, who had raised several children, could recognize the sincerity, the anguish, in a child's eyes.

He turned away and sped silently to the back trail, his great bow at his side, an arrow held easily in his right hand.

Ahead of him, Virginia Dare, the first English child born in the New World of Virginia, stumbled along numbed with fear, despair, and horror at the un-Christian nudity around her, and was unaware that she had made her first friend among the heathen savages.

2

They stopped at a small stream at noon, and the captives were each given a handful of crushed maize. Virginia watched through dazed eyes as the Indian girls knelt by the stream and mixed water with the almost powdery substance, kneading it into a porridgelike consistency. This they rolled into small balls that they popped into their mouths and chewed slowly, occasionally scooping up a handful of water and slurping it down.

Wolf watched the strange girl, the "child devil," as he found himself mentally referring to her. She appeared to have no difficulty in keeping up with the pace he had set for the captives, an alternate jog trot and quick walk. Keeping to the center of the group of captives, she seemed to be oblivious to her surroundings, trotting along in a jerky fashion.

When she jumped over a small rivulet, Virginia had raised her patched and tattered dress, made from one of her mother's petticoats, pulling it above her ankles, and Wolf saw that she was wearing rabbit skins on her feet, with the fur on the outside. His reaction was the same as Badger's: Why would anyone wear foot coverings when it was not winter? Unlike Badger, he did not come to the conclusion that they were worn to cover her tracks.

Wolf sat with his back against a tree, chewing on his maize ration, watching Virginia closely. She sat, cross-legged he thought, for he could not see her legs under the dress, and clutched the crushed maize given her, but seemed to have no idea what it was. She simply stared at the maidens by the stream, and it seemed to Wolf she was not seeing them. She seemed sunk in lethargy. He had seen that look in people hurt grievously in battle or in an accident. When the end was near, they went still and quiet and stared into the distance for some time before they died.

The tribe's holy man said they were looking into Heaven, where the Kewasowak, the gods, lived.

But Virginia was deep in shock. Her existence in the forest had been precarious at the best of times. She had often been hungry, often cold in the winter, and had sickened in the rains. And the summers could be so hot that she could have screamed and torn off her tight clothes to get relief.

She had known no other life. She had been happy with her quiet-spoken parents, content to forage in the woods for fruits and nuts and herbs and help her father set traps for small animals and birds for food. But the fear of discovery by the Indians had always hung over them. The whole point of life, as instilled into her by her parents, was to live from day to day, month to month, and year to year, until the English came to rescue them and carry them back to the glorious land of England across the great seas.

But the only life she had ever known had ended abruptly that morning. Snatched from the loving, gentle care of her parents and thrust into the hands of these brutish, painted savages, the horror was so great that her mind had retreated.

She was seven years old, she had lived all her life in this land. But in her living memory she had never seen an Indian, until that day.

Wolf wondered why she did not eat. The crushed maize was what the braves carried with them on war parties, and even on long hunting trips when they had no time to stop and cook meat, and it could sustain them for many days.

The maize ration was the only concession that prisoners were given on the march; a minimum sustenance was necessary to keep them on the move. Apart from that, it was up to them to keep themselves alive. There could be no stopping for sickness or any other weakness. Any prisoner falling by the wayside was promptly dispatched by the stone-headed tomahawks or wooden swords, edged with teeth of stone or bone chips, carried by the warriors bringing up the rear.

As the leader of the raiding party, it should have been beneath Wolf's dignity even to notice the gray-eyed girl's obvious inability, or unwillingness, to feed herself. But he felt compelled, in view of the agreement with Badger, to see that the girl stayed alive until they reached their tribe. If she did not eat, she would weaken. And Badger would find her body when he came up their back trail. Wolf did not want this, for he had seen the unusual interest his uncle had taken in the creature. Badger had shown no concern for any females, young or old, since his wife and daughter had died many years earlier. For Badger to say they would bring the girl before their werowance was tantamount to an order. Badger was a man of few words.

Wolf motioned to one of the maidens, a buxom girl of sixteen who was already showing signs of the heavyset, complacent mother she would one day become. He did not know the names of any of these girls, nor had he any particular interest in them. The raid had been carried out to replace the young girls stolen when one of the increasingly frequent wars among the True People had spilled over into their town. Several men had been killed too. That had happened several moons ago, but the grief of the girls' families would not be assuaged until the werowance, Nahyapuwa, had agreed to send a party to steal maidens from another tribe. A town could not do without girls to marry and have children, tend the crops, and look after the men, any more than it could survive without braves to hunt and protect the tribe.

Wolf and Badger had been chosen, as two of the tribe's wiliest and fiercest warriors, to lead the raid. A meeting of the tribe's elders had decreed that the raid would be made as far away as possible, to lessen the chances of their being followed, which could only result in more deaths.

The future of the tribe depended on the success of the raid, but Wolf, with a snug household of a wife and several young children, had no desire for a closer acquaintance with the maidens. He would leave that for the eager young braves.

The girl he had motioned to dutifully stood up and came over to him. She was sturdily built and would never be tall. Her pointed breasts were beginning to swell with young womanhood. She was tattooed on her arms and legs and a necklace was painted around her neck. Her hair was cut in a fringe on her forehead and coiled around her neck and held there by skillfully carved bone grips.

Standing in front of the reclining Wolf, she placed her hands on her shoulders, but not crossed over, the way a married woman would do. She put her left hand on the left shoulder, the right on the right shoulder, in an odd combination of awkwardness and submissiveness. It was a sign of virginity and calculated, as Wolf well knew, to bring out the male protectiveness in even the most narcissistic brave.

Wolf instinctively ran his eyes over her body—the sturdy legs, the rounded hips visible even from the front, the rather flattened features of her face. She was certainly not the most attractive. Some of the other captives were beauties, slim, seductive, and enticing.

Then she seemed to twinkle, and Wolf blinked. He knew the look immediately. His young daughters used it to turn aside his anger when he scolded them, and to get him to play their silly games for hours while his wife looked on, smiling complacently.

The captive girl's mouth barely moved, just a twitch at the corners, but the eyes shone merrily, a completely unseductive gleam of light. Her whole body seemed to twinkle.

Beneath his stern exterior, Wolf smiled to himself. This one would have no difficulty in finding a husband. She was made to make a man happy, to have happy children. Many braves would think her the choicest of the maidens.

"What is your name?" he asked her. The girl answered in a low, melodious voice.

"I am called She Smiles," she answered, and despite himself, Wolf smiled at her reply. The name was apt.

He pointed with his nose at Virginia Dare.

"That girl must eat," he told her. "Teach her."

Obediently, She Smiles turned and padded over to the English girl. She knew instinctively that she had charmed the fierce Wolf and was pleased. He was a superb man. Then she remembered the short, powerful man she had heard called Badger. Now *that* was a magnificent brave, she thought. She had almost to shake the sensuous thoughts from her mind as she squatted down by the girl in the strange coverings.

"Why do you not eat?" she asked.

Virginia stared at her uncomprehendingly.

She Smiles was startled by the strange eyes staring blankly at her, but was not repelled. She assumed simply that this girl child was from another tribe whose coloring, as well as clothing, was different.

She took Virginia's hand and pulled her to her feet.

"Come over to the water, little one," she said. Through the deep lethargy that had fallen over the child, the soft, sympathetic voice somehow penetrated. Perhaps, although she spoke in a completely alien tongue, the musical voice of She Smiles resembled that of her mother. Virginia allowed the Indian girl to lead her to the stream's edge.

Wolf watched as the older captive fed the young one, mixing the crushed maize first into a crumbly substance, then into a loose paste. She fed it into Virginia's mouth, and the English girl chewed obediently.

It was something she had never tasted before, and if she had had her senses about her, she would have spat it out immediately, for she had been trained by her parents never to experiment with strange foods. But she swallowed the maize balls and washed them down with water that She Smiles held to her mouth with cupped palms.

They traveled until dusk, crossing many small streams. Virginia, still staring blankly ahead of her, somehow managed to keep close to She Smiles.

At one point they traveled some distance along a rock-strewn river. When they eventually climbed back on the bank, Virginia bent down and slipped off her clumsy fur shoes, wrung the water out of them, and slipped them back on again. It was an instinctive gesture, smoothly done with the ease of long practice.

She Smiles noticed that Virginia's feet were startlingly white, the odd color marred by red blotches.

They ate again before dusk, then moved into the trees away from the stream so that its splashing would not drown the sounds of an approaching enemy, human or animal. The braves slept in a circle around the captives, and sentries were changed at regular intervals throughout the night.

As they drew farther away from their own town, the captive maidens showed distinct signs of relaxing. To them, abduction by another tribe had always been a possibility. They had been trained from childhood to be subservient to men and they knew and accepted that if captured, their fate would be to be married to one of their conquerors. Their only concern was that they would be treated well, not harshly, and would be welcomed into their new tribe and family. As these maidens had so far been treated properly, they had begun to anticipate their new life. The town from where they had been taken had suffered constant wars and many, too many, of the younger braves had succumbed to battle over the past few years. The older men had started taking two and even three wives so that the widows would not be without a husband and homeless.

The captured girls, ten of them, had been in the last year of their three-year incarceration in the maidens' long house, and had seen little to look forward to on their release except an aging husband or a return to their father's house. Then had come the raid.

And the young braves who had stolen them were handsome and vigorous. The girls were secretly thrilled.

o

On their back trail, Badger came to the shallow river and checked to make sure the party had given the impression it was going upstream, then actually followed downstream as arranged. When he came to where they had left the water, he saw where Virginia had removed her rabbit-fur shoes and replaced them. He thought again of the appealing look in those large gray eyes. No devil would have a look like that, he thought.

He found himself looking forward to seeing her again when they waited for him at the river with the copse of white ash on its bank.

There was no sign of any pursuit, which could mean that the town they had attacked either did not have enough braves to send a war party after them and leave sufficient numbers to guard the town, or that most of the braves had been out hunting when the attack had taken place. Unencumbered by the captives, Badger had been able to range well behind his own war party to check the pursuit, and had found none. He climbed a tall pine tree and perched until dusk, but saw nothing.

His long experience in tracking told him there was no pursuit. The next day, he decided, he would overtake the war party and its captives before they reached the rendezvous and give them his news.

They had come to more open country and Wolf had increased the pace. The sun came out from behind the clouds that had obscured it for the past several days, and the countryside began to show the incredible variety of its fauna.

Turkeys scuttled out of their way and mourning doves, already feeding their first offspring of the year, called *oooooo-oooo-ooo* to each other among the coniferous trees. Parakeets, with bright green bodies and yellow heads, flashed in flocks in the sunlight. A shy pileated woodpecker, its bright red crest extended as it scattered the bark of a rotting tree looking for grubs, vanished into the deep woods at their approach. Flashing patches of yellow, white, and red showed where flickers were busy searching for ants on the ground.

With the open country came increasingly large stretches of marshlands and the animal life changed. They left behind the large herds of white-tailed deer and the occasional black bear and began to cross the land of the muskrat and the beaver. Once they saw a pair of white-throated minks tearing apart a muskrat lodge in a shallow pond to get at their favorite prey with which to feed their litter of hungry kits.

The war party had been heading east. Now they turned

north, out of the marshlands, and the change of direction brought the first spark of animation to the English girl.

The group had paused for a moment after reaching slightly elevated land at the foot of a thickly forested area, and again Virginia had quickly squeezed the water out of her fur shoes. Her face was drawn and etched with lines of fatigue. But while the eyes had been blank before, now they suddenly lightened with understanding.

Virginia was educated. Her parents had told her so. Educated far beyond the capabilities of the savage of the New World of Virginia.

She knew the world was a globe. She could read, because she had been taught from the Bible that her parents carried with them always. Admittedly she could not write, for the paper and ink had been exhausted years earlier. But she knew about the sun and the moon. She knew the sun rose in the east and set in the west and where was north and south.

She also knew that east was where the great ships with the white sails would come from. She had been to the sea once with her parents. To a sea her father called a "sound," although she had heard no sound but the harsh cries of the gulls. Beyond that sea, her father had told her, were the Outer Banks of Virginia, which were islands on the way to England.

On the Outer Banks there was a place called Croatoan, her father had said. Croatoan was where an Indian called Manteo lived. Manteo was not a savage like the other Indians but a Christian who had been to England. Manteo had held Virginia in his arms when she was a baby and had vowed—he could speak English, too—to protect her if anything happened to her parents.

But in the exodus from Roanoke, Manteo and Virginia Dare and her parents had become separated. A small group of the English colonists had fled by Indian dugout across Roanoke Sound to the Indian village of Dasemunkepeuc. The villagers there, who were related to the treacherous Indians of Roanoke, had attacked them, killing several of them. The three Dares, Ananias, his wife Elinor, and the two-year-old Virginia, had escaped across the marshes and made their way into the heavily forested interior.

Two years later, when Virginia was four, they had their first—and last—trip to the coast. They had eaten mussels and other shellfish, raw, and Virginia had chased shrimp and tiny crabs among the rocks. She had smelled the powerful odor of the sea.

Her mother had found a large shell and told Virginia to listen at the opening. The sound she heard, said her mother, was the sound of the sea, and she could hear it anywhere. It was true, for she carried the shell for a whole year before it was left behind on one of their quick departures from "dangerous" territory—that meant where there were signs of Indians.

They had stared out to sea for days, but they had never seen the outer banks where Manteo lived. Nor had any great ship with white sails appeared.

Virginia had wanted to stay by the seashore. It was so wonderful to be able to sleep out in the open on the sandy beach, instead of in the damp earth. But her father, obsessed with capture by the savages, had insisted that they would be quickly seen if they ever dared light a fire to cook or warm themselves, and had taken them on the long trek back into the interior and the safety of the never ending forests.

He had promised they would return the next year, and every year after that until they found the great ships, but that autumn he had the fight with the great black bear and after that he was never the same. He read the Bible more frequently, mumbled to himself, and constantly looked over his shoulder. He was as kind as ever to his daughter but, young as she was, she knew some great change had come over him.

He talked more of Heaven and God than of England, and gradually he even ceased to talk of the great ships with the white sails. And when Virginia would remind him of his promise to take them to the sea again, he would only mumble, "Soon, my dear, soon." But he never took them again.

Now, as they changed direction, the memory of the sea came back to her. She looked around her in a panic.

"The sea!" she cried. "We must go to the sea!"

Wolf turned, his hand automatically going to the sharpened stone head of his tomahawk held at his belt. The group went still. Although the danger of pursuit seemed to have receded, they were still a war party, and silence had to be maintained.

She Smiles moved quickly. She stepped over to Virginia and clamped a hand over the little girl's mouth. Virginia struggled, but only briefly, then the fierce light went out of her eyes and her thin shoulders sagged. She Smiles took her hand away and watched for a moment, but the English girl made no attempt to call out again.

She Smiles looked at Wolf and he returned the look gravely. Then he took his hand away from his ax, turned, and strode away. The group started after him, but the smallest captive remained where she was, staring to the east. She Smiles took her hand. She felt the thin fingers grasp her own, and they trotted off together. Wolf, turning around to make sure all were on the move, saw what had happened and was pleased. The "child devil" would live until they reached their tribe.

He did not notice that the nostrils of the self-appointed chaperon were twitching in distaste.

The faster pace in the open sunshine had brought out a fine sweat over the bodies of the Indians, drying almost immediately in the cool spring breeze. But Virginia's body was tightly wrapped in her patched clothing and the perspiration could not evaporate.

She Smiles had no way of knowing that the English did not wash apart from their hands, face, and hair.

"Washing the body is forbidden," Virginia's father had instructed her. "A Christian has to care for his soul, not for his body."

Virginia Dare had never bathed in her life, and She Smiles, the savage, uneducated Indian girl who bathed and swam every day of her life, wondered what the stench was that arose in a cloud from the strange creature who was clutching her hand so tightly.

3

Badger overtook them that afternoon, an hour before they reached the river with the white ash trees. He went straight ahead to speak to Wolf, telling him there had been no pursuit. They could have found out the reason for this simply by asking the captives, but men could not lower themselves to ask women about matters that concerned warfare.

When they moved on again, Badger fell back as casually as possible until he was near Virginia.

When he had overtaken the war party, coming up on them so silently that he was in their midst before they knew it and could have wreaked havoc among them had he been an enemy, he had seen the Indian girl holding the hand of the strange creature the way a mother would a small daughter.

He drew near to speak.

"What do they call you?" he asked.

"They call me She Smiles," the Indian maiden said and, as though to justify her name, allowed a smile to brighten her face. Badger was surprised at the transformation. With just a little smile, this girl—plain was the only word he could think of to describe her—became almost beautiful.

Then his nostrils twitched, as hers had done earlier.

She Smiles anticipated him.

"It is this small one," she said, so quietly that Badger had to lean over toward her to hear. A voice from behind made him turn around.

"She is a devil. That is the devil smell."

Evidently She Smiles and Badger weren't the only ones with sensitive noses.

Badger slipped a few paces behind—and to one side to avoid the pungent odor—and examined the girl She Smiles.

Something about her had stirred memories of the wife he had never been able to forget. Like She Smiles, she, too, had been stolen by a war party, and she, too, had not been outstanding for her beauty. But she had given Badger, then a brash young brave, a single, sidelong look with her twinkling eyes, and he had demanded her instantly.

She had given him two strapping sons, fighting sons to be proud of, who had died gloriously in war.

And a daughter, the most beautiful creature Badger had ever seen. A delicate thing with large eyes who had followed him around from the moment she could walk. Tall Girl, they had called her, because she promised to grow up taller than both her parents. Then mother and daughter had both died in a raid, killed instantly by the axes of a band of marauding warriors seeking scalps and glory.

Badger went berserk that night, slaying six of the invaders with his stone-edged sword before they fled into the forest. And the tribe's storytellers always recalled that summer as the one when Badger was filled with the wrath of the gods.

Badger had not lamented his sons. It was decreed that a boy should grow up to be a warrior, to fight and to die, and if to die young, then preferably in battle, when his spirit would join the gods immediately.

But Badger, although he never allowed it to show, had been grievously hurt by the loss of his beloved wife and daughter. He had promised his child that when she grew up, he would rename her Tall Woman, and that she would marry a mighty warrior, a king perhaps, and she would become Queen Tall Woman and all of the True People would hear of her, from the marshes to the distant mountains.

But she had not lived to become Tall Woman, and Badger, inside, still lamented.

He looked at the odd pair ahead of him. He watched the rounded buttocks of the Indian girl and thought that they reminded him of his wife when she had been newly captured.

The excitement and success of the raiding party had made him feel manly and vigorous again and for a moment he entertained thoughts about She Smiles. But only for a moment, for he told himself that she was a girl, a mere child still, and much more suitable for one of the hotbloods of the tribe.

He slipped quietly to the rear and took up his position there.

When they reached the river by the white ash, Wolf paused for a moment to admire the tall, heavy-stemmed trees, with their graceful, drooping foliage and gray deeply ridged bark.

Then he raised his bow above his head and stepped into the water. Within a few steps he was up to his waist and began swimming easily and expertly, one hand keeping the bow out of the water, the other arm and his legs propelling him forward powerfully.

The captured girls were herded to the water's edge, and without a pause in their stride, they took to the water. Virginia, still holding She Smiles's hand, stepped into the river obediently and the Indian girl, assuming she could swim, let go of the small hand.

The cold water had reached Virginia's waist before she realized what was happening. Her eyes once more lost their glaze and she looked around in panic. She stumbled on a rock and went under. Thinking Virginia had started to swim, She Smiles struck out toward the opposite shore. Virginia surfaced with a scream, gasping and thrashing her arms. She went under again, and this time the current caught her and dragged her toward the center of the river, her ballooning skirts showing the others where she was.

She Smiles saw what was happening and turned smoothly to go after Virginia. But Badger was on the river's bank.

"No!" he shouted at the Indian girl. She Smiles recognized the voice for one that was obeyed, and in one supple movement brought her legs under her to change her direction and struck out once more for the far bank.

Badger handed his bow to one of the young braves, ran swiftly along the bank until he was level with the clump of multicolored clothes in the river, and dived in, a long, low dive that brought him up next to the girl. With one heavily muscled arm he lifted her completely out of the water, shook her to see if she was still alive, turned over on his back, and with casual ease and using only his legs, swam to the other shore.

He stepped up to the ash trees, the barely conscious girl suspended from his hand like a small animal brought down by the hunt, and dropped her in the tall grass. He looked around for She Smiles, for he had done his man's part and now it was woman's work, and she was there immediately, kneeling beside the prostrate girl. She pressed on the child's stomach, released and pressed again, as she had been taught by the women of her tribe, and the water bubbled out of Virginia's lungs. Then the English girl began to cough and splutter, and most of the party, who had crowded around, turned away. The small captive would live, and was of no more interest.

The braves carrying the crushed maize had held it clear of the river, along with their bows, while they swam across, and now they doled out the evening ration.

She Smiles took food for both herself and Virginia, mixed it with water, and started to feed the little girl. When she bent forward to put the first portion in the English girl's mouth, her attention was drawn to the tattered collar gathered tightly around her neck. It seemed to be moving to and fro. She peered closely, then sprang back with an exclamation of disgust.

Badger, who had eaten quickly and was standing nearby, pretending not to watch She Smiles and her charge, stepped up and looked down at the bedraggled figure sitting disconsolately on the grass.

Her hair was still dripping water and her clothes were plastered to her body. She had made no attempt—for the first time since her capture—to pull her dress over her ankles and feet, and her legs, thin and white, stuck out in front of her.

She Smiles pointed at her own neck, then at Virginia, and Badger bent down. He saw the collar weaving about and instantly recognized the cause. Vermin, hundreds of them, were crawling from the girl's clothes through the neck opening, escaping from the water. The collar wasn't moving, it was the gray mass that made it seem so. Badger had seen lice, but they were usually found on animal skins with the hair still on.

He gave an involuntary shrug of revulsion. He had never seen so many on a human.

"Perhaps they live like that on a devil," said Wolf, who had joined Badger, his eyes squinting at the loathsome sight.

Several others gathered around and peered over the heads of the two men crouched down beside the English girl, emitting various exclamations of repulsion.

Badger stood up suddenly and scattered them with a wave of his hand. He took Virginia's arm and jerked her to her feet.

"I have no fear of devils," he said to Wolf. "If this is a devil, I am going to see what it looks like."

He dragged Virginia away from the others, several yards downstream. He spun her around, looking to see where her strange clothing was joined together.

Down the back, from the neck to the waist, was a row of buttons, something he had never seen before, but which he recognized as some sort of fastening. He parted the long, wet hair, took the collar at the nape of the neck in both hands, and gave a powerful sideways and downward pull. The result surprised him. The material was old and almost rotting. The buttons flew in every direction and the cloth ripped past the girl's waist almost to the hem at her ankles. Virginia was knocked forward by the force of Badger's action and stumbled to her knees.

Her arms were still encased in the dress from her shoulders to her elbows and, dazed and completely bewildered, she clutched the clothing to her, her arms crossed over her thin chest.

But Badger, to whom a naked child was as natural as the sun in the sky, was determined to see what this strange creature was hiding under her equally strange garments.

He raised her to her feet by the hair and turned her around. Still holding her hair with his left hand, he seized the front of her dress with the other and tugged. The dress tore out of her hands and she stood there, naked.

Instinctively, Virginia covered her chest with her hands, and the Indians, who had quickly circled around to see what Badger was up to, gave a low hum of approval. For one so young, this girl was demonstrating in an oddly grown-up fashion that she was a maiden. Even the fierce Wolf nodded in approval. Perhaps Badger was right. A devil would not be so versed in the ways of the People.

Badger gazed at the girl with openmouthed amazement. She was skinny, almost emaciated, her ribs showed clearly. Her pelvic bones jutted out sharply and her legs and arms looked like reeds. Badger had not seen anyone as thin as that since a thief had been tied to a tree by his tribe many years ago and left to starve. When Badger had seen him several weeks later, the man had looked like this girl. But he had been dead.

This girl was healthy. They had been moving for days and she had kept pace with them, although it seemed to him now that she looked exhausted.

He was particularly intrigued by the color of her skin. It was a strange white, like that of a sick person. There were blotches of red all over her, but he saw the lice scurrying over her body in an attempt to escape from the sunlight and knew they were what had caused the angry blotches.

Badger squatted down and looked more closely at the girl's skin. He saw that her face and arms to the elbows were brown, the same yellowish brown of the People. It was only white where it had been covered by the strange material. *His* body was the same color all over, even where it was covered by his fringed apron.

Then he noticed that the skin was not really white, not like the white paste they made from tree roots for their war paint. It was a dull grayish color, with a rough texture. The girl stood numbly, her eyes on a level with his, but she did not seem to see him. Her gaze was turned inward.

He stretched out his hand and casually swept aside several lice. The skin felt dry to his touch, not glossy like a Person's. He touched it again, then scratched it slightly with a hardened nail. A piece came off and he raised it to his nostrils.

"Ai!" said Badger. "This creature has a skin that smells like death."

He looked around until he saw She Smiles and motioned to her.

"Take this creature into the river and wash her," he instructed the girl. "Wash her well and take off that foul skin." He looked across at Wolf. "If the skin does not come off, then we must leave her here. We must not take anything so evil back to our tribe."

Wolf did not reply, but turned and watched with interest as She Smiles led the child to the river's edge.

"Take those off," Badger commanded, pointing at Virginia's rabbit-skin shoes. She Smiles obeyed silently. "Throw them to me." The shoes were tossed on top of the English girl's torn clothing.

Badger picked them up. A glance showed him that the skins were badly cured. When he squeezed, they crackled. How could anyone walk in these things, he wondered. Only someone mourning the death of a close relative would inflict such pain on himself. He saw the lice crawling inside the shoes, and dropped them again.

She Smiles had taken Virginia into the water up to the child's knees. She began to splash water on the girl and rub with her hands, but evidently that was not cleaning her for she scooped up a handful of sand and began to rub it hard across Virginia's shoulders. The girl immediately began to struggle and She Smiles called out to the other maidens.

"Help me take off this devil skin! Quickly!" she ordered as the others hesitated. "It will soon be dark and we must purify her while we can still see."

Several girls rushed into the river and for the next thirty minutes they gave Virginia Dare her first scrubbing with water. The girl, awakened rudely from her lethargy, kicked and fought, but they were too many and too strong for her. Badger noticed that not once did she call out in pain or fear, and he was oddly pleased.

Then it was over, and Virginia once more stood before him. Her skin this time was red all over, a glowing red from the scouring with river sand.

He squatted down again to examine her. The gray outer skin had gone, to be replaced by one almost transparent. He could see the blue veins crisscrossing her body. What kind of a creature was this, he marveled to himself. First the skin of a lizard, now one that he could see through. A body so thin that a fully grown brave could not have survived with it. He was aware that her eyes were no longer blank, but were animated, and staring at him fiercely.

He stretched out a hand to touch her and Virginia jumped back quickly, clutching her hands to her bosom and shouting, in a high-pitched voice that was close to hysteria, "Don't touch me, you heathen savage!"

Badger did not understand the words, but their meaning was clear. He studiously ignored her, for it was not fitting that such a mighty warrior as he, to whom the wise elders listened with respect, should show any reaction to what a captive said, and a small and female one at that.

Instead, he picked up the discarded clothing and began to examine it. What the girl did then took him completely by surprise.

She sprang forward and began pummeling him with her sharp little fists. So amazed was he that he fell back on his haunches. There was a low murmur of surprise behind him.

Virginia grasped her dress and literally leaped backward with it, her eyes blazing. Without taking her gaze off the startled Badger, she scrabbled feverishly through her dress. She was searching for her one pocket. In the back of her mind was the realization that she had lost her knife, but she still had a weapon. She could not take her life with it, but with it she could fight back.

Still watching Badger intently, she found the pocket, pulled out the sling, and backed away slowly. She stepped backward into the river until she was up to her knees, bent down, and felt among the stones on the bottom. She found what she wanted, a smooth, round stone about the size of a wild turkey egg.

Badger and the others, including She Smiles who was nearest to her, watched her almost mesmerized. For two days the little girl had trotted silently among them, seemingly unable even to feed herself, covered in the strangest clothing any of them had ever seen.

Then, within the past hour, she had been found unable to swim, discovered literally crawling with vermin, had the clothes ripped off her to expose a skeletal body with a reptilian skin that had been removed by washing, had knocked a mighty warrior on his backside, and was now apparently about to do something else very odd.

Badger knew something momentous was about to happen. He made no attempt to rise, but simply sat where he had been pushed. A younger brave might have felt humiliated, but Badger was too well-known a warrior and too completely self-assured to feel loss of face. His eyes narrowed as he watched and wondered what the girl was doing.

Virginia fitted the stone into the sling and remembered what the Bible had said. This was the sling with which little David had slain the mighty Goliath. Her father had made it for her from a tanned hide they had carried from Roanoke. He had made many, and shown her how to use them, but this was the final one, the sling that she had learned to use with incredible accuracy. With it, and the proper stone, she could bring down a small bird at a full two rods, thirty feet away.

It was made of two leather thongs, each two feet long. The pocket for the projectile was a diamond-shaped piece of smooth leather with a small hole cut in it to hold the stone firmly. One thong ended in a loop that was threaded over the middle finger of her right hand and was held firmly when she crooked it. The other thong she grasped between the thumb and index finger of the same hand.

Badger watched, wondering what the girl would do. He surmised it was a weapon she was holding because of the stone, but he had no idea what it was. But Virginia simply stood there, glaring at the Indians, the sling held just out of the water.

It was the brash Runs-Like-Deer who broke the tableau. He pulled his tomahawk out of his belt and brandished it above his head.

"Ai!" he yelled. "Come, devil, do you want to do battle with a warrior?"

Some of the others grinned, for they knew that Runs-Like-Deer was only shouting that to make them laugh. But what happened next happened with such incredible speed that not even Badger, watching intently, saw just how it was done.

When she saw the ax raised in what she assumed was a threat against her, Virginia brought up the sling. It went around her head once, twice, thrice, in a blur of motion. On the fourth whirl, just as the stone in its pocket came level with her shoulder, she let go the thong imprisoned between her thumb and first finger, and the stone whistled through the air.

Badger saw the whirling sling, but not the released projectile. He described it later as moving faster than a striking snake. While his eyes were still on the sling, he heard a sharp crack and a cry from Runs-Like-Deer, and the tomahawk dropped to the earth beside the young warrior. Badger leaped to his feet and whirled around. Runs-Like-Deer was holding his right arm just below the elbow, his face a mixture of pain and outrage. Badger turned back to Virginia and saw she was fitting a second stone into her sling. Several of the young braves were pulling out their axes and one of them was running to fetch his bow. Wolf was standing with his mouth open foolishly. He obviously had no idea what had happened. Badger immediately took charge of the situation.

"Stop!" he roared and all movement ceased instantly. He turned to Virginia and raised both hands toward her, palms outward.

He watched the peculiar weapon with trepidation and a slight awe. He knew she could hit him with the stone before he could get his ax out of his belt. He kept his palms outward as he talked soothingly.

"Come, little warrior, do not be angry." He heard Wolf chuckle behind him and knew the spell was broken. "We know that whoever you are and wherever you come from, you must be esteemed a true brave. You do not know how to eat our food, but you survived the long marches. You do not know how to swim, but you entered the river without fear. You have been scrubbed with sand until your skin is transparent, and you did not call out. Now you have shown us that in battle you are as fierce as any of our braves. Let there be peace between us."

Many of the party were openly laughing now. They were highly amused at the spectacle of the renowned warrior Badger surrendering to the little bedraggled naked girl facing him. It appealed to their sense of humor. Only Runs-Like-Deer was still ruffled.

"She is a devil," he growled. "She used magic to bite my arm."

Without taking his eyes off Virginia, who stood unmoving, the sling weaving slowly back and forth, Badger told him, "That was no magic. That was a weapon. Not a weapon to kill, a weapon to sting and bite and distract a warrior. A child's weapon, but a weapon for a warrior child. Do not feel humiliated because a child made you drop your tomahawk, my son. Not even Badger could have moved faster than that stone."

Knowing that diplomatic remark would mollify the injured brave, Badger dropped his arms and unexpectedly turned his back on the English girl.

"There is no pursuit," he said to Wolf. "I say that we shall light a fire tonight to dry our coverings." He slapped the short, wet apron hanging in front.

"I, too, say we shall light a fire tonight," said Wolf, as he was the leader of the war party, setting the seal of approval on the decision.

Looking at the sea of backs as they all turned away from her, Virginia was puzzled. She had no idea what the short, thickset Indian had been saying to her, but she understood it to mean they would not kill her, as she had thought when the taller man had waved his ax.

She continued to stand in the river shallows, the chill of the swift water spreading up her legs. She became aware that one of the Indians had not returned to the ash grove. A girl was standing close to her. Virginia recognized her as the one who had been feeding her, the kind one.

"Come," said She Smiles, holding out her hand. Almost without thinking, Virginia put her left hand into the Indian girl's square, warm one and allowed herself to be led to where a fire was being kindled. None of the other Indians paid her any heed.

Later, when the pickets had been posted, Badger watched the little captive and her self-appointed protector. She Smiles lay a few feet from the fire, her body curled like a sleeping puma. Inside the crook of her arm Virginia slept, one spindly arm tucked tightly around the Indian's waist.

Badger left the fire and returned a moment later with the English girl's torn dress. He fed it into the fire and watched the lice scamper madly from the flames. None of them succeeded in escaping.

After he had made his round of the sentries, he thought about the morrow, when they would at last reach their own town. There would be feasting and dancing, and the captives would be made welcome by the love-starved women who had lost their own daughters.

He would show the little captive to the chief and the elders, and describe how she had faced up to the entire war party and offered battle. He would tell them that she may have been a devil but was no longer. The devil's skin had been scrubbed from her and the devil's clothes burned. He would say she was now one of the Lenapowaki, the True People, and if she were instructed and trained properly, she could become a Person.

He would give her a name. He would call her—no, she would have to become a Person first. He would call her Little Warrior.

Badger lay back on the cool grass and in a moment was asleep.

4

On the next day's march, Virginia Dare almost died.

Wolf and Badger were awake before dawn and doused the fire, which had been kept alight during the night by the sentries. Many of the party had slept naked, their leather aprons hung over bushes to dry. When they were shaken awake, these were quickly fetched and kneaded to soften them—many had become stiff from the soaking in the river the day before.

She Smiles had eased herself out of Virginia's grip, gone into the trees with the other maidens to attend to the needs of nature, then they had all plunged into the river to cleanse and freshen themselves.

Virginia, left on the dewy grass, woke up cold and stiff. When she tried to rise, she found her whole body a mass of aches. Then she remembered the terrible thing the Indian girls had done to her and was filled with outrage.

In England, she knew, only the crude people from the countryside, the lowest peasants, bathed openly. Gentlefolk and their children would never lower themselves to such filthy depths. Virginia's parents had given her a long list of things that gentlefolk just did not do.

She ran her hands over her painful skin and realized for the first time that she was completely naked. She sprang to her feet, crying out in pain as her abused skin protested.

At that moment, She Smiles and the other captives returned from the river, all of them completely nude.

Virginia stared. Now she understood what her parents had warned her would happen to any Christian taken by the savages. They intended to make her like themselves, naked, objects of sin. After the near drowning the day before, and the pummeling and scrubbing in the river, she had been too exhausted to realize what was happening to her, and had fallen into a heavy sleep snuggled up against the warm, soft body of the Indian girl who had appeared to befriend her.

But as She Smiles walked toward her, Virginia remembered there had been collusion between that painted heathen who had stripped her and this girl who had nearly ripped her skin off in the river. She pointed a finger trembling with righteous anger.

"You betrayed me!" she shouted. Every head turned in her direction and She Smiles, the cold river water dripping from her smooth skin, stopped in her tracks.

"You pretended to be my friend!" Virginia went on, her

voice still high-pitched and outraged. "And you let them take my clothes off and bathed me in front of everyone. You cannot do this! I am a gentlewoman!"

There was a sob in her voice as she uttered the last words and She Smiles heard it. She had no idea what the girl was shouting at her, but she had detected the outrage. She had done something that had offended this strange little creature, though she could not imagine what it could be.

She did the thing that came naturally to her. She dropped to her knees in front of the English girl, opened her arms, and Virginia sprang into them, threw her arms around the Indian girl's neck, and began to weep piteously.

Badger assumed from the little captive's voice that she was complaining bitterly about something. This pleased him, for the child's silence for days had been unhealthy. Children often complained to grown-ups. The fact that Virginia now seemed to be more like a normal child he attributed to the shedding of the devil's skin and clothes.

He patted Virginia on the head quite tenderly, and she stopped crying instantly and stiffened. He noticed the sling, which had slipped off her finger during the night, lying on the ground, picked it up and examined it. But he could not understand the principle. He pried one of Virginia's hands from She Smiles's neck and pressed the sling into it.

Immediately, Virginia turned around and stared up at him. He saw a wariness, an accusation, in her eyes, and was puzzled. The other captives were accepting their fate with equanimity, even relish. Didn't this child realize she would soon find a loving mother?

Badger remembered something else. He pulled apart the taut strings of the small soft leather bag fastened at his waist. The fire-making materials kept in it were useless at the moment, being soaked in the water. He had not had time to remove it, to hold it high as he normally would while crossing, when he leaped in to save the girl. But he had remembered something else in the bag.

He pulled out the tortoiseshell comb he had taken from the dead devil woman and handed it gently to Virginia. She looked at it and her eyes widened as she recognized it instantly as her mother's.

It was the first time she had thought of her mother, of her parents, in days, and the realization came crashing in on her that they had been left behind, that they were somewhere back in the trackless forests.

When she looked up to ask Badger where they were, the husky Indian had turned away. She Smiles, too, stood up and fastened her skirt around her waist.

"Let us eat, little one," she said quietly, taking Virginia by an arm. Virginia looked up at her. The animosity she had felt at this girl's betrayal had vanished with the tears. She examined the broad tattooed face, recognized the calm, sweet beauty of the girl within, and allowed herself to be led to the water's edge to be fed.

Two hours later, Virginia Dare was suffering her first sunburn, and her feet, which had never touched the earth uncovered, were becoming lacerated from stepping on the twigs and small stones that covered the forest floor.

When the party paused to drink at a stream, she sat down and examined the soles of her feet. She had taken the loss of her rabbit shoes as another violation of her person. She wanted to complain, but she felt too dizzy and hot.

She Smiles knelt down beside her and looked at the girl's feet. She said "Ai," and Badger went over. She Smiles held up the soles to him.

"This is truly a strange child," he said. "She wears foot coverings that would torture the bravest warrior, yet when she walks the earth like a Person, her feet split and bleed like a thief whose back has been thrashed by the birch rods of the women."

"There is a strange warmth from the girl too," said She Smiles, taking care to speak in a diffident manner befitting her station as a woman. Badger did not appear to notice.

He took the comb from Virginia's unprotesting hand and tried to fix it in her hair, but the hair was too soft and the teeth of the comb would not grip. She Smiles put out her hand, palm upward, and Badger handed it to her.

He watched as the young Indian girl took Virginia's long, silken tresses and in a few swift movements had arranged them in a knot at the base of the neck. Into the knot she pressed the comb and it caught firmly, holding the hair in position. She Smiles cupped her hand under Virginia's chin and lifted up the small face.

"You have beautiful hair, little one," she said softly and gave a dazzling smile. The pain of the sunburn was beginning to cloud Virginia's vision, but she caught the smile and her lips twitched in answer.

"Ai, she can smile," said Badger. "Perk up, Little Warrior, tonight we shall be home and you shall dance and feast all night."

A grown warrior did not tell a little girl about dancing and feasting, and She Smiles knew that he was obliquely flirting with *her*. She was pleased, and lowered her eyes so that he would not see the unmaidenly light in them.

By noon, Virginia was running a fever and was stumbling blindly, held upright only by She Smiles's arm. When Wolf called a halt by a tinkling brook, the little captive collapsed, moaning.

Although their path lay through the great forests, Wolf, who was leading them, knew every natural clearing within many miles of his town, and was deliberately wending through as many as possible to check on the game. He was keeping as good a tally as he could, considering he knew nothing of mathematics. But he would be able to describe one clearing as having sufficient white-tailed deer for the town to eat for three days, another with enough turkeys for a feast. Red and gray squirrels he could describe as being "many," or "more than many." The tribe would understand him.

It was passing through these clearings, where the sun shone bright and clear, that had played havoc with Virginia's sensitive skin. Had she been naked when they crossed the open marshlands she would have died of sunstroke. As it was, even with the limited exposure to the sun she had received, the girl was badly burned.

She Smiles, who had never seen such pale skin as Virginia's before, wondered at the way it had turned quite red. Fever she knew about, but she had no way of realizing that in this case it was a result of the sunburn. In fact, she had never seen sunburn before.

Badger examined the prostrate child and shook his head in puzzlement. Even Wolf, who was beginning to realize that the strange captive was going to be adopted into the tribe—he could tell that from the way Badger was always fussing over her—came and looked. But he, too, could not imagine what had happened to the girl who, only the day before, had been ready to fight the whole war party.

When they returned to the tribe, there were women there qualified to take away the fever, Badger thought, but would she live till then? That he was worried about the girl could be seen by all, and no one dared to anger him by making suggestions for her care.

It was one of the captured maids who plucked up the courage to speak, and saved Virginia's life. She approached the small group around the moaning child and paused, her eyes cast down, and waited to be called on to speak. Finally, Wolf condescended to notice her.

"You wish to speak?" he asked. He spoke harshly, but the girl appreciated that as the chief of a war party he was custom bound to talk to a captive in this way, especially a female.

"My mother—" she began, and stopped instantly. Her mother was no longer. As far as she, and everyone else, was concerned, her mother was dead. Soon she would have a new mother. She began again.

"Once when I was small, I was taken to a town where there was a boy with strange skin. It was not like a Person's, but pale. And his hair had no color, and his eyes were like the sky—"

Badger understood. He dismissed the girl with an imperious wave of his hand, and she backed away meekly. He turned to Wolf.

"She means an albino. I have heard of such a being. The sun burns their skin like the fire. But this one is not an albino. See." He pointed down at Virginia. "Her hair is black, and her eyes are like the fire smoke, not the sky—"

He stopped, for he had remembered the dead devil. Her hair had no color, and her eyes were like the sky.

Had that she-devil been an albino? Perhaps not a devil at all?

Little Warrior—he had quite definitely decided that would be her name—had gray eyes, like the one with the face of the bear, who must have been her father. He had assumed, naturally, that the one whose hair had no color could not be Little Warrior's mother because she had different eyes, and everyone knew that all creatures—Persons, animals, birds, or fish—had the same color eyes as their parents. But if the female had been an albino, then of course she would have different eyes, the color of the sky.

It was becoming too complicated for Badger. He was an Earth Person, as his name implied. His thoughts lived in the forests and streams, among the animals and birds. The werowance and the elders were there to handle complex matters requiring deep thought. He brought his mind back to the present. Although eye colors went from parent to child among the People, bodily characteristics did alter from parent to child and between brothers and sisters. All Persons were different in some way. That was easy for Badger to absorb for he could see it with his eyes. And animals and birds, too, had differences, although not so great.

He had it now! Children could have some physical characteristics from one parent, others from the second. Little Warrior had her hair and eye color from her father, and the albino skin from her mother. He sighed with relief at having reached that conclusion, and promptly put it from his mind. He turned back to the maiden who had spoken of the albino, a comely, slim girl.

"What medicine was used on the albino for the burning skin?" he asked her.

Both delighted and awed at being spoken to in front of all the others by an obviously senior warrior, the girl almost fell in her eagerness to rush up and speak.

"The skin was rubbed with oil from the walnut, or sunflower seed, or the root of the sassafras."

Badger nodded his acknowledgment, and the girl backed away. He was pleased. Walnut oil they had with them—already mixed with their warpaints. All the braves in the party carried some in the small pouches fastened at their waist. Each morning, after they bathed, they had applied fresh paint to replace that washed off. He would use the warpaint to cover Little Warrior's albino skin.

He explained this to Wolf and the others, and several of them immediately produced their carefully wrapped paints—black, white, red, and blue. While She Smiles lifted Virginia to her feet and held her up, Badger and Wolf set to work slapping the greasy paint all over her. There was not a great area to cover. In five minutes, the thin body was painted from the neck to the toes, the colors used haphazardly, in the order the braves pressed them on the painters. When it was done, Virginia looked like a tiny, grotesque Harlequin.

She stood swaying, wrapped in her fever, unaware of what was being done to her.

"I will carry her," said She Smiles.

She squatted down with her back to the English girl, reached behind her and expertly pulled her right hand over her shoulder and tucked Virginia's left leg under her left arm. It was the way an Indian mother carried a small child.

She Smiles stood up, and was astonished at the lightness of her burden. She waited patiently while Badger and Wolf cleaned the paint off their hands with grass and leaves, then they set off on the last leg of their journey. This time, Wolf made no detours to check on game but, guiding himself by familiar landmarks, stands of oak, walnut or persimmon trees, headed straight for home.

She Smiles soon found her burden, light though it was, difficult to carry. Virginia was by now barely conscious with fever, and hung limply on She Smiles's back, which had become slippery with paint. She called to her fellow captives and two of them, one on either side, supported the little girl by holding up her legs.

England's firstborn in the New World, raised to despise and detest the heathen, was unaware of their tenderness.

o

Virginia was unconscious when they arrived at the town of Askopo, which means magnolia and which was named for the huge sweet bay tree that stood in the center of the town. For twenty feet, the trunk was free of branches, but from then up it was in full bloom, a dense mass of creamy-white flowers. Had she been conscious, she would have been fascinated, as she always was by the beauty of the trees and the flowers among which she had spent her life.

She was unaware, too, of the welcome given the victorious returning war party. Wolf had sent messengers ahead to warn the town, and the entire population—all one hundred thirty-four of them—were spread along the last mile of the route. The women and children threw flower petals at them and the men whooped and cheered.

Under the magnolia, the chief awaited them. Nahyapuwa's name in English meant He-Frequents-The-River, which was the Indian way of describing the magnificent bald eagle. The werowance, a tall, handsome man in his sixties, had painted his cockscomb scalp lock white, like the head of his namesake.

He wore no feathers in his hair, nor was he tattooed or painted; the only sign of authority was the string of great pearls hung around his neck. His arms and wrists were also banded with pearls, and bunches hung at his ears. He wore a handsomely dressed and fringed deerskin, tied high up on his waist, which hung down both front and back. His arms were folded, which was a sign of wisdom.

Seated on either side of Bald Eagle were the elders of the tribe. They wore magnificent cloaks of skins, lined inside with choice furs, which were suspended over the left shoulder and hung down to their knees. The elders were smiling.

When the war party arrived, Bald Eagle and the elders squatted cross-legged on the woven reed mats spread under the tree. Wolf and Badger sat down facing them and the rest of the war party gathered around. The women captives stood in a group to the right, surrounded by women and children, the children jumping up and down, asking their names and grasping their hands, the women stroking their arms and faces, remarking on their beauty. The welcome was so overwhelming that the captured maidens blushed and giggled in mingled pleasure and embarrassment.

She Smiles had been taken off along with her burden by several old women known for their skills in medicine. Badger did not deign to look around for them.

A leather bag of the precious *uppowoc*, tobacco, was produced, along with a supply of *uppowcan*, clay pipes, and the squatting group smoked quietly for a while. Wolf and Badger, deprived of the sacred herb while on the raid—war parties never made smoke, which could give away their location to the enemy—sucked greedily on their pipes so that the *uppowoc's* strong medicine could circulate through their bodies and expel any foul vapors that had entered while they crossed through enemy territory.

Then Bald Eagle asked them to relate the story of the raid, and the whole town crowded around to hear.

Wolf gave a description of how the enemy town had been scouted out the day before the attack and the location of the maidens' long house marked. The absence of so many braves was also noted, and it was decided that Badger and a few warriors would take care of the others while the rest, led by Wolf, would steal the maidens. The plan had been successful, and once outside the town, the youngest of the girls had been set free. Only those whose appearance showed they were almost ready to leave the long house and be married were taken away.

Bald Eagle and the elders discussed this for some time, and the werowance decreed that for the time being the captured maidens would be put in the maidens' long house of Askopo, until it was decided which of the bereft mothers would be given which girl.

This decision was greeted with low murmurs of approval.

Wolf then told of the journey back and the encounter

with the "devils." The braves who had killed them and taken their scalps were told to describe the event and they did so with many gestures and exaggerations, causing the crowd to give voice to many exclamations of awe.

Then it was Badger's turn to describe the strange girl they had captured. He talked gravely, and at length, and Bald Eagle and his elders showed their approval of his reasoning about albinoism by nodding sagely.

There were more calls of "Ai!" and slapping of hands together in wonderment when he described how the little prisoner had faced up to the war party with her strange weapon, and Runs-Like-Deer held up his arm to show where he had been struck by the projectile. Badger ended by saying he had decided to give the girl the name Little Warrior.

"Where is Little Warrior now?" Bald Eagle asked, deliberately setting the chief's seal of approval on her name and thus her acceptance into the tribe. Bald Eagle was very fond of Badger who, as a child, had followed him around continuously.

Several women pointed to the lodge where Virginia had been taken and the werowance, followed by the elders, then Wolf and Badger and the war party, and finally by the rest of the tribe, walked along the main eating area and among the wooden-framed, reed-mat-covered lodges until they stopped at one on the outskirts of the little town.

The whole front of the lodge was exposed. The mats had been removed to give light and air to the interior. Virginia lay on the elevated sleeping bench, surrounded by several old women.

The werowance called out to them, and one of them, who was called *Namankanois*, the Swallowtail Butterfly, because when she had been young she had been brightly painted and lovely to behold, came forward.

She did not address the chief with awe, for she had known him since childhood and was his cousin. Her deerskin mantle was hung over one shoulder, like the elders', leaving one shriveled breast exposed.

"The child is very sick, O son of my father's brother," she said in a high-pitched voice. Swallowtail was very experienced in the mysteries of medicine.

"The skin is strange, like the albino, and is burned as though by the flames of the fire. The war paint that was put on her"—she gave the war party a withering glance to show her contempt for their presumption in trying to administer to a sick person—"has been removed and her body covered in oil from the crushed sunflower seed.

"When that has soaked in, her body will be enclosed in *wapeih*, the healing clay. Then the priest will drive away the evil spirits that have entered into this girl."

She half turned away, then remembered something. She spoke again.

"What is happening to the maidens who were captured and brought here?"

"They will reside in the maidens' long house until after the homecoming victory celebrations are finished, then they will be distributed to mothers without daughters," Bald Eagle said evenly.

The Swallowtail cackled loudly. She saw through the edict immediately. The feasting and dancing that would follow for the next few days would lead to high excitement and there would be much running into the forest and women would return with their buttocks muddied. Most of such traffic would be made by husbands and their wives, but the girls who had already passed their three years in the maidens' long house would be free to take lovers, and some would. But if the newly captured maidens were allowed to attend the roistering, and lost their virginity, there would be much argument over whether they had been deflowered prematurely, with some thwarted would-be husbands demanding they be made into prostitutes as was the law. The very reason for the celebration—the successful abduction of maidens to swell the town's depleted supply of future wives—could be the instrument of civil war.

Swallowtail was highly amused. There would be a small army of old women and widows put to guard the maidens' long house for the next few days.

"I would ask something concerning one of the new maidens," she said, and went on without waiting for an answer. "The one called She Smiles looks on this sick child as a sister and wishes to remain with her until the sickness is passed, or until she is dead."

The werowance hesitated. He did not want to make special concessions for one person and risk having a barrage of requests for others. Many of the young braves would be headstrong tonight. Badger spoke.

"Who will be responsible for this maiden?" he asked.

"I will be responsible, O Badger," said the Swallowtail, surprised at the warrior's interjection and putting two and two together as fast as her nimble, gossipy old mind could. "I and my sisters in medicine here. She will not be allowed to take part in the feast."

"It is good," said Bald Eagle, with obvious relief, and turned away.

The huge baked clay pots were kept boiling on the fires for two nights and a day, constantly refilled with choice cuts of venison, ripe maize, and freshly caught fish. The stew was ladled onto small wooden plates or large platters made from woven reeds from which everyone ate with their fingers.

There were roasted swan, geese, turkey, and mallard duck, and the long, narrow feeding area between the lodges, covered with reed mats, was piled with fruits—strawberries, raspberries, and mulberries. And there was cold, clear water from the river to wash it down.

But Badger ate sparingly. He partook of some of the game and fruit, and squatted as inconspicuously as he could near the lodge of the Swallowtail.

The first night the priest came. He wore the distinctive short cloak of the holy man, made of fine hares' skins with the fur outside. It was tied around his neck, with an opening to allow his right arm free, the left arm kept inside the cloak. It came no lower than the middle of his thigh, and he was naked underneath.

During the night, he sang over the prostrate body of Virginia Dare, waving his rattle made from an empty gourd filled with pebbles. He puffed tobacco in his pipe and blew the smoke over the English girl. At dawn, he said the girl would be cured, and left.

Virginia slept all that day and the next night, while the feasting, singing, and dancing went on. Many wives were taken into the woods and returned laughing and muddied. No braves violated the sanctity of the maidens' long house. And Badger sat there silently, moving away only to eat and drink, then returning to his vigil.

On the second dawn the feasting was over. The whole town had exhausted itself, with the exception of the girls in the maidens' long house, and some of the old men and women who preferred to watch and laugh at the antics of others. And Badger.

Badger stretched himself at dawn and went down to the river to swim and cleanse off his war paint.

When he returned, the Swallowtail was beckoning to him. She waited until he was close before she spoke. The town was silent and voices carried, and she wanted no one else to hear the conversation. She wanted all the enjoyment of gossiping about it later.

"The evil spirit has left the girl. She is well."

Badger went into the open-fronted lodge for the first time since his vigil began and looked down at Virginia. She was sleeping peacefully, her features beautiful in repose. Badger stretched out a callused hand and stroked the pale cheek. The girl was thin, even thinner than when she had first had her devil's clothing removed.

"You behave like a father," said the Swallowtail. She was not in awe of Badger or any other man. Her prowess in medicine gave her immunity.

"I shall be her father," said Badger, and surprised himself more than he surprised the old Indian woman.

"You will need a wife, then," she said, with another cackle.

"There are many who would gladly be my wife," said Badger stiffly, angry at being maneuvered into such a conversation with a woman.

"Then why not a young one? A maiden. There is one here who would gladly be your wife. There she is!"

Badger looked up, surprised, and saw a figure standing quietly in the shadows. It was She Smiles, her hands placed on her shoulders, her eyes downcast in maidenly modesty.

"She is a child," he said. But the Swallowtail was too far into her matchmaking to stop now.

"She will warm your bed, Badger, and give you many fine children. And this one is strong and will work well in the fields. And she will be a loving mother to this child, whom she already regards as her own."

Badger was silent for a few minutes.

"A girl as young as that does not want an old man," he said. The old woman cackled. She knew what Badger was asking.

"This one does. She told me, 'Ai! That Badger is a magnificent creature, a mighty warrior. What young virgin would not want to be his wife and have his children.'"

Badger was satisfied. He turned again to look at She Smiles.

"I will tell the werowance that you do not need to go to the maidens' long house," he told her, and saw her face light up with pleasure.

She Smiles came forward slowly. The Swallowtail watched closely, determined not to miss one gesture, one nuance.

"What will my husband call our daughter? Little Warrior is surely a name for a man child." Swallowtail held her breath. She had told She Smiles of the tragedy of Badger's beloved daughter.

Badger was silent. He picked up Virginia's small, thin hand and held it gently. As though something in him had communicated itself to her in her sleep, her fingers slowly clasped around his. To Badger, it was an omen. He made up his mind.

"In our lodge, she will be *Mato-aka*, first-born daughter. In the tribe, she will be called Tall Girl."

The Swallowtail clamped her hand over her mouth to prevent herself interrupting this glorious moment that she would tell over and over to the other old women by the evening campfires.

She Smiles moved close to Badger, allowing her body to touch his lightly.

"It is a good name, my husband," she said softly, and Badger smiled for the first time in more summers than he could remember.

Virginia Dare slept on peacefully, unaware that she had been legally adopted into a new family among the savages of the New World.

5

Virginia slept most of the next few days, tended constantly by She Smiles and the Swallowtail. Several times a day, the medicine woman fed her a tea brewed from the dried rootstock of the sweet flag plant she had collected in the swampy areas the previous fall.

This magic plant, she explained in whispers to She Smiles, would take care of *all* the child's sicknesses at once.

"This child," she said, "suffers from a loss of appetite, as you can see from how thin she is. Ai, she is like one who has been dead many days."

She Smiles shuddered.

"She probably has indigestion, which may be the cause of her loss of appetite," the Swallowtail went on. "You cannot eat if what you eat causes the stomach pain."

She Smiles nodded silently. She was the perfect audience for the old Butterfly, who was growing to like her more each day.

"Then, as you can see, she is suffering from weakness and exhaustion. And, if I am not mistaken, she has trouble with the liver."

She Smiles nodded almost violently, making it clear that, in her eyes, the medicine woman could *never* be mistaken.

In appreciation, the Swallowtail showed her how she made the medicinal tea. She covered the bottom of a cup, made from a hollowed-out deer horn, with shredded sweet flag root—the root bark having been first carefully removed—and poured boiling water over it. It was then left to stand for fifteen minutes to infuse, and fed to Virginia when it was still lukewarm.

The result was miraculous, at least to She Smiles. A day

or two after the treatment began, the Swallowtail suddenly rose from her squatting position next to the sleeping bench where Virginia lay. She raised the soft skin that covered the child and placed her ear on the girl's stomach.

She cackled and motioned for She Smiles to do the same. When she did, she heard the distinct growling from Virginia's flat belly.

"You see," cried the Swallowtail, "she is hungry again. Now she will eat." And she set about preparing a broth made from boiled venison. Without opening her eyes, the child drank greedily.

Virginia had been washed and cleansed by the two women, and her hair had been cleared of lice by rubbing tobacco juice into her scalp.

And She Smiles, with the Swallowtail's smiling approval, had prepared an aromatic wash made from soaking crushed rose petals in water which she gently rubbed over the child's body.

When she finally woke up and looked around her, Virginia's first impressions were of the coolness of her skin, and the wonderful scent of wild roses.

Then she saw that she lay in a house. She had never seen a house before, but she knew what they looked like, for her parents had made little models of them for her to play with.

Was she in England at last? Had the tall ships finally come and taken them to the great city of London?

But she could not recall the sea voyage, the months sailing across the great ocean she knew lay between the civilized Christian world and the heathen land where she had been born.

And the wall opposite where she lay was open, not covered like the houses in London were. And through the wall she could see other buildings, like arbors, covered in bark and reed matting, and she could smell wood smoke, and there were people moving about, naked people—

Indians! The word exploded in her brain, and she opened her mouth to scream, then suddenly there was a hand, a soft hand, against her cheek. Another arm slid under her head and drew her close to someone's face, and a voice murmured words in her ear, words she did not understand but knew were soothing.

She lay awhile and let her heart stop its pounding, then turned and looked at the face next to hers.

It was a strange face, a savage one. The eyes were large, black, and slightly slanted, the eyelashes long. The nostrils were flared, giving the nose a flattened look. The lips in a generous mouth were full and voluptuous.

The skin was light brown with a reddish glow. From the ears down the cheeks to the corners of the mouth were twin rows of dots. Virginia knew what they were for her parents had described such markings. They were tattoos, made by pouncing the skin. Under the chin was another design, three vertical stripes, also in a blackish-blue color.

The woman's jet-black hair hung in a fringe to her thick eyebrows and thickly down each side of the rounded face and then, just before it reached the shoulders, it was gathered behind the head.

Something stirred in Virginia's memory. She vaguely recalled a long walk through the marshlands, of falling in a river, of being stripped of her clothes and brutally scrubbed—

It was this woman! Then she recalled someone feeding her, comforting her.

Virginia looked again at the eyes. They were deep and the expression was of mingled tenderness and humor.

It was not a pretty face, she decided, not compared to her mother's blonde beauty, but there was something in it that arrested her panic.

Then the savage woman smiled, and Virginia's fear subsided. It was a warm, beautiful smile, showing the white even teeth.

Despite herself, despite the fear of the savages that had been instilled into her ever since she could remember, Virginia felt herself smiling back, a thin, tremulous smile, and immediately the woman was hugging her and laughing softly.

The woman leaned back—she must have been kneeling low beside her, Virginia realized, for her bed was near the floor—and examined her, still smiling. She wore a double necklace of some kind of colored stone, Virginia saw. The upper arms were also tattooed in blue and red designs.

Then Virginia saw the naked breasts and recoiled in instinctive horror and disgust. She knew it was sinful to expose them. She had never seen her mother's breasts, or any part of her body except her hands, feet, and face. The Christian religion forbade nakedness, she knew.

She Smiles immediately saw the reason for Virginia's flinching and, equally instinctively, covered her breasts with her arms, her hands resting on her shoulders.

They stared at each other for a full minute. Then She Smiles lowered her hands and pointed at her breasts.

"*Ot-us,*" she said. Female breasts. "*Wingan.*" Good. She nodded her head several times in emphasis.

She was using the pidgin language that tribes spoke to each other when their dialects were too diverse for normal speech.

She pointed to the sky.

"*Nepaush,*" she said. The sun. "*Ahone.*" The god. The sun god.

She raised both arms high.

"The sun god is good."

She lowered her arms languorously, her hands stroking her face down to her waist, then crossing over to stroke her arms.

"*Wingan. Nepower, wingan.*" Good. Naked, good. "*Cup-peh.*" Yes.

Then She Smiles pointed below her waist and gave Virginia a conspiratorial grin.

"Here, naked, good, no."

She shook her head decisively.

"*Mattah, mattah.*" No, no.

She held up the edge of the soft leather apron fastened around her waist.

"*Pagwantawun,*" she said, giving the name of the covering. "*Wingan, cuppeh.*" Good, yes. She nodded again.

She raised her eyebrows at Virginia.

"*Kennehawtowskear?*" Do you understand?

Virginia knew this strange creature was explaining something to her. The words, spoken softly, meant nothing by themselves. But, without realizing it, these two from different worlds did have a language in common. Sign language.

Virginia knew that a nod meant yes, and a shake of the head meant no. So the woman had told her *yes*, her breasts should be exposed, and *no*, her private parts should not be seen. She disagreed, but she understood.

"*Kennehawtowskear?*" She Smiles asked again, this time giving the little tweak to her lips that lit up her face, the glow that, until now, no child had been able to resist.

Virginia, still fixing the Indian woman with her calm, gray eyes, knew she was being asked one of two things. Did she agree, or did she understand. The woman's face was so warm and friendly that her own lips twitched in response.

She nodded, and the woman again reached for her and hugged her.

At that moment the Swallowtail returned from one of her herb-gathering expeditions and began to fuss over Virginia.

"We must make her beautiful for her father's visit," she told She Smiles. "Now that she is awake, everyone will want to come and see her."

Between them, they fed the little girl a bowl of meat broth, washed her, combed her hair with a comb made from a fish skeleton. And then they showed her the dress that She Smiles had made for her while she lay unconscious. It was a beautiful, soft sueded doeskin. She Smiles had measured the child carefully with a knotted *rahsawan*, a leather strip.

Virginia looked at the dress with wondering eyes. It was a sleeveless shift with long fringes at the shoulders and hem of the skirt. She did not protest as the women lifted her to her feet and slipped it over her head. They stood back and made approving sounds.

Then She Smiles produced a wide doeskin belt, crafted with brightly colored beads made from stones, and tied it around Virginia's waist. The Butterfly pointed at the belt, first one side, then the other.

Virginia looked down. There were two small purses hanging from the belt, skin bags drawn tight with rawhide strings.

"*Raragwunnemun*," the medicine woman told her. Without looking up, Virginia sensed she was being told to open them. Slowly she undid the one on her left side and groped inside. She took out the tortoiseshell comb her mother had worn in her hair. She looked at it slowly and, still not looking up, unloosened the other purse. She pulled out her sling. For a moment longer she stood gazing at the objects in her hands.

These were her possessions. Her mother's comb and the sling her father had fashioned for her. She was aware of the soft feel of the dress, the long fringes faintly tickling her arms and legs.

They had covered her. They themselves went naked but somehow they knew that as a Christian, she must be covered. She looked up, and there were tears in her eyes, tears of bewilderment, for she could not understand these people, these naked, painted, heathen savages.

When they saw the tears, the two Indian women knew immediately what had caused them. The girl, this strange little creature, couldn't help her gratefulness showing in this way. She was obviously overwhelmed by the beautiful dress they had made for her, the dress they had decided, after much discussion with Badger, would cover her body and protect it from sunburn until her skin grew strong enough to absorb the life-giving rays and turn a ruddy brown like her arms and face.

And the gratitude was in her eyes because they had carefully preserved her only possessions brought from her other life. Females liked personal possessions, they knew. Even little girls.

The tears melted their hearts and they swooped down on Virginia Dare and gathered her up into their arms, both of them holding on to her and making clucking, soothing sounds. After a while, they sat her down between them, holding her hands while they talked softly about their small charge. Eventually, weak from her illness, and exhausted from the emotional strain of finding herself with, actually *living with*, Indians, Virginia Dare fell asleep in the arms of She Smiles.

When Badger visited her that afternoon, Virginia was sitting up, She Smiles squatting on the ground beside her, the Swallowtail hovering in the background.

Badger had his bow and quiver of arrows with him, and he placed them on the ground beside him as he listened to She Smiles's description of the conversation with the girl. She seems to undertand the language of the People, the Indian girl told him. At least, some of it.

Badger sat looking gravely at Virginia, and she returned his gaze evenly. She understood now that the two women, the old one and the young one, were not her enemies. In fact, they seemed to be her friends. But this was a man, an Indian man. And Indian men, she knew from her parents, tortured and killed English people.

This man did not look fierce, however. She remembered now the ones who had captured her. They had been painted devils. This one had no paint on his face or body, nor was his skin pounced to make tattoos.

On his head he wore long feathers, turkey feathers daubed red. There was one on each side of his head fastened somehow in the long hair coiled behind each ear. The third and largest stood straight up from where the savage cockscomb met his forehead. She found herself staring at it, and realized that the skin there had actually been pierced and the feather quill inserted neatly into the hole.

The man's face was calm, dignified, and showed no sign of the savagery she had seen on the faces of the ones who had taken her prisoner.

As she stared, his wide face slowly creased into a smile, and he pointed to his bare chest.

"Badger," he said. "Badger."

Then he pointed at Virginia.

"Tall Girl."

The Indian words meant nothing to her. The glottal stop that characterized the Indian speech was unknown to her. It made the words sound like little short barks, even though the voice was soft and resonant.

He pointed at himself again.

"Badger," he said and, pointing at her, he asked, "*Kwe kwoi ternis kwire*?" What is your name?

There was no mistaking his meaning.

"My name is Virginia Dare and my parents are Ananias and Elinor Dare," she answered, her face expressionless.

"Ai," said Badger, rolling up his eyes. "That is indeed a great name." He tried to repeat it but could not. It was a very long name. He had another thought and picked up his bow.

"*Hawtop*," he said. He held it toward Virginia. "*Kwe kwoi?*" What is this? The girl answered immediately.

"That's a bow," she said in her clear voice.

Badger's eyes lit up. He looked at the bow wonderingly.

"*Hawtop*," he said. "*Datsabo*."

He turned to the Swallowtail.

"Is this a language of the People she speaks?" he asked excitedly. "Does it not sound so? *Datsabo?*"

"It sounds so," said the medicine woman, but doubtfully.

Badger snatched an arrow from his quiver. He held it up to Virginia.

"*Askwe-owan*," he said.

"That's an arrow," she answered.

Badger was delighted.

"*Datsanro*," he said. "*Datsanro*."

He stood up.

"I will fetch the priest," he said to the women. "Perhaps he will be able to understand this language."

A few minutes later he was back with the priest in tow.

The priest was named Screams-Like-Wildcat, for he had been born with a severe case of colic, and had yelled with pain for the first few weeks of his existence.

Later, his family had wanted to change his name, for he had developed into a serious, rather introspective child, but he had been pleased with it and clung to it, for it made him sound fierce.

He sat down and immediately found himself under the intense scrutiny of the strange child. The priest was a highly sensitive man and, by virtue of his training for the priesthood, understood something of psychology.

A priest's position in the tribe was more than making magic. He prevented crime within the tribe, especially theft, to which all the People were addicted. Everyone knew that a priest knew when a theft had taken place and who was the guilty party. That was magic, and therefore no one stole within his own tribe, only from other tribes, which was not a crime.

There were other crimes a priest had to root out *after* they had been committed, unlike stealing, which his magic prevented. These were crimes of omission, where people avoided their share of chores, of lying and slander, sex crimes, as when a bachelor slept with a married woman, or a girl had sex before she was released from the three years' stay in the maidens' long house. Sometimes the crime was murder.

It was here that psychology came into play. The priest knew the right questions to ask to trip up the most confident of liars, how to read expressions, eyes, tones of voice.

But despite his powers, Screams-Like-Wildcat was too gentle a man to be really feared, even by children, though the tribe held him in great awe and respect.

He knew this strange girl was summing him up, wondering who he was and why he had been brought here. She showed no fear, and that pleased him. He carefully turned his head so that she could examine him better.

The first sight of the priest was frightening to Virginia. Apart from the stiff cockscomb and a fringe over the eyes, his head was completely shaven. The fringe in front must have been stiffened with some material, she thought, for it projected almost like a hand shading the eyes from the sun.

His face was finely featured, with furrows across the forehead like her father had. "Thinking lines," her father had called them. The nose was thin and sharp, the lips molded as gently as a woman's, and the chin had a cleft. Colored ornaments dangled from his ears. He was not painted or tattooed.

Screams-Like-Wildcat told Badger to repeat his question-and-answer experiment with the girl. When it was over, and Badger asked him if Virginia was indeed speaking some unknown dialect of the True People, the priest continued to look silently at the child. He did not know if she was speaking a dialect. He could not even imagine who she was or where she came from. But he realized that this was a highly intelligent girl. He stood up in one supple movement and spoke to the three adults.

"This is a child," said Screams-Like-Wildcat. "What person can understand a child best?"

He looked at them in turn, but no one answered, for they knew he would tell them.

"Another child," said the priest, and the others said "Aah" in unison.

"I will bring the daughter of Wolf," he went on. "The little one that is called Chipmunk."

The Swallowtail clapped her hands delightedly and She Smiles, who did not know Wolf or Chipmunk, looked inquiringly at Badger, saw that his face had lit up at the name, and was pleased. She would like a new friend for her new daughter.

When the priest returned he was accompanied by the tall, haughty Wolf, who looked down at Virginia and was quite startled at the unwavering gaze given him in return.

Then, from behind his back, came a little elfin creature. She was brown and completely naked, except for a leather string that ran between her legs and was tied around her waist. At the crotch it was padded with moss. Prodded by her father, Chipmunk dutifully walked up to Virginia and sat down in front of her.

Virginia Dare was frightened. All her life she had known only two people, her parents. She had seen no others. Now they were all around her, examining her, questioning her. And now this little naked creature. She had never seen another child before.

They examined each other carefully. Chipmunk saw a thin girl, taller and probably older than herself, with peculiar gray eyes and long, glossy hair. A serious-faced girl. A beautiful one.

Virginia saw before her an exquisite creature, almost a doll. She had had a doll once. Her mother had brought it from London because she was pregnant before she set sail and had hoped her child would be a girl. The Indian girl had a rounded face with huge black eyes and a wide mouth. Her hair hung thick to her shoulders.

Chipmunk was frightened, too. The whole town had

talked about the strange little captive and she had been almost in tears about visiting her.

"Speak to her," said the priest.

Chipmunk fixed her eyes on Virginia's, pointed to her breast, and said, "*Near.*" I. Then at Virginia. "*Kear.*" You.

Back to herself. "I Chipmunk. You Tall Girl."

She waited, but there was no response from the stranger. She tried again.

She pointed to herself, and held up her other hand with the fingers outstretched.

"I am five years old," she said, enunciating clearly. "*Paransk.*" Five.

Virginia's face lit up. She held up one hand, the fingers and thumb splayed, and two fingers of the other hand.

"I am seven!"

Chipmunk laughed with delight and clapped her hands. "*Toppawoss. Kear toppawoss.*" Seven. You seven.

The priest spoke: "Let us leave the children. They will talk together best when there are no adults to listen."

He saw Virginia look up at him with that penetrating stare and smiled at her, a sudden smile that softened the austere, almost harsh lines of his face, then turned and left the lodge.

The others followed, leaving the two girls examining each other, wide-eyed. After a while, Chipmunk rose from the floor and sat down beside Virginia. They started counting again with their fingers, Virginia trying to repeat the Indian words, with their difficult glottal stops and half-swallowed vowels.

Nekut, one. *Ningh*, two. *Nuss*, three. *Yowgh*, four. *Paransk*, five. *Comotinch*, six. *Toppawoss*, seven. *Nuss-wash*, eight. *Kekatawgh*, nine. *Keskeke*, ten.

Chipmunk was a natural teacher. She started holding up so many fingers and asking, "*Kase?*"—how many?—clapping her hands if Virginia got even an approximation of the sound of the number, and shrieking with laughter when the English girl stumbled over the word. The little Indian was so obviously enjoying herself that Virginia couldn't help smiling.

When Chipmunk tried to count higher, it was Virginia's turn.

"*Ninghsapoioieksku*," said Chipmunk, raising her ten fingers twice, but the word sounded so alien and impossible to pronounce and the expression on the five-year-old's face so solemn that Virginia burst into laughter herself, and Chipmunk immediately joined her.

When they had subsided, Chipmunk pointed at both of them and said "*Chammay*." She took Virginia's hands and said it again. "*Chammay*."

"Chummy?" asked Virginia. The Indian girl nodded violently. "*Kear, near, chammay*." You, me, friends.

"Chummy," Virginia said again. It felt good to say. Virginia Dare had made her first childhood friend. She had also used the first New World word to be adopted into the English language.

Two days later, she was judged by her new "family" to be strong enough to be taken on a tour of the town of Askopo. Her tortoiseshell comb was carefully fixed at the back of her head, her lips were brushed lightly with red berry juice to relieve the pallor that persisted from her sunstroke, and the Swallowtail put two strands of her finest pearls around her neck.

With Badger leading and She Smiles and the Swallowtail behind, Virginia and Chipmunk, hand in hand, were paraded before the tribe.

Chipmunk waved her free hand toward the women and dozens of children, even some of the braves, as they came out of their lodges and from the gardens to stare at Virginia.

"*Chesk chammay*," she cried. All friends.

"Chummy," said Virginia, and the women clapped their hands, for the word "friend" was also used as a greeting.

"Ai," they cried, "look at her. She is beautiful." And Badger was pleased.

But someone else said that she was too thin and should be fed more, at which an old woman ran to the cooking pot and came back with a piece of steaming meat impaled on a short stick and held it out to Virginia.

"*O-iaw*," she said. Lean meat. "*Pa-angun*." A little piece.

Virginia took it hesitantly. She turned around to She Smiles, who nodded encouragingly. Virginia put the morsel to her tongue and licked it tentatively. It was the most delicious thing she had ever tasted in her life!

Virginia Dare had eaten meat before. Although her father knew of the bow and arrow, and how to make them, he was a native of the great city of London, had never been trained in archery, and was unable to become even the least expert with them.

But he taught himself to make traps to catch small animals—cottontail rabbits, red squirrels, and even tiny creatures like the deer mouse and the jumping mouse that could leap five or six feet in one leap. They were never able to trap the bigger, stronger animals.

At one time her mother had been able to make birdlime to catch small birds. She had come from a country called Ireland, which was across a small sea from London, she had told Virginia, and she had been taught some of the things her husband could not learn in a city.

She had made the greenish, sticky substance from the inner green bark of the holly tree. She had boiled it in the small iron pot they had managed to salvage after the ambush.

The substance was spread on twigs, about two feet long, which were then placed in bushes where birds frequented. Once they landed, the birds' feet became firmly stuck and they were easily captured.

But then, when Virginia was still very small, the bottom of the pot had fallen out, and they were unable to make fresh birdlime. That was when Ananias Dare had made a slingshot. He was a poor shot himself, but Virginia became expert and eventually could not only hit perched birds thirty feet away, but could knock down the flying squirrels that abounded in the forest and sailed gracefully from tree to tree.

The meat had always been roasted furtively over tiny fires to escape the watchful eyes of the savages. Virginia had liked it, even though it had usually been roasted too crisply to retain any of the juices.

But this. This tender, juicy, spicy thing, was a taste such as she had never experienced before. She Smiles and the Swallowtail had been feeding her strength-giving meat broth, but it had been heavily dosed with bitter-tasting herbs to drive away the evil spirits that entered the body when a person was sick. This was the first meat she had tasted since her capture.

Virginia ate greedily, then licked her fingers carefully as she had been taught. She made a little curtsy to the old woman and said, "Thank you."

The old woman, who was so aged everyone had forgotten her name and simply called her *Tumpse-is*, Old Woman, cackled with glee and covered her face with delight, and embarrassment at her own effrontery, then ran off to tell everyone who would listen of the strange and beautiful girl who showed such appreciation for even a morsel of food.

In the evening, the Swallowtail brought a huge steaming platter of stewed venison, maize, and tender roots to her lodge, and Virginia, Chipmunk, the two women, and Badger squatted in a circle around it and ate. Virginia gorged herself. She had never eaten so much at one meal. Then she crawled to her bed and lay down, stomach distended, and promptly fell asleep.

Badger was pleased. He had been worried, first that she would not survive at all, and then that she would not be happy with her new family. It was obvious she had accepted her new life.

"She is becoming a Person," he said, and the others agreed.

Virginia Dare, had she been awake and had she thought about it, would have realized that she had not thought about her parents since she had met Chipmunk.

That night, Badger took Virginia Dare with She Smiles and the Swallowtail to one of the large communal fires. The little girl watched, mesmerized by the slow chanting, wondering at the children scrambling over and clinging to the men, who appeared quite unperturbed by it. How could this be, Virginia thought, when it was a known fact, as the English had learned at great cost, that Indian men, being heathen, had no Christian attitude toward children, and massacred them without conscience.

She felt herself lifted gently from the shelter of She Smiles's arms onto the lap of Badger, and held there casually. She studied his features in the flickering firelight, the high cheekbones, the slightly hooked nose, the jutting chin.

Badger looked down and smiled at Virginia, an oddly sweet smile for such a fierce warrior. He began to rock back and forth to the singing's cadence and soon the little English girl, tired out from her day's adventures, began to doze. She fell into a deep sleep snuggled up to the bare chest of a man whose race her parents had taught her to despise and fear.

6

It had been ruled by the werowance, Bald Eagle, that the spring planting of *pagatowr*, the Indian corn, would be made before the marriages of the captured maidens, and the men had already turned up the earth with their crude mattocks made from a forked branch of a tree.

The women did all the planting and, helped by the children, all the extensive weeding during the six- to seven-month-long growing and harvesting season of the three corn crops.

On the first planting day, Chipmunk took Virginia to the fields where they joined her mother. Virginia had seen the woman before and knew who she was. She was a comely creature with flashing black eyes and a ready laugh.

Chipmunk pointed at her and said: "*Nek. Nek-near.*" Mother. My mother. Virginia smiled and said, "*Chummy*," and the woman laughed and patted her head.

They played for a while in the freshly turned ground until Chipmunk saw a group of braves passing by. She called to Virginia to follow and ran up to them, stopping in front of the tallest and fiercest-looking.

Wolf laughed when he saw her, bent down and swept her high in the air, shaking her playfully for a moment, then depositing her on one of his wide shoulders.

Chipmunk waved down to Virginia and called out, "*Nowse. Nowse-near.*" Father. My Father.

Virginia understood. *Nek*, mother. *Nowse*, father. They were easy words. Not like the Indian word for "twenty," which she knew she would just *never* be able to pronounce.

Wolf lowered Chipmunk to the ground and the men strolled away. Chipmunk turned to Virginia.

"We will go and see your mother and father," she said. The sentence was too long for the English girl and she replied with the expression Chipmunk had taught her.

"*Matta-kennowntoraw.*" I do not understand.

Chipmunk tried again. She pointed at Virginia.

"*Nek-kear. Nowse-kear.*" Your mother. Your father.

Virginia's face fell. Her mother and father. Where were they? What had happened to them? When she had regained consciousness in the Swallowtail's lodge, the horror of her capture had been pushed into the background of her mind, and she had unconsciously suppressed the memory each time it had tried to surface.

Although she found herself comparing whatever she saw in the Indian town to things her parents had told her, or warned her about, she had not deliberately thought about them since her capture, for she knew something was wrong, very wrong, and she dared not think about it.

Now Chipmunk had forced her to think, to remember. She still could not recall her mother's scream or her father's roar. The memory was still too traumatic for her mind to bear.

But the pictures of her "previous" life, as she was now beginning to think of it, flashed before her. Her father, with his beard and gentle hands. Her mother's golden hair that had prematurely turned gray. The songs her mother had taught her.

A great sadness filled her. Where were they? Where were the great ships that would carry them back to England?

She allowed Chipmunk to take her hand and lead her through the little town. At some distance from the Swallowtail's lodge, Chipmunk stopped and pointed. Virginia looked and saw She Smiles hunkered down, evidently working at something.

"*Nek-Kear*," said Chipmunk. Your mother.

Virginia stared silently. Somehow, she was not surprised. She had sensed that the attention She Smiles had been paying her was more than that of just a friend. But if She Smiles was now her mother, that meant—

Chipmunk was speaking again.

"Badger," she said. "Your father. Badger."

Suddenly, Virginia understood. She had been adopted by the Indians. She had new parents. A new father and a new mother. And that meant only one thing.

She turned and ran away from the lodges and into the trees. She ran a long way, then she crawled through the thick undergrowth to the bowl of a tall oak. Huddled there, she cried. She sobbed out her hurt and her sadness and her loneliness.

Virginia Dare was seven years old. She had just lost her parents. And she would never see them again.

o

Virginia cried herself to sleep. When she awoke, it was afternoon, and she was hungry. She was about to rise when she realized she had nowhere to go. She had run away from the Indian village, from the people who wanted to adopt her and make her into an Indian. Where would she go now?

She sank back onto the bed of crushed ferns that she had wet with her tears and stared up at the trees. Suddenly she became aware of a faint humming noise interspersed with mouselike squeaks.

She used to lie like this for hours—when her parents deemed it safe for her to be out in the open—watching the antics of the exquisitely tiny ruby-throated hummingbird, hovering in midair, suspended by an almost invisible ring of whirring, purple-feathered wings, the iridescent green body and brilliant metallic red throat flashing in the dappled sunlight under the trees.

A cock bird, unaware of her presence, came into view, darting hither and yon like a large, jewel-colored insect. It was soon joined by its mate and together they flashed in and out of the flowers, hovering as they inserted their long, thin bills deep into the heart of a flower.

Virginia forgot her hunger and her troubles in the delight of watching these beautiful birds. But her newfound sense of peace was interrupted by a harsh chattering. Frightened, she pressed herself against the tree and searched the area around her with wide eyes.

The hummingbirds had been disturbed, too, and darted back and forth like angry bees. Then she saw what had upset them. Into her view came a parrot, about a foot long, green with a bright yellow and red head. She had seen many of these noisy, cheeky, gregarious creatures. Then came another parrot, and another, until about a dozen of them had descended through the branches of a cocklebur, searching for any seeds left in the spiny pods from the previous fall.

She watched amazed as the hummingbirds hurled themselves at the parrots, darting at their heads and hovering within inches of the powerful curved beaks, their whirring wings ruffling the yellow throat feathers of the larger birds. The parrots scrambled uneasily through the tangled branches, chattering raucously to each other. Their racket prevented Virginia from hearing the calls of the search party passing only a few hundred yards from her hiding place.

o

Chipmunk had been nonplussed when her new friend ran away. She had followed slowly to the edge of the forest, calling tentatively, "Tall Girl? What is the matter, Tall Girl?"

She had poked haphazardly under the trees with a stick, dropping her voice to almost a whisper when she thought she heard adults nearby. Until she found Tall Girl, she did not want anyone to know that she had run away. Chipmunk realized that the strange new girl had been adopted by Badger and She Smiles, and she knew it was something she herself had said that had caused Tall Girl to run. She was afraid Badger and She Smiles would blame her for the loss of their new daughter.

As she continued to wander in the woods, Chipmunk became more and more certain that her friend had gone back to wherever she had lived before she had been captured, but she was unwilling to tell the village this and run the risk of punishment.

Thus it was several hours before anyone knew of Virginia's disappearance.

"How long ago did Tall Girl run away?" Badger asked Chipmunk when the child finally returned to the village. Palefaced, the girl stammered out that it had been before noon. Badger looked at Wolf. Tall Girl had been missing for four, perhaps five hours.

"Bring more braves," Badger snapped, and Wolf turned away immediately, running toward the river, where a group of men were fishing. Badger strode off in the direction of the trees, waving his arm at the children.

"Come," he said. "Help me find Tall Girl."

The children scattered into the trees, running ahead of Badger. At the forest edge, Badger stopped and turned around. She Smiles stood a few yards away, her face creased in worry. He motioned to her to join him and she ran after the group.

They spread out in a long line, several children between each adult, searching the undergrowth, looking into hollow logs, even climbing trees.

It was Wolf who first heard the chattering and held up his hand. Gradually, the noise made by the searchers died out and they all listened.

"Parrots," said Wolf, disgustedly, and the line moved on.

The parrots grew increasingly uneasy as the hummingbirds continued to harass them, and eventually, at some unseen signal, they took noisily to the air and flew off.

Virginia lay for a few minutes longer, then remembered her predicament, and sat up. The hummingbirds, becoming aware of her for the first time, whirled about in panic, then they, too, flashed out of sight in a red and green blur.

The child stood up, brushing bits of broken fern from her hair, realizing how hungry and thirsty she was. She looked around her, but had no idea where she was or how far she had run before collapsing.

Where would she go, she asked herself once more. Could she live in the forest by herself? She had her sling for hunting, but how would she make fire to cook and keep away the wild animals at night? At the thought of wild animals, Virginia shivered and looked around her fearfully.

Where were her parents? She pushed the thought away. She knew where her parents were, for Chipmunk's words had told her. She could not have a new father and mother unless her other parents had gone to the place they called Heaven, where all good Christians went when they . . .

She thought of little Chipmunk, who was her friend, and She Smiles, who was so kind to her, and Badger, who looked very fierce but was really gentle, and the old woman called Swallowtail Butterfly, who fussed over her. She thought of the delicious meals the two women cooked and her mouth watered involuntarily.

The light was just beginning to fade and the shadows under the trees were starting to lengthen. "Please, somebody, help me," she whimpered softly. She thought of her comfortable, safe bed in the Swallowtail's lodge and her misery increased.

"Please, She Smiles, please, Chipmunk, come and take me home." The word "home" had slipped out and she found it somehow reassuring, for she began to repeat it.

"Please take me home, please find me and take me home." She was wringing her hands in despair now. "I want to go home! I want to go home!"

There was a noise behind her, the noise of feet moving across the litter of the forest floor. They had come for her!

She turned around with a cry of joy on her lips and froze.

The bear, a three-hundred-pounder and twice as tall at the shoulder as Virginia, was annoyed. He had spent the morning turning over rocks and tearing old logs apart in his search for ants and beetles. He had destroyed a few ant hills and eaten many of the inhabitants. The morning's foraging hadn't been too bad, and he had enjoyed his sleep at noon in the heat of an aspen thicket.

But the afternoon had been frustrating. He had dug up several burrows of little animals, but found too few of their owners at home. Then he had spotted a bees' nest and had clambered up the tree, about to plunge his claw-armored paw into the crevice where the delicious honey was stored when he heard the advancing line of beaters searching for Viginia.

He feared and hated humans. He carried an arrowhead in his side in memory of an encounter with these noisy, evil-smelling creatures.

For a moment, the exquisite memory of the taste of honey fought with the memory of his painful encounter with man, but the memory of pain won, and he slipped down the tree in a cloud of angry bees and loped away.

He was growling to himself as he crashed through the underbrush, the thought of the delicious honey turning his frustration into anger. Then suddenly there was a small creature in front of him, and he skidded to a halt, raising his brown snout to sniff. The wind was away from him, which was why he had not smelled this being before. If he had, he would have recognized it for a hated human and given it a wide berth.

Virginia was terrified. She recognized the black bear immediately—it was the beast her father had fought that had so changed his personality.

The bear was twenty feet from her, squinting at the child with its little red-rimmed eyes, its long nose sniffing the air.

Almost without thinking, Virginia pulled her sling out of her purse, slipping a stone into it. Then she waited, near paralyzed with fear, the sling dangling from her hand, swinging gently back and forth.

The bear noticed the moving sling. Some ancestral memory told him it was a weapon, and he raised his head and snarled. Virginia's arm swung the sling in a blur and released the stone.

It hit the bear on the tip of his snout and he bellowed in

pain and anger, rearing upright on his hind legs and roaring once more.

Virginia screamed.

Both Wolf and Badger heard the bear's snarl and stopped to turn in the direction of the sound. Then they heard the girl's scream, and Badger ran, scattering children and braves as he sped in the direction of the sound, Wolf hard on his heels.

As they vanished through the trees, She Smiles started after them, fear clutching at her heart.

Virginia stared at the bear in terror. It was as tall as the one her father had fought. Its red tongue lolled out of its slavering jaws, the long teeth gleaming savagely in the semidusk under the trees. It threshed its forelegs, warning the creature in front of it to step aside, to flee, but Virginia stood transfixed, unable to move.

The bear dropped back on all fours and bunched itself for the charge. It hunched forward just as Badger charged through the thickets, bow in one hand, an arrow, ready for nocking, in the other. Still moving at top speed, he tried to set the arrow in place but it caught in an overhanging branch and was whipped from his fingers.

He stopped his rush next to Virginia and the girl flung herself at him, her thin arms circling his waist, almost knocking him off balance. The bear was starting to move. In desperation, Badger drew his tomahawk from his rawhide belt and threw it underhand. The weapon struck the bear on its already smarting nose and the creature again rose to its full height, glaring in fury at this new enemy.

Wolf appeared to one side, his stone ax in his hand, ready to leap to the attack, but Badger had already diverted the animal from its deadly charge and had slipped another arrow from its quiver. He nocked it expertly, pulled and released it in one fluid motion; almost miraculously, the arrow appeared in the animal's small white breast spot.

The bear roared in mingled fury and pain, realizing that this creature, this human, was responsible for the sudden, red-hot pain in its chest, but not understanding the arrow's fast flight.

Virginia still held tightly to Badger and felt the man's muscles tense and relax as he shot another arrow, and a third, and saw them all appearing in the same white spot on the bear's breast.

Mortally wounded, the animal was still clawing the air, but its roars and snarls had altered. Along with the blood frothing from its jaws came moans, wails, sobs, and howls, astonishingly like the anguish of a man in deep agony.

Then it simply collapsed, the arrows protruding from its breast snapping as the great weight came down on them. Badger sighed, lowered his bow, and looked down at Virginia. A moment later She Smiles burst into the little clearing, throwing herself beside the girl and scooping her into her arms. Virginia, trembling, released her tight grip on Badger and threw her own arms around the Indian girl's neck. She Smiles rocked back and forth on her haunches, cooing and patting the little girl.

Badger gazed for a few moments at his new daughter and his wife-to-be as they clutched each other fiercely. He smiled.

He touched She Smiles lightly on the head, and she rose from Virginia's side. Without a word, they each took one of the little English girl's hands and started back to the town.

It was the Swallowtail, who had seen many captured children raised by her people, who understood what the incident in the forest meant to the strange, gray-eyed girl.

"She knows now. From now on she will remember no more of her past. And she will weep for it no more."

The Swallowtail was a wise woman, and everyone who heard her soon marveled at her wisdom, for indeed there was a change in Tall Girl, who had been Virginia Dare.

She laughed easily. She played with enthusiasm with Chipmunk and the myriad other children that seemed to infest Askopo. She learned to swim. She was curious about everything and began to acquire an Indian vocabulary at an amazing speed. She loaded her sling and amazed everyone with her marksmanship.

She Smiles was delighted. Badger was openly proud.

She followed Chipmunk eagerly as the Indian girl led her away from the lodges and into the woods. Virginia watched with interest as her friend bent her knees and walked crouched almost to the ground, peering into the undergrowth. Then Chipmunk signaled her to stop, took her hand, and pulled her down among the weeds and wildflowers.

She pointed to the base of a tree, and Virginia saw a tiny animal she recognized immediately. Her parents had called it a squirrel mouse. It was about six inches long, a mixture of brown and gray color. But what made it noticeable were the black and white stripes across its eyes and down its sides. Its tail, which was bushy like a squirrel's, was almost as long as its body.

Her father had caught one in a trap once, but it had looked so pretty Virginia had begged him not to kill it for food. When he had gone to the trap to release it, the small animal had chattered furiously at him in a squeaky voice.

The little Indian girl pointed at the creature, then at herself.

"Chipmunk," she said.

Virginia gazed first at one, then at the other. The same bright, inquisitive eyes. The chatter. She burst out laughing, and the little animal flickered out of sight.

Chipmunk jumped to her feet and danced through the underbrush chanting, "My name is Chipmunk" in her high-pitched voice. Virginia joined her, but her pronunciation of the name, which she was saying for the first time, amused Chipmunk so much that she fell to the ground and lay there, giggling hysterically.

Virginia lay down, too, realizing that for the first time in her life she was completely happy and carefree. The fear that had hung over her like an evil thing, the fear of the savage, had lifted. Already she was beginning to forget, as only a child can, the physical hunger that had dogged her and her parents ever since she could remember. And no longer had she to force herself to crawl into their burrow and skulk underground. Now there was daylight every day, and cool fresh air, and the beautiful stars every night.

"Come, I will teach you more names," Chipmunk said,

and she led the older girl back to the lodge of the Swallowtail. There they found the medicine woman fussing with her herbs and She Smiles pounding maize ears in a stone mortar into a milky paste, preparing it for baking into cornbread.

She Smiles looked up as they entered the lodge, laid down the elongated stone she was using as a pestle, and held out her arms to Virginia. The English girl hesitated shyly, but Chipmunk, who had been accustomed her whole life to being fussed over by adults, pushed her forward, and she found herself hugged by her new mother with the strangely sweet smile.

The Swallowtail left her work to squat beside them and asked Chipmunk what they had been doing. The little girl, always eagerly accepting any opportunity to chatter, immediately went into details of how she had made Virginia understand Chipmunk's name.

"Tall Girl," Chipmunk said, crowding close and pointing to She Smiles. "Do you understand *her* name?"

When Virginia looked blank, Chipmunk said, "She Smiles," but the English girl shook her head.

Then Chipmunk began to pantomime the name. She pressed her lips together, then opened them in a big smile. "Smile," she said.

The Swallowtail called out, "Look, Tall Girl," and pulled her mouth open with her fingers to show all her teeth. It was more of a grimace than a smile, and Chipmunk screamed with delight.

Finally, She Smiles motioned Virginia to look at her. Slowly, her sensuous lips moved into the gentle smile Virginia had come to anticipate on the young Indian woman's face. She Smiles pointed to her mouth.

"Smile," she said.

She put her forefinger on Virginia's mouth, but there was only puzzlement on the face of the gray-eyed girl on her lap. Then she slowly tickled Virginia's lower lip, her own smile expanding, until at first a small, then a wider answering smile appeared. She Smiles pointed directly at Virginia's mouth and said again, "Smile."

Virginia suddenly realized what they were trying to tell

her. This woman was called Smile. Her eyes widened with recognition and she said, "Aah!" Chipmunk and the Swallowtail cried out happily, clapping their hands.

Virginia had a sudden thought. She turned to the medicine woman and asked, "What is your name?"

The Swallowtail, taken aback by the strange words, and also at being addressed by the adopted girl directly for the first time, sat with her mouth open in surprise.

Virginia decided, on the spur of the moment, to try out some of the Indian words she had been learning from Chipmunk. Taking a deep breath and summoning all her courage, she pointed to the small Indian and said, "Chipmunk." Then she pointed at the Swallowtail and asked, "You?"

The old woman gasped for a moment, then her face lit up with pleasure. She got to her feet, went outside the lodge, and began yelling for someone. Within seconds a boy of about ten, wearing a loin covering made of rabbit skin, appeared. The medicine woman gave him some instructions and he sped off, she calling after him, "*Uttek, a peya weyack wingwhip!*" Go, and come back quickly.

The boy was back in ten minutes, both hands cupped together in front of him.

Carefully he handed what he was carrying to the Swallowtail and ran off again.

The medicine woman came over to Virginia and squatted down beside her. She held her hands up close to Virginia's face, said, "*Namankanois,*" and opened her hands.

The large butterfly, its color a variegated yellow and brown, clung to one palm, its wings closed. Then it opened them and fluttered them to dry off the moisture caused by the enclosed human hands. Virginia recognized it immediately.

"It's a tiger swallowtail!" she exclaimed. She knew its name because her parents had described how her grandfather, John White, who had been governor of the English colony on Roanoke Island, had made paintings of the creatures in the new land, to take to the great queen of England. One of the paintings had been of this butterfly. She turned to the old woman.

"Your name is Tiger Swallowtail?"

There was no mistaking her meaning, although her audience could not fathom the actual English words. The Swallowtail nodded vigorously several times, pointed to herself.

"*Namankanois*," she said, and when Virginia repeated it, the three Indians clapped their hands. Virginia Dare smiled back in delight.

With the resilience of a child, and a child's need for love and affection, she had accepted her new life.

She wept no more for her past. But, despite the Swallowtail's prediction, she never forgot it.

7

Virginia was in the woods alone, hunting for squirrels with her sling, when she saw the attackers.

The movements in the trees caught her attention and she froze, thinking she had come across a gray-squirrel nesting area. But that couldn't be, for squirrels were noisy animals. If she had stumbled onto them, they would have signaled danger with a rapid *kuk*, *kuk*, *kuk*. Even if they did not think she was an immediate threat, there would have been a drawn-out *ku-u-uk* at close intervals.

These were silent movements and all of them, she realized with growing concern, came from around the base of the trees, not in the branches. Could they be caused by animals? Slowly and carefully, Virginia began to back away.

She had gone only a few yards when she saw it.

Through a gap in a clump of bushes a head appeared, the head of a beast. One side of the face was yellow, the other a bright red. There were great white circles around the eyes.

From the head sprouted horns. Three of them. One on either side of the head, the third growing straight out of the forehead.

Virginia stood petrified. The head moved from side to

side, peering, then it vanished. Her heart was pounding in her narrow chest and nausea stirred in her stomach. She was transfixed with terror, unable to move.

Then a noise pierced her fear-dulled mind. The harsh, strident call of the red squirrel announcing a trespasser on its territory. It was followed almost immediately by the danger calls of its gray cousin, a sharp *kuk-kuk* here, another over there.

The racket finally penetrated her paralysis, and she realized what she had seen. Indians! Painted like the ones who surrounded her the day . . .

The head she had seen would be attached to a body, a muscled body, hideously painted with whorls and loops. The horns were not horns at all, but feathers. And the alarm signals of the squirrels told her that there were many of them, skulking in the undergrowth.

She turned and ran. She ran as she never had before, her head and arms pumping, her bare feet barely touching the earth.

She tore into the little town of Askopo and past the first few empty lodges. When she came to the main eating place where the great fire was kept smoldering all day, the scream burst from her lungs.

"Badger! She Smiles!"

Several braves appeared before her. One of them dropped to his knees and caught her as she ran full tilt into him. Before he could question her, she pointed back the way she had come and shouted:

"Nimatewh! Matta wingan! Matta chummy!"

It was not properly articulated Algonkian Indian, but the braves understood. Man! Not good! Not friend!

The Indian let go of Virginia and bounded away, shouting at the top of his voice. The others with him sped in different directions. The girl flopped to a sitting position, breathless and panting.

She looked around, wondering why there were no women and children to be seen. But of course, they were all at the corn planting. In the lodges there would be only very small babies and old people.

And the men, the warriors? She looked again, this time

in panic. If the warriors were out hunting, apart from the few who had stopped her . . . And where were they now? Had they run away? Where was Badger, her new father?

Virginia got to her feet. From one of the purses tied to her belt she took out her sling and a stone. It was not the type of stone she used for knocking down birds and squirrels. She had found it on the bed of the river, where there were lots of them; round, flattened stones with edges worn smooth from the centuries of water flowing over them.

She had sharpened the edges to use them in competing with the boys at their morning arrow target practice. Supervised by the mothers, boys who had reached the age to be taught the bow had to show a certain expertise in shooting at an old warrior bark shield before they were allowed breakfast. Virginia's sharpened stones had pierced the shield every time.

Now she fitted one into her sling and faced the forest from where the attackers would descend upon them . . .

o

Out in the woods, the leader of the band of raiders was snarling in fury. He had brought his twenty braves clean through the land of the Moratucs without once being spotted. He had found the tribe that had dared steal maidens from a Secotan village—they had taken the choice beauties, he had been told—and now, at the last moment, discovery!

It was one of the Secotan maidens released by Badger and Wolf as too young for marriage who had revealed where the abductors had come from. She had heard one of them boasting of the reception they would get on their return to Askopo, and this had been relayed to the nearest large Secotan town.

From there, the word of the maiden-stealing had spread and, by coincidence, reached a man who had actually been to a Moratuc town called Askopo when he had been trading north of the river.

There had been weeks of talk of revenge, and finally, with the man agreeing to act as guide, a war party had been organized.

They had not intended to attack Askopo that day, merely to scout it out and see where the bachelors' long house was, for that was where the main opposition would come from. Then, at dawn, they would attack, killing the bachelors before they were properly awake. After that, the subjugation of the town would be easy, and they would return loaded with scalps, choice furs, pearls and beads, the stolen maidens, and any other women they fancied. They would be acclaimed as mighty warriors, and they would have taught the insolent Moratuc a lesson . . .

But they had been discovered! How, he could not understand. The noise of the squirrels could not have done it. Those noisy animals would raise a racket if one of their own kind trespassed on another's territory. No experienced brave would alert a whole town because of squirrel talk.

But someone had. The town just ahead was buzzing with alarm.

The leader of the war party could hear the shouting. Yet no one had seen them. He was certain of that. They had seen no one spying on them. In his frustration, he ground his teeth and beat his fists on his forehead. The young braves around him stood back warily.

There was nothing they could do now except retreat into the forest, to remain hidden there for a few days until the alarm had died down and the town was lulled into carelessness once more. Then they would attack.

But even as he thought this, the leader knew it would not happen. The town had been alerted, and if the expected attack did not come, the Moratuc would send small parties of braves to seek out the enemy and harry them, wearing them down until they finally fled ignominiously.

The only thing to do was depart immediately, before they could be humiliated, and head south to their own lands. Perhaps they could find another Moratuc village isolated from its neighbors and small enough for them to attack. Then all would not be lost and they could still wrest glory and booty from this war expedition.

But he was afraid to return to his own town and admit failure. He was a junior chief and he had made many speeches before the war party had left, many promises. He would be disgraced. The other chiefs would jeer at him. Even the party he was leading now would laugh at him behind his back.

He looked once more in the direction of the town. The blood lust rose in him. He wanted to kill those people, to humiliate them, to show them they could not steal from his people and live to boast about it.

It had been only minutes since the town had been alarmed. He turned to the men nearest him.

"Bring the others. We will attack!"

The painted warriors around him laughed with glee.

The men of Askopo were rushing to its defense. The braves to whom Virginia had given the alarm had spread the word quickly. A large group of the men, including Badger, Wolf, and the priest, Screams-Like-Wildcat, were at the river, fishing. Others, and that meant most of the young men, were at the cornfield, watching the young women doing the planting and, in the case of those betrothed, keeping a proprietary eye on future wives.

Now they charged back into the town to get their weapons. The elders, who were no longer expected to fight, were rounding up the women and children and herding them back into the town in case an attack was made on the planting field.

Badger was first into the bachelors' long house. He snatched his bow and quiver from where they hung over his sleeping bench. He scrabbled for precious seconds underneath the bed and produced his *monohakan*, his sword, a long flattened stick of hardwood, the edges serrated with tiny sharp stones, so uniform and firmly inserted into the wood that it could almost be used as a knife.

Then, with one bound, he leaped over the bed, through the open wall, and ran into the town, the war cry screaming from his lips, followed by the young bachelors, the ones who had made up the band that had captured the Secotan maidens, the young men who would follow honored warriors like Badger and Wolf to the death.

This group arrived at the eating place at the same time as Wolf, at the head of another band.

The braves who had given the warning were already in place, erect, arrows nocked, bowstrings taut.

The attackers burst out of the trees, screeching and yelling. The sight and sound would have quailed the hearts of inexperienced braves, and indeed, the bowmen standing there, who had not yet been bloodied in battle, wavered as though struck a physical blow. Then Badger, the mighty warrior, was among them, and they steadied, letting loose the deadly arrows, the three-foot-long, stone-tipped willow rods that could pierce three bark targets tied together.

Six of the attackers stumbled and fell. And then the rest of them were racing at the defenders, swords and stone axes raised, death cries screaming from their open mouths.

Battle fury blinds men. A red mist clouds their vision and they see nothing but the object of their attack—a thing, a creature, another man. And they charge at the object, blinded to all else, sometimes oblivious to their own death, in their primeval urge to reach their lethal target.

The battle rage had taken over Badger. He was growling and snarling as he reached the front rank of the defenders.

The familiar red mist—which the old warriors tried to describe to the novitiates—was descending on him. He saw the line of attackers—but there was something else. A small figure. Something clad in a doeskin dress, with long fringes and a daintily worked belt.

The red cloud cleared from his eyes. That was a child there, right in front of the attacking enemy. His daughter.

The enemy warrior in whose path Virginia stood swung back his sword, a cruel thing serrated with human teeth. In a moment it would crush her skull and toss her aside.

Badger drew back his own sword and threw it with all the force of his mighty arm. It flew between the Askopo bowmen and struck the enemy brave in the face. His head went back with a loud snapping noise but his legs continued to propel the body, and the dead man fell among the archers, knocking their ranks askew. Then the front rank of the charging enemy was among them.

Badger ran forward to retrieve his sword and had actually bent down and grasped it where it had fallen when he saw Virginia facing him, her expression taut, her face a deadly white. Her sling was in her right hand and, as he watched, her arm swung it. In a blur it went around her head once, twice, three times, and something whistled over his stooped head. Behind him he heard a sickening, soft *blup*!

Badger was a superb athlete, with hair-trigger reflexes. He pivoted, his sword swinging for a deadly backhand blow. And stopped. The man behind him, his *tamahawk* still raised, was dead. There was no need for Badger's death blow.

The man's left eye was a crimson blotch. The blood had just begun to squirt out onto the white paint circling it and its twin. The yellow and scarlet painted face of the leader of the attackers had frozen in shock before he fell dead. Badger could see the edge of a stone protruding from the eye.

Somewhere to Badger's right he heard someone crying "Tall Girl! Tall Girl!" and he saw She Smiles running toward him.

He grabbed a handful of Virginia's dress and, as She Smiles drew nearer, threw her to the stricken woman. The girl sailed through the air and into the arms of her Indian mother. Then She Smiles turned and ran in the opposite direction almost without a pause.

The next few minutes were savage and bloody. The fighting was now hand to hand, the arrows had stopped flying. The air was filled with screams of fury and anguish, the sound of blows and bodies striking the hardened earth.

From their position at the edge of the great crowd of women and children packed against two of the larger lodges, She Smiles, Virginia, and the Swallowtail, holding on tightly to one another, watched Badger in his splendid killing fury.

In and out of the embattled warriors he charged, keeping low, avoiding the whistling swings of tomahawk and war club from enemy and friend alike, slashing at the unprotected and vulnerable lower parts of the attackers.

His serrated sword ripped through kidneys, intestines, and hamstrings, wreaking terrible havoc on legs and thighs.

And then it was over, as suddenly as it had begun. The enemy was down, strewn across the great communal eating and dancing area. But fallen among them were Moratuc defenders, wounded and dead.

The women broke from their huddled ranks and rushed onto the battlefield. Moments later, adding to the confusion and din that followed the slaughter, their loud lamenting echoed through the town as they extricated their dead from the bloody piles.

Three families were bereft, one of a husband and father, two of young sons who had borne the brunt of the first brutal assault. There were several wounded, some badly but none fatally, and these, to the accompaniment of much wailing, were carried or helped to their lodges by their womenfolk.

Badger and Wolf were picking their way through the gore when they were given the news—stunning for the whole town, a shocking personal bereavement for Badger. The werowance, Bald Eagle, had been killed.

One of the elders told them what had happened. They had gathered around the women and children, armed with clubs, to protect them if the enemy should break through the defenders' ranks.

But Bald Eagle, a warrior of great renown, had been unable to stand by while others fought to the death for the town of which he was the elected chief. He had rushed into the fray but, in his late sixties, he was not as agile as the foe. He had struck one blow, and one of the enemy had tumbled to the ground, and then he in turn had received a tomahawk blow he was unable to dodge.

He had been killed instantly.

They gathered around the body of their fallen leader. His two wives, old women now, had thrown themselves down beside him and their cries added to the general clamor.

Badger was crushed. From childhood, from the moment he had understood what a warrior was, Bald Eagle had been his hero. When Bald Eagle had returned from a war sortie, Badger had helped him dry his scalps.

Bald Eagle had repaid Badger's hero worship by taking him on his first raid, and had praised him before the whole town afterward.

Their friendship had matured over the years until they became like brothers. Badger was shattered by his dearest friend's death. It was Wolf who truly understood Badger's feelings, for he felt the same hero worship and brotherly love for Badger that Badger had felt for Bald Eagle.

Among the People, there could be a brotherly affection deep enough to transcend the love of a woman.

A brave broke into Badger's reverie to tell him that one of the enemy had been found alive, though badly mutilated.

He had volunteered to tell, on promise of being killed quickly and not tortured, where the raiders had come from and how they had tracked the maidens to Askopo. Badger agreed. He ordered that first the man be taken among the bodies to identify the leader.

But by now all was chaos. The enemy had been scalped and among the victorious braves some bitter quarreling over ownership of the trophies had begun, their raucous roars adding to the din of the wailing women.

And when word of Bald Eagle's death spread, the women went berserk among the enemy dead. With sharp-edged clam and oyster shells used in scraping the hair from hides and the skulls of their menfolk, they tore the flesh from the bodies. Small children with sticks ran in and out of the cacophonous melee, defiling the uncaring dead. Steam rose as entrails spewed out of ripped stomachs.

Badger, leading two men carrying the wounded Secotan brave, pushed and kicked his way through the turmoil. The blood lust in the aftermath of battle scarcely affected the warriors themselves, but seemed to be an affliction visited upon the women.

Eventually, the leader was found. It was the man Virginia had killed. Badger was satisfied. If any of the attackers had escaped, they would be leaderless now, and could be counted on to return to their own territory as fast as they could.

He gave a signal. The Secotan brave was dispatched and scalped, his body tossed to the women, who received it with jubilant cries. Then Badger went in search of Virginia and She Smiles.

Virginia had watched it all, from the charge of the enemy out of the woods to the sickening orgy of mutilation. The Swallowtail had been called to administer to the wounded, so Virginia and She Smiles remained alone, holding each other close in mutual fear and shock.

The young Indian woman had never witnessed a battle, and consequently had not seen its aftermath. And having no blood relatives in the town of Askopo, the revenge lust had not affected her. The thought of what she would have done if Virginia or Badger had been killed did not occur to her.

Virginia trembled and She Smiles held her tighter.

"It is over, little one," she said soothingly. "They are all dead, the evil men, and they will never frighten you again."

Although she did not understand what She Smiles said, Virginia was thinking along the same lines.

She saw again the long line of hideously painted men running at her, their weapons held high, their devil tails lashing behind them, just like those other painted men with tails who had captured her . . . She pushed the memory away.

Again she saw the savage about to kill Badger, her new father, and she distinctly remembered what she had done to *him* with her sling. She had struck him with all her might, and he had fallen to the ground.

She remembered the way Badger had grabbed her and thrown her to She Smiles, who had taken her to the safety of the women.

And the battle itself—she could recognize the "bad" Indians, the painted ones. And the "good" ones, the ones like Badger with no paint. The *good* ones had won, that she knew.

Now she watched with horror as the dead were torn to pieces. But she did not feel the same paralyzing fear she had when she had first sighted the painted enemy Indian head. It was the *bad* Indians who were being punished. And they *should* be punished. They had tried to kill her, and Badger, and all the people in this town who were so kind and good to her . . .

8

It took two days for the clamor to die down, for the enemy dead to be burned, and the Moratuc braves to be buried. The body of Bald Eagle would be preserved and kept in the temple of the werowances, a lodge on stilts at the outskirts of the town.

On the third day, the whole town congregated to discuss the successor to Bald Eagle. Normally it would have gone to his brothers, and on their deaths, to his sisters, and from there to his sisters' children, but never through his own children. This was the law of succession.

But Bald Eagle had no brethren. His brothers were dead, either in battle or in accidents. His sisters were married in other tribes, either traded or stolen. The line of succession was broken. The town elected Badger werowance.

He protested vigorously, for he did not wish to sit and dispense wisdom while others enjoyed the happy life in the woods and on the rivers. He protested that he did not have the wisdom necessary to be chief, and that one of the elders should be elected.

But it was, in fact, the wisdom shown by Badger in describing the future of the tribe in the wake of the bloody battle that had made the people, led by the elders themselves, acclaim him.

In an emotional speech, Badger had said the tribe could not absorb another raid like the one they had just survived. Too many warriors had been slain in battles during the past few years, and there were now almost too many women and children for the remainder to protect.

The reason they had captured the maidens, he told them, was for the tribe to produce more sons who would grow up to replace the warriors they had lost. But this would take years—the new maidens weren't even married yet. Look what had happened already, due to the lack of braves. He bent down, picked up Virginia, who was standing between him and She Smiles, and held her high.

"This girl child fought the enemy like the bravest warrior," Badger cried, and a loud sigh swept across the packed crowd. The story had been told and retold by witnesses.

"Shall we train little girls to take their place alongside braves because we have not enough warriors?"

There was a chorus of "No, Badger! No!"

He put Virginia back on the ground. The Swallowtail, Wolf, the elders, and many others exchanged glances. Never had they heard Badger speak so eloquently. Never had they heard Badger speak in public! He was known for keeping his own counsel.

There was a silence, and Badger realized that he was expected to provide a solution. He knew what his solution was, but was unsure what the reaction would be. No True People, not even the women, would run away from battle. But he had to tell them his thoughts, even though they disgraced him.

He told how scouts had discovered that three of the enemy had made their escape. Would they return with another expedition to seek revenge for their now twice-affronted people? Badger did not know, but if they did, they would surely come with a much larger force to overcome the Moratuc village. And next time they would make sure they were not discovered by a little girl hunting squirrels. They would choose their time, wait until some of Askopo's braves were away hunting, until they were certain of their superiority, and then strike.

And that would be the end of their little tribe. The men would die, the women would be taken away, some to be married, the rest to be servants and field workers, and the children—the tractable ones—given away to other parents.

Badger waited until he was prompted by cries of "Tell us what to do!" before he told them his plan.

"We must leave this place. We must find a new home where the Secotan will not find us, where the hunting will be good and the earth fruitful for our crops, and yet peaceful enough for our boy children to mature and take their place alongside the warriors. That will take years of peace."

He looked around, expecting opposition, but there was none.

"It is good that warriors fight and die in battle. It is the way of the True People. But sometimes the People need a period of peace, for children to grow up, for boys to become warriors and girl children to be wives."

The roar of acclaim told him his argument had succeeded.

They would move from here, travel north, to a place where there were many small streams, for that was where the deer grew most. He had not meant, however, that the tribe should call on him to lead it.

He protested in vain.

The crowd began to murmur its acclaim of him, the murmur grew to a hum, the hum to a roar. Badger had no choice but to accept the office of werowance. She Smiles, as soon as they were married, would be his werowansquaw. Tall Girl, his daughter, would be the tribe's first princess for many, many winters.

o

They wandered for three weeks, following streams, plodding along silent forest trails. Then one day Wolf came rushing back to tell Badger he had found the perfect spot for their new town, at the confluence of two medium-sized rivers.

A town had stood at this spot many winters before and

the forest had not yet grown back. There were great open spaces where the cornfields had been and even now pumpkins, gourds, peas, and beans were growing haphazardly. Not far away, said Wolf, were marshes with plenty of wildfowl and edible roots; other braves reported an abundance of white-tailed deer, bear, and other game.

The tribe looked over the place Wolf had found. Women tested the soil, men checked the rivers for fish. They spent three days there before Badger would decide. He insisted on thoroughly surveying the area. They estimated that the place was about halfway between the midreaches of the Chawan River in the east and the Moratuc in the west, where it turned north into Iroquoian territory.

The nearest towns, as far as they could figure, were weeks in either direction—the Algonkian Chawanoac and the Iroquoian Mangoak. There was no sign of any tribes that inhabited the north.

Finally, Badger called the tribe together and asked them if they would take this place for their new town. The answer was unanimous.

The only question left now was what to call their new home. It could not be another Askopo, for there was no sweet bay near where the center of the town would be. There were many suggestions, some serious, some joking, some ludicrous, and some bawdy.

An exasperated Badger turned to Virginia, who was standing next to him solemnly watching the proceedings.

"What shall we name our town?" he asked her. She shook her head; she did not understand. Badger spread his arms wide, smiled, and said, "Name!" and Virginia said "Chummy." Friend.

So they called the town Chammayoac.

The next few weeks were ones of feverish activity. First the corn planting had to be done. Later, the fields would also grow pumpkins, squashes, gourds, and sunflowers. The gourds would be emptied and used as water containers and rattles, and the sunflower seeds would provide both flour for bread and oil.

As soon as the first plantings were made, the whole tribe turned to house building.

Badger would have been happy with a lodge the same size as the Swallowtail's old one in Askopo. After all, he reasoned, then they could use the bark and mat coverings they had brought with them, instead of making new ones.

But he was overruled by the elders. As the werowance, he would have to receive visitors—strangers, perhaps—and he and the elders and priest and leading warriors would meet and talk in his lodge. He also owed it to his people to have a more ostentatious residence than that of a simple brave.

So he built a lodge sixty feet long and thirty wide. Virginia and Chipmunk tried to assist by dragging the poles into place, and were a source of great amusement for Badger and Wolf, who was helping him.

Virginia couldn't really grasp how quickly a lodge could be built. When she saw the height it would be—eighteen feet—she was astonished. It must be like the tall houses in London, she thought. It would be airy during the long, hot, humid summer.

Badger measured out one end of the lodge for the Swallowtail, to be divided from the rest by roll-down mats, as the place where the old woman could store her medicines, mortars and pestles for crushing dried herbs and roots, and keep her many plants hanging in various stages of drying.

The Swallowtail would also have her own fire for preparing her cures, and two sleeping platforms so that she and Virginia, her apprentice, would have privacy during teaching periods.

Virginia's instruction by the Swallowtail started as soon as the town was built. At the insistence of She Smiles, she was also taught to perform menial work, though as a princess she would always have servants. How could she tell if a chore was performed well or badly if she could not do it herself, She Smiles asked Badger and the Swallowtail. As Badger had no brethren, his daughter would be queen one day, and a queen should know all the work of a town.

And so Virginia learned to cook at the same time that she was taught medicine, hunting, and that elusive quality called leadership.

9

It was in the winters that Badger had most of Virginia's time. There were no gardens to tend, the Swallowtail's foraging trips for her medicines and potions had ended for the year, and She Smiles was happy to see father and daughter go off, hand in hand, for lessons in archery, tracking, and woodlore in the great, primeval forest.

The first winter of her new life with the Indians, he made her a willow bow and a quiver of reeds covered with rabbit skins. He fastened a deer-hide bracer at her left wrist to absorb the thwack of the bowstring when it was loosed. He made her arrows of reeds, canes, and hazel sprigs. He showed her how to form the bow, thick at the middle, slim at the ends, by scraping the wood with a sharpened shell. He taught her how to get the arrows perfectly straight by peering down them, spinning them in her hands, then working out the bends with the scraper.

The arrowheads were made from a variety of objects—a splinter of stone, the sharpened tip of a deer horn, the beak of a bird. These were fastened onto the arrow with a glue made from boiling deer sinew and deer horn.

The arrows were nocked with a beaver's tooth fixed on a small stick that Badger gave to Virginia to keep in one of her pouches.

The arrows were fletched with goose and turkey feathers, slit with a splinter of reed that Virginia found to be the sharpest knife she had seen, even sharper than the shiny, forged-iron knife her father had. This reed knife could joint a deer and cut leather clothes to shape.

Badger took his teaching seriously, not smiling even at Virginia's first hilarious attempts to shoot an arrow. But when, tired of constantly missing a squirrel that cheekily came back to its perch after each shot to scold her, she dropped the bow, took out her sling, and dispatched it with one shot, he finally laughed uproariously despite himself.

Virginia had heard something about archery in England from her parents, who had told her that until recently, archery practice there was compulsory and took place on Sundays and holidays.

They'd said the extreme range of the English longbow was over four hundred yards and King Henry had decreed that no Englishman over twenty-four years of age was allowed to practice at a range of less than two hundred and twenty yards.

She had asked if that was a very long distance and they had said it was, but it meant nothing to her for she did not know what a yard was.

Virginia learned to hunt the loon, with its eerie laughter, and the pied-billed and the horned grebes. And the snakebird that swam under water with just its long neck and head showing. And the turkey and the bobwhite, birds that were with them all year.

There was also the white-tailed deer, which supplied most of the tribe's venison, and the much larger *wapiti*, the elk. In the fall rutting season, Badger often took Virginia to see the elk bulls fighting over cows, sometimes to the death.

There were racoons, squirrels, and opossums. And the cottontail rabbit. And beaver. Virginia was fascinated by this rodent and spent days watching them building their dams. Equally intriguing were the otters, those superb swimmers, when a whole family of them played at sliding down a muddy river bank into the water.

She asked Badger why the People did not gather more of the riches around them. He seemed genuinely surprised at her question.

"Do you not have enough to eat?" he asked her. She nodded. "Do you not have sufficient to cover your body from the weather?" She nodded again. "Is our lodge not great enough?" She agreed that their lodge was the finest in the town.

"Then why should we want more? There is food when we are hungry, the waters of the rivers for our thirst, the skins of the animals for our bodies, and the trees to build lodges for our protection." He watched her for a moment, then asked:

"Are you not happy, Tall Girl?"

"I am very happy, Father," she replied immediately, with a smile.

"Then why do you ask such questions?"

"I must ask questions if I am to learn how to become a Person."

Badger smiled with contentment. She had given him the perfect answer.

As Virginia grew, Badger fashioned new bows for her, longer and harder to pull. By the time she was twelve years old, she was as tall as Badger and could use her bow alongside any young brave.

The priest, Screams-Like-Wildcat, taught her to fish. He scorned the weirs built on the rivers to trap them. It was a simple but highly effective way of fishing, for almost any time of the year, the traps had some fish in them.

But the priest preferred to use skill. He taught Virginia to shoot at fish with an arrow that had a line attached to it so it could be retrieved. It took her years to master this technique.

He taught her spear fishing, using a long, slim pole with a barbed point made of stone or bone. And he taught her angling. They made hooks from bone and the line Virginia fashioned herself as she had been taught by She Smiles, using shredded bark, deer sinew, or grass to spin a thin, highly durable thread.

The priest was also passing on to Virginia his knowledge of psychology. It was not a formal training, however; she learned simply by being near him, watching him study the everyday, normal behavior of the tribe, spotting an aberration then working out a logical answer as the reason for it. His was essentially a practical science, based on shrewd observance of his fellow man. There was no magic, but the tribe could not know this, or his powers would fail.

Virginia learned to detect lies by facial expressions, verbal evasions, even by the way a person would walk. Indians had little to lie about, so that when a person did invent a lie it was generally to cover up some minor wrongdoing.

Screams-Like-Wildcat explained that laws, made by wise chiefs in the Beginning Time, were for the preservation and happiness of the tribe.

Thus, it was the law that men go to war and hunt, for a good warrior and hunter would attract women as wives and even a small tribe would become a great one with the coming of many children.

Virginia learned it was the law that women were not responsible for their infidelities. Her English mother had told her about Indian women. They were sensuous, she said. Voluptuous was the word she used. They trapped men with their nakedness and their bold eyes and their seductive ways.

Long before she reached puberty, Virginia was aware of the charged sexual atmosphere of Indian life. The braves, attired and painted for hunting, were a thrilling sight to the women, young and old. Even when they just wandered around the town, they were aware of the effect of their smooth-muscled torsos and taut hips.

And the women exuded a femininity that hung over the town on sultry evenings like a tingling diaphanous blanket. Virginia saw the glances exchanged between the sexes, the furtive look that mirrored the illicit thought, the bold, possessive stare of the established claimant.

She noticed the way Badger and She Smiles secretly—or so they thought—touched each other in passing, and how they gave each other private smiles when their glances crossed.

But despite the open sexuality, Virginia's own emergence into puberty held more than the usual problems.

She had always been tall for her age, and many of the women were sure she was mistaken about the number of her years, that she was older and that, actually, her first menstrual period was long overdue.

In preparation for the woman's sickness, as it was called, young girls were given a tea made from the steeped flower heads of the pennyroyal plant. As they approached menstruation, they were given sage tea to drink. These two drinks were to regulate the periods.

But when Virginia continued not to menstruate, a worried Swallowtail fed her mint tea, a mixture of black corn and skullcap herbs, and kept her drinking until, at last, the first cramps came.

She had no doubt overdosed the child, for the cramps were severe and unusually painful, causing a high fever in the girl. The frightened medicine woman now prescribed hot elder bark tea and a drink made from spicebush twigs, which alleviated the pain somewhat.

Virginia had thought herself prepared for her first menstruation. She knew what happened and how women were treated for it. There were certain tribal rules for the woman's sickness. The woman concerned had to keep herself indoors as much as possible, away from the gaze of others, especially men. In some tribes, menstruating women stayed in a special lodge; in Chammayoac, the woman stayed in a screened-off part of the lodge that her children, but not her husband, could enter.

Meals prepared by a menstruating woman had their taboos too. After eating such food, its ill effects were counteracted by a decoction of skullcap used as a wash.

Badger never had to resort to this cleansing, for the Swallowtail had ceased to menstruate and took over the cooking when She Smiles was "sick."

So Virginia had been taught all about the peculiar illness that would be with her most of her life. Nevertheless, she was unprepared for the pain. Becoming a woman was far more hurtful than she had been told.

A year after She Smiles and Badger had married, the young Indian woman gave birth to a son. Badger named him Little Deer. When his eyes opened, they were black, sparkling, and mischievous. Virginia adored him from the start, and as soon as they were permitted, she and Chipmunk were carrying him all over the town.

Two years later, She Smiles produced a daughter. The moment the baby smiled, everyone knew she would grow up just like her mother. Virginia called her Owl because of her huge eyes.

The years went by quickly, it seemed to Virginia. There was so much to do, so much to study and learn, that she never seemed to have a moment to spare. But it also seemed her life was full of friendship and love and happiness.

In 1601 she was fourteen years old. Virginia knew she had been born on August 15, 1587, that she had been seven and a half when she had been taken by the Indians. She knew from She Smiles and Badger that over seven years had passed since then, and therefore this was the year 1602; since summer was ending, sometime soon—she no longer knew the English months—she would be fifteen.

She was tall and beautiful, and supremely happy. She loved her parents and her brother and sister. She loved her friends, especially Chipmunk, who was now twelve and a lovely-looking child herself.

Virginia played her flute and dreamed. Alone in the dappled forest on this warm, lazy day, she dreamed of growing up and becoming the greatest medicine woman the tribe had ever known, marrying the most handsome brave she had ever seen, having such beautiful children that . . .

A hand came from behind her, tearing the flute from her lips. Hard fingers clamped over her mouth. Another hand encircled her waist and she was dragged to the ground.

She looked wildly around her. She was encircled by tall painted men with tomahawks and wooden swords clasped in their hands.

She had never seen them before. The right side of their heads was shaved, like the men of her own tribe. But these men had not touched the left side, so that the hair hung long there, like a woman's, to the shoulder.

But they did not look effeminate. On the contrary, their strange hair made them the most fearsome-looking creatures she had ever seen.

One of the Indians motioned for silence, and the grip on Virginia's mouth tightened. The deathly stillness continued for long minutes. Then she heard it. War cries. A moment later came the shattering screams of women.

The warrior who had signaled for silence waved his hand

and the others glided silently into the trees bordering the path to the town.

The noise of the fighting rang through the forest. Then the first of the women and children fleeing to safety came running along the path. Horrified, unable to cry out a warning, Virginia watched helplessly as the strange warriors fell on them, clubbing with their stone axes.

She fought and struggled to get free from the encircling arms. If only she could get to a bow, if she could get her sling out of her purse . . .

The man moved the hand over her mouth and she bit it. He let her go with a cry, but before she could move he struck her a great blow across the side of the head with his other fist and she collapsed into darkness.

The carnage continued.

10

Virginia slowly gained consciousness, aware of a bruised and aching head. She realizd she was clutched in someone's arms and started up, but the Swallowtail's voice urged her to keep still. She looked around slowly and saw that they were crouched against the side of Badger's lodge.

There was a tremendous tumult all around them, and Virginia struggled again to rise, but the old woman held her tightly.

"Don't look," she whispered fiercely in Virginia's ear.

Virginia stared at her and for the first time remembered what had happened to her in the woods. The last she recalled was being struck on the head.

"How did I get here?" she asked. "Who are those men?"

"One of them carried you here," said the Swallowtail, and her voice was loud in order to carry over the whooping and shouting. "I told them you were the chief's daughter and they left you here with me. The town has been attacked and we are defeated and captured." The Swallowtail lowered her head so the girl could not see the fear in her eyes.

Virginia tore herself loose and sat up. Now she could see across to the communal eating and dancing places and to the lodges beyond.

The strange Indians were everywhere, running in and out of lodges, carrying out pelts and sueded skins. Screeching and yelling, they smashed cooking pots and threw the few valuables the town possessed over the ground. Watching the cushions and bedding mats scatter, Virginia saw that the ground was covered in mounds.

Puzzled, she watched and saw one of the mounds move. Instantly, one of the painted strangers dropped the loot he was carrying and leaped onto it, his stone tomahawk crashing down again and again.

It was a body. Virginia looked around wildly. They were all bodies. The ground was covered with them. She grabbed the Swallowtail's arm fiercely.

"Where are our braves?" she shouted. The old woman simply shook her head silently. A terrible thought struck Virginia.

"Where is Badger? Where is my father?"

The Swallowtail pointed to one of the lodges.

"He is alive in there. He was wounded. Some of our braves are kept prisoner with him."

Virginia saw now that groups of women and children were crouched, like themselves, against the lodges, watching silently the orgy of mutilation and destruction. One or two of the lodges had been set afire, either deliberately or accidentally, and women and children were running to shelter at other houses.

She asked who the attackers were.

"They call themselves the Opossum," said the Swallowtail. "They come from the north."

Virginia realized that she and Swallowtail were alone at the werowance's lodge, and she went faint at the implication.

"Where is my mother?" she demanded. But the Swallowtail looked away and did not answer. Virginia clutched at the medicine woman's face and turned it around to look directly at her. Her voice held a note of hysteria.

"Little Deer and Owl? My brother and sister? Where are they?"

The Swallowtail looked at her with infinite sadness, and two tears welled out of her eyes and rolled slowly down her cheeks.

With a cry, Virginia pulled free of the old woman's arms and ran to the entrance of the lodge. The Swallowtail stumbled after her.

"No, Tall Girl!" she cried. "No!"

But Virginia stepped into the relative gloom inside. She looked around, her heart pounding with terror. She ran into her parents' sleeping alcove, calling, "Mother, Mother!"

Then she stopped suddenly. There was something lying on the floor. Something grotesque. Something that had been She Smiles. Lying beside the obscenely mutilated body were those of Little Deer and Owl.

Virginia screamed and started forward, but she was grabbed by the Swallowtail, suddenly and fiercely strong, and pulled back.

The medicine woman held her close.

"They did that after she was dead."

"Why?"

"Because your father killed many of them, even though he was taken by surprise. When he was knocked down with a blow on the head, they revenged themselves on his queen and their children."

After a little while, Virginia asked:

"Did you see this, Swallowtail?"

"Yes, my child."

The old woman led her from the lodge.

"I have gathered our herbs and medicines to take with us. They will not harm us, for we are medicine women.

"I will kill them!" Virginia said fiercely. "I will poison them. All of them."

The Swallowtail stroked her soothingly.

"It is the way, child."

"Then the way is wrong!"

The Swallowtail did not answer. They stood and watched while women and children were herded off to the fields to harvest the grain, the ripe and the green. They would be forced to carry this along with the other loot. The invaders pointedly ignored the two medicine women.

Virginia noted dully that the women all seemed to be the young ones. She asked why.

"They came for war and wives. They have no need for old women—or old men."

Virginia asked where all the old people were, but the Swallowtail again did not answer.

"And the children? Did they kill many children?"

"Many children. Yes."

Virginia could not absorb what she was being told. Only an hour or two ago she had left a bustling, happy town to walk in the forest. Now it was all gone. Chammayoac was no more. Nothing but dead bodies. Bodies of old women and men, and braves and children.

Dazedly she looked around at the awful carnage. Smoke from the burning lodges drifted across the open square and into the trees. There were so many things she wanted to ask. Why, why? Then she remembered.

"Chipmunk? Where is Chipmunk?"

"Chipmunk is dead, my child. All her family is dead. And the priest, Screams-Like-Wildcat. He tried to fight, but he was too old."

Virginia sank into a horrified stupor. She was only vaguely aware of being prodded into the long column of women plodding slowly north, bowed down with their loads. She did not see Badger. Behind her, the town of Chammayoac was put to the torch.

o

Virginia squatted with the Swallowtail and the other women captives and watched the torturing of the braves who had survived the destruction of Chammayoac.

She had almost no recollection of the forced march through the marshes and swampland into the territory of the Opossum people.

They had crossed the northern reaches of the Chawan

River where it divided, one branch turning west to become the Meherrin, the other north to be called the Nottaway. Dugouts had been waiting for them and they were ferried to the northern bank. Half the captors had stayed with the canoes, now piled with loot and scalps, while the other half escorted the laden captives along the marshy bank of the Nottaway.

The Swallowtail said later there must have been well over a hundred Opossum warriors in the surprise attack.

The captives had arrived the day before and had been led to a corner of the great square of the Opossum town. There they had collapsed with exhaustion, too weary to lament their sorry situation.

They were not unkindly treated by their captors, they were fed, and allowed to the river to drink and wash.

Dazed with shock throughout the long trek, Virginia had stumbled alongside the Swallowtail. The old woman had seen the looks the captors had given her ward and had kept her close by her side.

Although many of the captive women were attractive, Virginia's beauty stood out. She was almost as tall as a man, with straight shoulders and a tiny waist. Her glossy hair hung to her shoulders and was kept in place with a headband of plaited colored leather thongs. Unlike the other women, who wore only a fringed apron in front, Virginia was still attired in full-length clothing. When She Smiles had attempted to wean her from her dress to the moss crotch strap worn by girls up to ten years of age, Virginia had again become sunburned. So her new family had decided her body would have to be always fully covered.

What she now wore were several beautifully prepared skins sewn into one long piece with a hole in the center and fringed all around.

It slipped over her head, falling down to her knees at the back and front, and was tied at her waist with a leather belt stitched with colored beads.

When Virginia asked why all Indian clothes had long fringes around the edges, She Smiles had taken a piece of unfringed buckskin and started to rub it against the girl's leg. After a few moments, Virginia had called out in pain and looked ruefully at the red mark. Then She Smiles drew the fringe of Virginia's dress across her other leg. The fringe did not burn.

With her distinctive clothes, her uncut hair, her strange gray eyes, and her beauty, Virginia was the center of attraction for many of the Opossum braves.

But her chaperon, the Swallowtail, had no fear for her safety. She had told their captors that Virginia still had to pass through the maidens' long house. She would be given immunity.

Virginia was not thinking of herself or her future as she sat in the center of the group of women and saw the young Opossum girls make savage sport with the last of the Chammayoac braves.

Six had been taken prisoner, two were dead, and the third was being tied to the stake in the center of the square. About fifty feet from the stake sat the werowance and his elders and chief warriors. Beside them were the chief's wives and children, and all around clustered the rest of the tribe, children held on their fathers' shoulders for a better view of the spectacle.

Virginia looked at them listlessly; there must have been between three and four hundred people crammed into the square—it was a large town, she thought, with many warriors and lodges. Compared to it, her own town of Chammayoac was small, so quiet and so poor.

There was some commotion at the chief's dais, and for a moment his eyes turned to the corner where the captives sat despondently.

He made a sign, and a brave approached the captives. "Which one is Tall Girl?" he demanded harshly.

The Swallowtail rose to her feet.

"Who seeks her?" she asked. She had no intention of allowing these people, although her conquerors, to address her as though she were a common field worker.

"The werowance of Chammayoac, Badger, wishes to commune with her before he dies," the brave answered. "My chief has given permission."

Virginia threw off her lethargy instantly and bounded to her feet.

"I am Tall Girl," she said.

The brave looked at her with some surprise. He had not expected one so young. But he simply said, "Follow me," and turned away.

Virginia, without a backward glance at the Swallowtail, wended her way through the seated women and hurried after him.

At a small lodge behind the killing post he stopped and spoke to the sentry. Then he gestured her inside and stalked away.

Virginia stepped gingerly through the doorway. In the gloom she could see three figures lying on the floor, bound hand and foot. It was easy to recognize Badger's squat, muscular frame, and she rushed forward, throwing herself down beside him and cradling his head in her arms.

"Father, Father," she whispered. "I will help you to escape and we shall flee from this place—"

But Badger cut her off. "No, my child. I cannot escape and leave my braves here to face death alone. It is the fate of the captured warrior to die, otherwise my spirit will not rest."

She argued and pleaded with him but he kept repeating, "Listen, you must listen, I have something to tell you," until finally she fell silent.

Then he told her of her past, of finding her alone in the forest, of knowing she belonged to a distant and very different tribe. He lowered his head when he told her he did not know what happened to her first parents, not meeting her eyes as he spoke.

They talked for a long time, not needing to keep their voices low because the torture outside had begun and the crowd was roaring its applause and merriment, oblivious to all else.

The third captive had been tied to the stake. Two girls about seventeen approached him, holding skewers, to which long rawhide thongs were fastened. One of the girls slipped in the pool of blood and entrails around the stake and the assembly shrieked with laughter.

The captive stood unmoving as they pinched the pectoral muscles of his breast with the fingers of one hand while with the other they ran the skewers through the fold, deep into flesh and sinew.

Then they pulled the cord through to the halfway mark.

The crowd grew quiet, enthralled, wondering how this prisoner would comport himself. The first two had died without begging for mercy.

The girls looked at each other and smiled. The prisoner tilted his head back and looked at the darkening sky. His song grew louder.

The girls turned and ran full tilt toward the chief's dais, thin ropes held over their shoulders. When the ropes tightened, they came to a complete stop, falling suddenly on their backs. The thongs had come loose, torn right through the prisoner's breasts. The crowd roared. Two other girls approached the brave and the ritual began again. The prisoner continued to sing his death song, and the throng went still again, awaiting the next part of the ceremony.

Inside the lodge Badger talked quietly, calmly, as if he were in his own lodge. As he spoke the name Manteo, Virginia started.

"I have heard of him. My parents said—" She stopped, confused.

"You remember your past, Tall Girl?" Badger said, pained at this revelation.

"Yes, Father. I remember where I was born, where my people came from across the great sea, in a town where the lodges are built seven and eight upon each other. So high that when they sit in rows, the top ones meet the sky."

"You have always known of this other life?" he asked.

Virginia started to explain all she had hidden in her heart for so many years, but Badger interrupted.

"You must escape from here, Tall Girl. That is why I called for you. Find Manteo and go back to your people. Do you know where Manteo lives?"

"On an island called Croatoan across a great salt lake. It lies in the path of the sun from Askopo, the town where first you brought me."

Outside, the crowd was howling. The captive at the stake had been rent from breast to genitals. Now his fingers and toes were being cut off.

"Then go there, Tall Girl. Go south to the lands of the Moratuc, where you will be received because your father was the werowance Badger. If they cannot help you to find Manteo, go farther south to the Secotan tribe and tell them She Smiles was your mother. They will help."

"But how can I do it without you?" Virginia asked, holding close to him.

"By doing all I have taught you," Badger said. "Were you not taught the bow by the great warrior Badger? Did he not make you a great hunter and tracker? Did not the priest teach you to speak the language of the birds?"

She said nothing, and he spoke again.

"You must steal a bow and a full quiver of arrows. If you must kill a brave to get your weapons, hide his body so that it will not be found. Take also a knife and tomahawk. And your healing herbs and potions, for a medicine woman is always welcome in a town."

Outside, the roaring continued but neither Virginia nor Badger paid any mind.

"I cannot do this alone," Virginia said.

Badger closed his eyes. He had lost his wife and two younger children. Soon he himself would die. He wanted this daughter to survive. She *had* to live.

"Do you have your knife?" he asked her.

From one of her purses, Virginia withdrew the stone knife she used for chopping herbs.

"Here is what you will do, my daughter. You will cut the bonds that tie my hands. As the chief, I shall be the last to be taken to the torture post. When the next two braves are gone—and that shall be soon—I will cut the bonds around my ankles and free the one remaining warrior.

"Together, he and I will overpower the guard, take his weapons, and kill the Opossum werowance.

"Then his guards will slay me, but I shall die in battle as befitting a warrior, not tortured to death by women like some creature of the field.

"When you see me come out of this lodge, you must

make your escape. All eyes will be on me and you will be able to get away. Do you understand, my child?"

"They will follow me, Father."

"It will be many hours before they notice your absence. In the forest, you will use your rabbit shoes to hide any traces of where you have gone."

She nodded, looking fearfully toward the entrance of the lodge. The guard was mesmerized by the death spectacle. Badger turned on his side and Virginia quickly cut his bonds.

"Go now, my daughter. Go quickly, for the end has come."

At the stake, the victim had finally died. He was cut down and thrown aside to be tossed into the fire later.

Virginia slipped her knife under Badger's body and held him tightly.

"Good-bye, Father," she said. Despite all her training, tears were pouring down her face.

"Good-bye," whispered Badger.

She rose quickly and stumbled to the door.

Her head held low to hide her face, she crossed the entrance and hurried back to where the Swallowtail anxiously awaited her.

But no one noticed her passage. The mob was howling for the next victim.

11

Virginia and the Swallowtail divided their herbs and medicines into two hide satchels, the old woman insisting Virginia take all the copper and shell beads the Swallowtail kept in a pouch tied inside her skin wrap.

"You will need them to pay for canoes to cross rivers, and for guards to escort you through countries where there is war. But use your skills as medicine woman so that you are well lodged and fed—and do not hesitate to demand payment in beads, copper if there be any, for it will sometimes be necessary to pay for your survival."

As the Swallowtail rattled on with advice, the enormity of what she was about to attempt began to penetrate Virginia's numbing sorrow over Badger's death.

How could she disarm a brave and travel weeks, months, perhaps, across unknown territory? She had never been without parents to protect her before. She tried to communicate her fears to the medicine woman.

The Swallowtail took both Virginia's hands in hers and spoke urgently.

"Listen, Tall Girl. You must obey your father and go. You will live to find whatever it is you have come among the People to find."

As she said the last, she gave the girl a shrewd look that made Virginia think the medicine woman knew more about her than she had ever let on.

"Now, choose the brave whose weapons you will take. Quickly, for the time is near." The Swallowtail pointed. "Look!"

Virginia glanced in the direction the Swallowtail was pointing and saw the guard go inside the lodge where Badger was held prisoner.

"Quick, Tall Girl. Let us move in back of the women."

They crawled to the rear and squatted while Virginia looked at the braves guarding the women. There was one standing almost directly behind the group.

"That one, she whispered.

"Then quickly, my child, for soon Badger will sing his death song, the death song of the Opossum werowance."

Virginia hugged the Swallowtail close to her.

"One day I shall come back for you," she said.

The Swallowtail smiled.

"I will stay alive until then, Tall Girl."

Virginia rose and, without a backward glance, strode up to the guard who stood nearest, heavily armed with bow and quiver, tomahawk and wooden sword. He put his hand out, indicating that she must stop.

"Where are you going?" he asked.

"*Sheik-in,*" she answered, using the crude word for relieving oneself.

The brave smirked.

"I will accompany you to see you do not try to escape," he said. This was exactly what Virginia had wanted him to do.

She led the way into the trees.

"Why do you go so far?" he called after her.

"Because I am a virgin," she said over her shoulder, and he laughed.

She stopped eventually next to a tree and lowered her bag to the ground. She stepped behind the foliage, withdrawing her sling and slipping a heavy, round stone into it. Then she stepped out again.

"Watch me, brave warrior," she called, and swung the sling.

The stone hit him between the eyes and he slowly fell backward onto the ground. Virginia dragged his heavy body into the undergrowth, pulling the full quiver off him and tearing the ax from his belt. She hid them with the bow and sword and her own bag in a bush. Then she returned to examine the brave.

A large lump on his forehead was rapidly turning blue. How long would he remain unconscious?

She decided it would be long enough, and slipped back to the edge of the crowd of women, where she sat down behind the Swallowtail.

The old woman reached back to touch Virginia's leg.

The girl had returned just in time. The crowd was applauding the death throes of the victim at the stake when two men burst out of the prisoners' lodge. Virginia's heart began to pound.

One of the men carried the guard's bow, with an arrow already nocked. He loosed it at the nearest Opossum brave and the man screamed and grabbed with both hands at the shaft protruding from his belly. The prisoner slipped another arrow from the quiver as Badger, sword in one hand, tomahawk in the other, started across the square.

He leaped over the blood and gore surrounding the killing stake as he headed for the dais of the Opossum werowance.

The chief rose to his feet and tried to leap aside, but Badger was upon him, the sword slashing the man's throat open, almost decapitating him with one mighty backhand blow. Then Badger was among the elders and other warriors, hacking and slashing, the war cry bubbling from his open mouth.

There was instant pandemonium. Two hundred braves rushed to the dais to avenge their chief and stop the killer. The guards around the women ran forward to help.

"Go now, my child," said the Swallowtail. "Go, hurry."

Virginia hugged the old woman.

"*Nouwmais, Namankanois*." I love you, Swallowtail.

She ran into the woods, collected her bag and weapons, and made her way through the trees until she found a path leading north.

From the purse at her waist carrying her English mother's tortoiseshell comb, she withdrew a pair of moccasins made from rabbit skins with the fur outside.

She tied her bag securely at her shoulder, the quiver at her back, the ax at her waist. She threw the sword into the bushes. It was too long and unwieldy for her. With the bow in one hand and the slippers in the other, she walked along the path, thumping her bare feet down hard, leaving distinct impressions.

She walked this way for about fifty feet then stopped, slipped on the moccasins, and walked backward for a few yards, treading very carefully, looking at the ground as she did so. Satisfied that the soft rabbit-skin shoes had left no tracks, she stepped into the trees and headed in a wide circle to take her clear of the Opossum town.

Anyone following her would see her footsteps vanish suddenly and completely in the middle of the path.

That night, as she lay by a stream, lonely and hungry, thinking of Badger and She Smiles, Little Deer and Owl, Chipmunk and Wolf, Screams-Like-Wildcat, all dead, and the Swallowtail she had left behind, she sobbed bitterly. Terrified and alone in a strange place, she cried herself to sleep.

In the lonely days ahead, as she thought of where she was going, to find Manteo, who had known her as a child, and enlist his help to seek the great ships with the white sails that would take her to the wonderful land called England, her spirits gradually lifted.

She had a vague idea that her trip would take her at most a few months. It was two years before she was to reach Manteo's home on the island of Croatoan.

There was a profusion of dugout canoes beached near one of the towns she passed, and Virginia was able to push the smallest one into the river and paddle downstream. She hid by day and paddled by night, making, by necessity, slow progress.

She shot small game, by arrow or sling, and cooked them at night before returning to the river. She made fire by rubbing a pointed stick furiously into the specially made hollow in a piece of dry tinder. When the wood began to glow, she pushed dry moss onto the incandescence and blew it alight. She had made fire for many years and now did it almost effortlessly.

As the river widened, she picked up speed and, feeling she was now outside the reach of the Opossum people, began to travel by day. Almost immediately, she paddled around a bend in the river and into a host of fishing canoes and found herself taken to Chawanoac, the main town of the Chawan River people.

She was treated kindly and was the object of much curiosity because of the color of her eyes. But they would not allow her to continue south to the Moratuc tribe. They said she was too young to travel alone and should stay until she was older.

When she insisted that she was a medicine woman, they refused to believe her, but it was agreed that she could live with an old medicine woman of the tribe, a woman called Otter for she had once been a renowned swimmer. As soon as Otter discovered that Virginia did indeed understand the use of herbs, drugs, and potions, she eagerly accepted her. Virginia had found another home. But the drive to continue traveling until she found the big ships was all-consuming.

Compared to Chammayoac, Badger's town, and even the

larger Opossum town from which she had escaped, Chawanoac was a mighty city. She learned that it could field seven hundred warriors in battle.

It was so large that she never saw the werowance, who was called a king, nor was even allowed in the vicinity of his great lodge.

When she told Otter she was a princess and added, lying, that the weapons she bore were those of her father who had died in battle, the old woman smiled.

How many warriors did her father's town have, she asked. When Virginia told her, she said:

"My child, a town so small is hardly a town. The werowance of such a town is only a small chief. The daughter of such a werowance is merely another girl. Do not be angry, child," she added as she saw the light of outrage in Virginia's eyes. "You loved your father, and he was a great warrior, but you are not a princess here. If you are a good assistant to me, you will be happy."

During her stay at Chawanoac, Virginia came to understand what Otter had tried to tell her. She was from a very small town and would not be accepted as a special person. But while she was under the protection of Otter, she would be treated with respect.

On her own, she was just a girl without a family, a nobody. When she thought of the dreams of glory that her family and friends in her beloved Chammayoac had held for her, her heart ached for those who had never known how lowly they were regarded in the great towns of their neighbors.

One night the following spring she stole a dugout and escaped downriver. In the town of Tandakwomuc, at the confluence of the Chawan and Moratuc rivers, she paid a handful of her precious copper beads to be ferried up the swift-flowing Moratuc River to the town of Moratuc itself.

There, the name Badger evoked more interest than it had done in Chawanoac, and they insisted she stay.

She stayed only long enough to earn more strings of beads by her healing arts and fled at harvesttime, near her sixteenth birthday. Two months later she reached the main town of the Secotan, the people of her mother, She Smiles.

She was received with great kindness and sympathy. When she said her mother had arranged that she be trained in healing by a medicine woman, they believed her and allowed her to practice her art. She was careful not to mention Badger, or say she was a princess, and tried to be as unassuming as was possible for someone with her beauty.

She had taken Otter's well-meaning advice to heart.

She discovered the Secotan knew of Croatoan Island, that it lay east of the mouth of the Secotan River, but that no canoe was large enough to attempt the journey across the great bay at that point. The only route was through the lands of the Pomouik and the Neusiok to the south, where the islands approached the mainland.

It would take many beads to be guided through this unknown territory, so Virginia worked hard to earn them. She exchanged all her payments of skins and cooking pots for beads—copper ones whenever she could find them.

She remained until the following summer, then arranged and paid for an escort through the great marshes of the Pomouik and to be ferried across the mighty Neus River.

At last Virginia turned east and made her way to the coast. Croatoan lay some distance to the north and she pledged the last of her beads to the ten-man crew of a large dugout to take her there.

She arrived on Croatoan in August 1604, just a few days before her seventeenth birthday.

Manteo, the chief of the Croatoan, was amazed when Virginia told him who she was. He stood speechless, staring at her. Finally, he asked:

"You are truly the grandchild, born on Roanoke Island, of my friend John White?"

When she said again she was, he engulfed her in his arms and she shed tears of joy. Later, she asked him where the great ships were that would take her to England.

"There are no ships, Virginia," he said. It was the first time she had been called by her English name in ten years. "Your grandfather went to England just after you were born to fetch food and supplies, but he never returned. And we have never seen the ships again."

Virginia Dare was aghast.

"But how will I go to London?"

"Most of the English on Roanoke—those still alive—left to sail to Chesapiuc in the north with the small ship they had. That was where they talked of going when your grandfather left. So that is probably where the ships have been sailing to all these years."

"In the north?" Virginia said. "But I have come from the north, and the journey has taken me two whole years. How can I go back again?"

Manteo took her hands and spoke soothingly.

"My child, you will stay this winter with me on my island. In the spring, when the winds and the seas are calm, I will send you with an escort to find your people in the north.

"Until then, you will tell me of your life since I saw you as a baby, and I will tell you about England."

12

Virginia sat in the center of the great dugout as it was paddled smoothly north up the great sound, staying close to the shores of the outer bank islands.

There were twenty rowers, and each had his weapons beside him. It was the largest and deepest canoe Virginia had ever seen. Manteo told her it had sailed many times across the sound to the mouth of the Secotan River. They were passing Hatarask Island and were nearing Roanoke, the island where she had been born. Soon she would be with the English, the people she had yearned to see for so long.

The months on Croatoan had been exciting but disquieting, and she had left puzzled and apprehensive.

Manteo, whose name meant Hawk in English, had treated Virginia with great respect as well as affection. She was given young women to look after her needs, soft cushions to relax upon, and the finest skins to sleep on.

He took her into the very bosom of his family, two wives, several children, and a host of relatives.

There was a feast in her honor the first night she arrived. Then, with his entire family gathered around, Manteo insisted she tell all that had happened to her since she could remember.

It took several days for Virginia to tell her story, for she was surrounded by avid listeners who constantly asked her to repeat parts that they particularly liked.

Then it was Manteo's turn to speak, to tell Virginia of his travels to London, a town with more people living in it than all the True People together.

Virginia was spellbound. She had been told many things about London by her first parents. She knew the river on which the great city stood was called the Thames, that there was a great bridge across it called London Bridge, that a great Christian church called St. Paul's Cathedral stood high over the city, and that a mighty edifice called the Tower of London dominated the river.

But she had been a child when she was told these things, and she no longer knew what a cathedral was, or understood how a bridge could be built over a wide river, or what they meant by the Tower. She pressed Manteo to tell her over and over of these things.

She was intrigued by the houses built one on top of the other, and demanded to know if the dwellers ever fell through the floors onto the people below, or if they had to tread very lightly to avoid such a calamity. Perhaps they wore rabbit-skin shoes, she suggested.

Manteo answered all her questions, but she felt he was holding something back, and pressed him to tell her what it was. But it was several weeks later, after she had settled in with his family, before he told her things that were to upset and even frighten her.

"The English people, the Christians," he began, "are not like the True People."

Virginia said she already knew that, and that the Iroquoian people were different from the Algonkian, too.

"It is because you wish to find the English and return with them to their country that I must warn you what they are like," Manteo went on as though she had not spoken. It was evident that what he was about to say had been on his mind for some time.

"I have seen that you are now a Person, one of the True People. If, after I have told you about the English, you decide to remain here and not seek them in Chesapiuc, you may stay as my daughter and be a princess of the Croatoan people."

He took some time trying to find the right words, but eventually it burst out of him.

"The English God, the Christian God, is *evil.*"

Virginia turned pale. Evil? How could Manteo, the friend of the English, who had been given the great honor of being taken, not once but twice, to the very heart of the English homeland, London, dare say such a thing about the Christian God! She found her shock turning to anger. How dare this untutored savage—

Sitting in the dugout traveling swiftly north to where she hoped to find the Christians from the Roanoke colony, Virginia remembered the angry scene that had followed.

"My father told me that the great Englishman Raleigh made you an English lord after you became a Christian," she told Manteo. "How can you turn against people who are your own?"

"It is true they made me a lord," Manteo said. "Lord of Roanoke and Dasemunkepeuc. Empty words, my child, for these places were not the property of the English to give. They belonged to the People who lived there.

"Can I make you queen of the Chawanoac people? No, for their land is not mine to give. But everywhere the English went, they declared the land to be theirs in the name of their queen and their Christian God. And the people who lived there had to leave and go elsewhere, leaving behind their hunting grounds and the good soil that grows corn."

"Perhaps the English who did this were simply bad people, different from the English in London and England," Virginia argued.

"They do the same in England, Virginia."

He tried to explain the class system to a girl who knew only that everything was shared. He told of the abject poverty he had seen in London, of the incredible filth.

"Everywhere there is disease and hunger. People who are crippled and deformed sleep in the streets because they have no lodges. And children beg for food."

"Why have the children no food?"

"I do not know," said Manteo. "I only know that the rich have food and the poor do not. And when the poor do not have food, they die, and their children are left in the streets to beg."

"Cannot the poor grown corn in the fields?" Virginia asked.

"They have no fields."

"Cannot they fish in the rivers and hunt the animals for food?"

"Only those who own the rivers and the lands and forest may hunt and fish in them."

"And the sea? Do the rich own the sea?"

"No, it is permitted to fish in the sea. But few people live near the sea. Before you came here to Croatoan, Virginia, did you live near the sea?"

He told her about prisons, and tried to explain the inconsistency of the debtors' prisons, where people who owed money could languish until they rotted if they could not pay their debts. The English did not understand, he said, that a man could not find the wherewithal to repay his debts unless he was free.

The very concept of debt, and money itself, bewildered Virginia.

He told her of the punishment for stealing. A hand or an ear cut off. Or branding with a hot iron.

"The Christian God is a cruel god, Virginia. He thinks only of punishment."

Virginia argued against this.

"My English parents told me that the Christian God is one of mercy. If your enemy strikes you on the cheek, you must forgive him and turn the other cheek so that he may strike that also."

That was true, admitted Manteo. That was what the Christian God said and what the Christians themselves boasted they would do, although he had not actually seen it happen.

They talked for days, Virginia becoming more confused and uncertain and, as a result, more adamant that Manteo had somehow misunderstood the English.

He told her how two ships had visited Croatoan in the English year 1584—Manteo remembered the date clearly—when his mother was queen. Manteo's tribe made friends with these English strangers, and Manteo himself agreed to accompany them back to their land across the great sea. On the long journey he was befriended by a man called John White, Virginia's grandfather.

"He was a good man," said Manteo, "and I met other good men, also. They taught me their language and I told them all I could about the land of the True People. In particular, they wanted to know what things could be taken from this land and sold in theirs.

"I did not understand then that the things they wanted to take were all the things belonging to the People."

He returned with another expedition the following year, when John White was the official artist. This was a large expedition of many ships and, Manteo estimated, about six hundred men, mostly sailors and soldiers, bringing about one hundred to settle in the new land under Governor Ralph Lane. Lane was a soldier, and a brutal one, said Manteo.

"The English were welcomed to the island of Roanoke and given land by the people there. But they did not grow corn and always expected the People, whom they called Indians, to feed them. When the People had no more corn to give, the English took it by force.

"All the English wanted to do was find *wassador*, copper, and pearls and other things they esteemed of value to take back to England.

"Because they were Christians and the Indians were not, the English thought the People should work for them, hunt and fish for them.

"Governor Lane ordered me to tell the People that if

they became Christians, they would be allowed to work in the fields to grow food for the English. This, he said, showed how merciful the Christian God was."

Wingina, the king of the Roanoke tribe, Manteo went on, grew tired of the brutal English treatment of his people and conspired against them. Lane retaliated savagely and Wingina and many of his braves were killed in a treacherous ambush.

"Everywhere they went, the English killed and spread disease."

The year after they arrived, the colony sailed back to England, unable, Manteo said, to coexist with the natives. He went with them, for now the Roanoke and other tribes considered him a renegade. The year after that, he sailed back, this time with John White as governor. White was bringing his pregnant daughter, Elinor, and her husband, Ananias Dare. The colony was supposed to go to the Chesapiuc, where the Indians were friendly.

But in July 1587, the one hundred fifteen colonists—including seventeen women, two of them pregnant, and nine children—were left on Roanoke Island, where they had landed through a navigational error.

The island was deserted, said Manteo. After the bloody reprisals against them by the former Governor Lane, the surviving Roanoke Indians had gone to their mainland town of Dasemunkepeuc.

But when they saw the old colonial village once more inhabited by the hated English, the Indians began slipping secretly across the water. Six days after the colony landed, George Howe became the first colonist to be killed by them.

White tried hard to make peace with the Indians, Manteo said, but they refused to come and parley with him. Their memory of their experiences at Lane's hands was still too strong. Manteo's own people, the Croatoans, had suffered because of their alliance with the bloodthirsty strangers. They had lost the friendship of many of the neighboring tribes, even as the English, eager to ambush and shoot Indians at the slightest provocation, had killed and wounded several of Manteo's own people.

Manteo was christened and made an English lord only a few days before Virginia Dare was born.

"There was a great feast in your honor," Manteo told her, "and another feast when a second child was born, although I forget to whom."

"He was the son of Dyonis and Margery Harvie; they called him John," said Virginia. "My English parents told me."

Shortly after Virginia's birth, Governor White sailed back to England to fetch more supplies. He never returned.

Manteo described the two years that followed White's decision to leave.

The English tried hard to survive on Roanoke, but Indian raids and disease reduced their strength by a half in the first year. Because of the hostile Indians, the colonists found it increasingly difficult to grow crops and hunt, especially since they had little expertise in either activity, being in the main builders and metal workers, not farmers or even country men.

Many wanted the colony uprooted and reestablished on the Chesapiuc, where the English originally intended to settle.

But the boat that had been left them, a pinnace, could carry only forty persons. With their supplies, arms, equipment, and livestock—poultry, pigs, and cows—moving would have meant at least three trips north.

It was pointed out that while the party at the northern landing stage would be growing in number, with scant means of feeding or taking care of itself, the group left behind would become steadily smaller and increasingly vulnerable to Indian attacks.

Faced with this dilemma, the remaining colonists did what men unsure of themselves have done since the world began. They did nothing. They voted to wait for the return of John White and his relief ships. But White did not come.

During the winter of 1588–89, they ate their livestock. Manteo managed to get supplies of corn from Croatoan, and several of his kinsmen stayed to fish and hunt for the colonists.

By the end of that winter, more had died, this time of starvation as well as disease.

As summer approached, with still no sign of John White, the Roanoke Indians recommenced their depredations. By this time the colonists had deserted their houses, withdrawing into the fort area, cutting trees to heighten the pallisade around it.

Then the Indians literally besieged the colony, shooting arrows over the ramparts constantly, attacking anyone who dared set foot outside.

The number of English was now down to twenty-seven souls—a dozen men, five women, and ten children, some of them babies, all of them weak from hunger and deprivation.

Belatedly, they realized they should have sailed away to the Chesapiuc the year before, when their number was double and they were much more fit.

Nevertheless, it was decided to attempt the trip at last.

This time, Virginia's parents were the only ones who refused to go. They would go to Croatoan and live with Manteo's mother's people until John White returned. Ananias Dare pointed out that if White returned to Roanoke and found no one, he might simply sail back to England, stranding the colonists on Chesapiuc forever. On Croatoan they would surely spot any relief ships and be able to contact them. Then they would sail to aid the rest of the colony.

The plan met with approval. The pinnace was loaded with whatever could be carried overland from the disembarkation point to the Chesapiuc, for there was no one with sufficient navigational skills and seamanship to dare risk taking it out to sea and into the bay of Chesapiuc.

Besides the twenty-four colonists and whatever food supplies remained, they took the rest of the copper, a couple of the small cannons, called falcons, and all the firearms, powder, and shot they could carry.

Ananias Dare carefully carved on the palisade entrance post the word "Croatoan," so that White would know where to look for him.

They waited until nightfall before setting out so that the

Roanoke Indians hiding in the forest would not see their departure and try to prevent it with a last-minute attack.

There were two small rowing boats with sails that the Dares and Manteo and his men would use to sail to Croatoan. The Dares loaded their equipment in one of the small boats. Manteo and his group were to row out at the head of the pinnace to lead it into the channel and point it in the direction where the Chesapiuc lay.

"Your parents were to wait until we returned," Manteo told Virginia. "But as we led the pinnace to safety, we were seen by lookouts of the Roanoke Indians. They must have known we were escaping, for they yelled in fury, running up and down the shore.

"I knew that once the pinnace was well offshore and its sail unfurled, no Indian canoe could catch it. So when the sail was let down, we called our good-byes, and hurried back for you and your parents.

"But you were gone."

Virginia explained what happened. Seeing the pinnace escape, the infuriated Indians had come running to the fort. Ananias Dare had only time to push off the boat and jump in after his terrified family.

In the darkness he lost all sense of direction and, after hours of sailing, they had grounded.

"We went ashore to hide, carrying our few possessions and gun, powder, and shot. At dawn, my father saw strange Indians examining the boat. Across the water he saw Roanoke Island and realized we had accidentally landed at Dasemunkepeuc, the Roanoke tribe's town on the mainland.

"He fled with us into the interior."

"If only I had returned to your father in time," Manteo said, his hand gently touching Virginia's hair. "How different it would have been."

"Yes," Virginia said, but her mind was on Manteo's description of the Roanoke colonists; evil, he had called them and their Christian God—but why? Although some Englishmen had behaved very badly toward the True People, she could not grasp all of Manteo's meaning. Surely, in the face of great adversity, during the last days of the colony, the English had behaved with special bravery.

"You must tell me what you mean by evil," she insisted to Manteo. "If I am to meet the English who were on Roanoke, I must know what they have done."

And Manteo told her. He described the last winter on the island. The corn was severely rationed by Ananias Dare and the other leaders. People were too weak to tend to the fish traps. No week passed without someone dying. The dead were buried outside the stockade, in shallow graves because no one had the strength to dig deep.

"It must have been going on for some time before your father and the others noticed that the graves were being opened and the bodies removed. At first, wild beasts were blamed. But there were no wolves on the island, the bears had all been shot and eaten, and small animals could not remove large human bodies.

"Then the English said it must be the Roanoke Indians. But the True People never violate the resting place of the dead, as you know."

Virginia nodded.

"The next time someone died—a woman—a watch was set near the grave. Your father and the other leaders concealed themselves behind tall trees and waited.

"It was a bitterly cold night with strong winds. They waited for hours, chilled to the bone, not daring to move lest they reveal their hiding place. Some of the men could hold out no longer and returned to their homes. But Ananias Dare and two others would not give up.

"It seemed near morning when finally a shadowy movement was detected near the grave. At first, they could not tell if the shapes were animal or human. Then the predators began to dig up the corpse and it was clear that men had come to desecrate the newly buried body.

"Your father and the others watched. There was no sound except for the wind howling in their ears and the shovels hitting the hard earth covering the coffin. Then Ananias Dare opened fire and the two men with him quickly followed. Several of those digging up the grave fell, although one man was able to drop his shovel and escape.

"Your father and the others ran to the grave. When they lit the torches, they could clearly see that the men around the burial site were English colonists.

"The following morning a search of all the living areas brought forth the remains of several corpses. A limb, a hand . . ." Manteo swallowed, his gorge rising, unable to go on for the moment.

"The English were eating their own dead," he burst out finally, not looking at Virginia as he spoke.

Virginia could not believe what Manteo had just told her. The horror of the act was beyond anything she had known from either her English parents or the Indians who had taken her as a child.

She shook her head no—no!—then angrily faced Manteo. "Did you see this?" she demanded. "Did you see it with your own eyes so you know it is true?"

"Your father told me what happened at the grave," Manteo said. "And I went with Ananias Dare the morning he and the other leaders searched the living places. I saw that, Virginia, and I will never forget it.

"Stay here with us," he pleaded once again. "You shall be my daughter. I promised your parents I would take care of you. The daughter of my friend Ananias Dare will be as my own. Are you not happy here? Do I and my people not treat you with kindness and respect?"

"Yes," Virginia said, "yes." She was very tempted to accept Manteo's offer, for indeed her days in his village had been very happy. And she was tired of running, searching for a place that could become her home.

But the English were *her* people. Even her Indian father told her to return to them. Now that Badger and She Smiles were no more, now that Virginia could never return to the home she shared with them in Chammayoac, she wanted to be with the English.

She had never lost the memory of her first parents, their warmth and kindness, the love they had given her. Her first parents were English and what they had said about the colonists and England and London was so different from what Manteo told her.

Perhaps Manteo had seen matters through the eyes of a stranger. Hadn't Virginia herself considered the behavior of the True People peculiar when she first found herself among them? The colonists could not have done what

Manteo said, not the people her English parents spoke about.

And hadn't her English father denounced the Indians as cannibals?

Now, as the dugout was rounding Roanoke Island, Virginia remembered once again her first father's words about the Indians. Cannibals, he had said. Heathens. Unbelievers in the one true God.

The paddlers were pointing out the spot where the fort had been, where Virginia was born seventeen years earlier.

Virginia stared at the spot until the canoe turned the bend and she could no longer see it. Her birthplace confirmed the rightness of her decision. She *was* English.

As the boat carrying Virginia moved up the Currituck River, the Indians paddling the dugout were becoming unaccountably nervous. They paddled until the banks were so close it was obvious they were nearing the source of the river. The leader ordered the canoe ashore. Fires were lit and fish cooked while some of the braves reconnoitered the area.

When they came back, their leader sat at the main fire and talked in low tones with his braves, looking several times in Virginia's direction.

Finally, he approached her.

"I do not recognize this region," he said. "Tomorrow, we shall go back down the river to seek the correct landmarks."

Virginia nodded. She realized he had lost his way but was not perturbed. It had been so many years since she had seen her English kinsmen, a few more days could cause no harm.

She awoke the next morning alone. The canoe with its twenty rowers had gone. They had slipped away in the night, leaving her only a platter of broiled fish and crushed corn.

Virginia's initial shock at being left on her own was quickly replaced by a determination to get to the English by herself. But her anger at Manteo's braves did not dissipate even as she tried to puzzle out a reason for their odd behavior. What could have made them desert her, disobeying their chief's orders to take her to her destination? What had they seen during last night's scouting expedition that could account for this? What would they tell Manteo—lie that they had left her with the English?

She was not afraid to be on her own, only angry at finding herself in this predicament. She had traveled to Manteo's village alone and she was certain she could find the way to Chesapiuc. Still, she churned with her betrayal by Manteo's people.

She decided the way to go was still north and, as the sun was rising on the horizon, she set off, her sack firmly strapped to her back, her quiver and bow in her hand.

She was chewing on moistened crushed corn, her noon meal, when she saw the hunters. They saw her at the same time, and came charging toward her with whoops and yells, gathering around her. They were tall, heavily muscled men, fiercely painted, with the hair on the left side of their heads falling to their shoulders, the other side shaved so as not to interfere with their bowstrings.

Now she understood why Manteo's braves had run away. They were clearly outnumbered by these fighters and did not want to face certain death.

The strangers took away Virginia's bow and quiver, but nothing else, taking her with them as they traveled slowly through the great swamps. They would eventually deliver her to their chief, the great king Powhatan, who ruled a vast empire surrounded by his wives, nobles, and bodyguards, and to whom tribute was sent from all his vassal tribes.

13

He was a handsome, well-built man in his sixties. His face was round and fat, and lined by many winters. His expression was sad rather than stern, as Virginia had expected.

He wore only a fringed apron, like an ordinary brave, but had many ropes of pearls and copper beads strung around his neck.

Virginia looked down at the three egret feathers that showed her own rank, then at the group of men in front of her. Her face was utterly without emotion, her eyes gazing directly at the king.

Powhatan was surprised at the captive girl's serenity. People in audience before him were inevitably frightened of his power and savage reputation, groveling and trembling before him. He stared at the girl, trying to decide her fate.

He could not know that Virginia's heart was beating wildly inside her body, could not guess that she had to summon all the cunning taught her by Screams-Like-Wildcat to remain passive before this fierce warrior who could end her life by a careless wave of his hands.

She had told Powhatan that she was the daughter of a werowance, explaining what had happened to Badger and his tribe. She said she had been wandering the forests since her escape from the Opossum. She offered her considerable knowledge of medicine in exchange for her life.

She had not begged, not groveled, not pleaded with the great chief for mercy. She had stated her case quietly and now waited for him to speak.

She had been told where she was: in the center of an empire of thirty tribes, every one of whose members was committed to obeying, on pain of death, the great king Powhatan. He ruled over some ten thousand people, with more than three thousand warriors at his command.

Virginia had tried to imagine ten thousand people and failed. She had grown up in a tribe of one hundred and fifty, knowing everyone by name. When she remembered her old town of Chammayoac and Badger's thirty warriors, she felt dwarfed and especially helpless in her new surroundings. But none of this showed in her face or her bearing.

At last Powhatan spoke.

"You will live in my household and be handmaiden to my daughter Pocahontas."

A guard led Virginia away.

She would learn much from the little girl who seemed to be her father's favorite. Within the household Pocahontas was called *Mato-aka*, Favorite Daughter, and her mother, Winganusquaw, which meant Good Woman, was also greatly in Powhatan's favor although the king had many wives.

She Smiles and Badger had been monogamous parents, and they had raised their children in a tight family circle. The Swallowtail was a sort of grandmother and various aunts and uncles formed an extended family.

Some of the men in Chammayoac had more than one wife, but Powhatan kept a dozen wives at any one time. Pocahontas said they all went with him on hunting expeditions, accompanying the king when he traveled inside his domain, gathering tribute from his vassal tribes.

When he became tired of a wife, he gave her away as a present to a deserving minor werowance or to a warrior, Pocahontas told Virginia loftily. "My father has had at least a hundred wives," the child added, "but my mother is the favorite."

At first Virginia thought the nine-year-old's chattering was mere boasting, but she gradually came to realize that Pocahontas had no reason to try to impress her. The little girl saw Virginia as merely the daughter of a petty chieftain while Pocahontas herself was the child of a mighty king and therefore a true princess.

Pocahontas often took Virginia to watch her father receive visitors. Some of these chiefs and their attendants wore animal heads fitted over their own, wolves and cougars being the favorites. Others wore tiny colored snakes around their necks, the snakes kissing their masters' lips from time to time.

These fierce men groveled abjectly before Powhatan, amply demonstrating the king's power over them.

Virginia saw some of Powhatan's summary justice, and

quailed at the thought of what might have happened to her had the king been offended instead of merely surprised at her seemingly insolent calm when they first met.

A man who interrupted Powhatan while the werowance was speaking was beaten unconscious with clubs by two bodyguards. The king ordered men executed regularly, the method depending on how deep their transgression or perhaps simply the depth of Powhatan's displeasure. Virginia never quite grasped the reason for the sentences.

Some of the condemned men had their heads placed on a sacrificial stone and their brains beaten out. For certain criminals a more elaborate death was prepared. A shallow round pit was dug and filled with burning wood coals. Then the condemned, bound hand and foot, were thrown into the red-hot pit and burned alive.

A third method was reserved for any well-known enemy. He was tied to a tree and the executioner cut off his arms and legs with sharpened mussel shells or razor-sharp reeds. After the skin was sliced from the man's head and face, he was disemboweled, and finally burned along with the tree.

Pocahontas found Virginia pale and trembling after seeing such an execution, and Virginia confessed she was afraid of the king's wrath.

"Why should you be afraid of my father?" the child asked. "I told him I like you. As long as you are good to me, I will see that no harm comes to you."

Virginia knew this was not meant as a threat, but was a statement of fact. Her charge was not malevolent, merely aware of her position and power.

Pocahontas was a lively, spirited child. She kept Virginia occupied from early morning on, demanding stories, walks, and games, ever new songs and dances. She did not make Virginia's life especially miserable, but neither did she help it become happy or serene in any way.

As her days of captivity grew into weeks and then months, Virginia's bouts of nightly depression and daily frustration grew. She could see no way out of Powhatan's empire, yet her yearning to escape never left her. She wanted desperately to go to Chesapiuc; she had not traveled so far, faced such difficulties, to be thwarted now.

But she was never alone. She slept in Pocahontas's lodge, next to the child. During the day Pocahontas seemed scarcely able to leave her alone. Virginia realized that the constant attention was a sign of the little girl's affection, but she could not bring herself to feel warmth toward the self-important, endlessly chattering Pocahontas.

Every time the girl airily summoned Virginia to fetch some water or move a mat, the young woman remembered with a pang the slow, sweet smile she used to see on the face of her Indian sister, Owl, when little Owl wanted something from an adult.

Remembering Owl, not much younger than Pocahontas when she was killed, brought tears to Virginia's eyes. She would turn quickly so Pocahontas wouldn't notice but at night, in the dark, the memories would come flooding back and her eyes would fill to overflowing. She would burst into sobs remembering the family she had lost.

Her Indian mother, She Smiles, so loving and patient with the lost, frightened child Virginia had been. And Badger, fearless and brave, a pillar of strength to his tribe as well as his family. And the Swallowtail—where was that kindly old woman now? Did the Opossum treat her well? Was she able to accept a lowly station in life?

It was in the Swallowtail's lodge that Badger had first tried a game with Virginia in an effort to form a bond between himself and the little stranger.

Fresh tears sprang to Virginia's eyes as she remembered the usually somber Badger getting down on all fours and crawling along the smooth floor, pretending to sniff under the sleeping benches.

Chipmunk had run up to the crawling Badger and given him a playful though none too gentle whack across the buttocks. Still on all fours, Badger had whirled, hissing and snarling, pretending to charge at Chipmunk. The little girl dropped her stick and with a shriek leaped on the bed where Virginia was sitting, throwing her arms around the English girl in mock fear.

She Smiles and the Swallowtail had both been helpless with laughter at Badger's antics until the younger woman suddenly noticed that Virginia had not entered into the spirit of the fun and was, in fact, frightened.

She shouted "Stop!" above the din, and went over to the bed. Virginia was trembling as She Smiles picked her up and held her. Badger got to his feet, signaling the end of the play.

"She did not understand that it was only a game," She Smiles told Badger.

Badger stroked Virginia's hair gently. He saw the tears in her eyes. She was frightened of *him.* Later, he would tell Virginia that somewhere deep in him there was a pain when he realized this. He did not want his new daughter to fear him. Only warriors should fear warriors.

Virginia smiled at the memory. How dear Badger had been, how kind and gentle despite his stern exterior. How different from Powhatan, who seemed to enjoy cruelty.

Virginia had been captured by Badger as she had been by Powhatan. But Badger had taken her into his family while Powhatan made her a slave. It was a long time before Virginia was able to fall asleep that night.

Then another prisoner was brought into Powhatan's town, different from any man Virginia had ever seen.

Pocahontas told her of the stranger. Virginia had not been allowed near the king's lodge this time and had not seen when the captive was brought before Powhatan. But his daughter had mingled with the others and had come rushing back to tell Virginia her news.

"He has hair of no color, like the healing clay, and it is not cut off on one side, like a warrior's—"

Virginia interrupted. "His eyes. How do his eyes look?"

Pocahontas looked carefully at Virginia.

"He has strange eyes. You have strange eyes, too, Tall Girl. But you are a Person and you told us all your tribe have eyes like you. He is very tall, but his skin is not like a Person's. It is not of our color, Tall Girl.

"It is like"—Pocahontas tried to find the words—"like the magnolia flower."

The magnolia flower, thought Virginia. White and pink. Could it be? She grabbed Pocahontas's hands.

"I want to see this stranger," she said. "Take me to him.

Please," she added, when she saw the rebellious pout starting on the little girl's lips.

"He has been taken to the prisoner's lodge," Pocahontas said, "to await my father's pleasure." She had become haughty. Virginia's heart sank.

"What will they do to him?"

"Execute him, of course."

"But why? What has he done to anger your father?"

"He is a trespasser. He was captured on my father's land without permission."

Virginia wondered desperately how she could get the child on her side.

"Where is he from, this stranger?" she asked.

"He comes from Menapacant, the town of my father's brother, the King Opekankano, who sent him here for my father to see."

"Where did he come from before that?"

"No one knows, for no one can understand his language. But Opekankano sent word that he was found on the shore of the great sea of the Chesapiuc."

Was he from a ship, Virginia wondered. A great ship with white sails?

"If *you* ask to see him, the guards will not refuse you," she told Pocahontas. "They dare not refuse you, the favorite daughter of the great King Powhatan."

The little girl's chin rose with pride. "Yes, they cannot refuse *me*," said Pocahontas. "Come, Tall Girl, we shall inspect the stranger together."

The child gave imperious orders to the huge, painted warrior guards standing before the prisoner's lodge, and the captive was brought out. At the sight of him, Virginia melted with pity.

He was dressed in the ragged remnants of what appeared to have been a shirt with a ruff, and balloon trousers that ended at the knees. But only someone who had seen such clothes before would have recognized them for what they were.

Virginia's English father had worn similar clothing.

His legs and feet were bare, scratched with thorns and bitten by mosquitos. The arms of his shirt had been torn off, and his wrists were cut and bleeding from the leather thongs that had bound him and had obviously just been removed.

He was taller than she was, as tall as his guards, who were the tallest men Powhatan could find in his kingdom. But he was stooped with fatigue, and he held his hands crossed in front of him, as though to ease the pain.

Then she looked up at his face, and the pity was replaced with something else, something that made her heart pound alarmingly.

His hair was unkempt and hung to his shoulders, but through the dirt its color shone through—the color of the morning sun. The golden color of her English mother's hair. And his eyes were the blue of the empty summer sky. Her mother's eyes.

He looked at her and in his face, and in his eyes, she read the hopelessness of his situation.

In his look she saw the appeal, not for pity, for his eyes were too fierce for that, but for understanding.

She felt the pulse beating at her throat. She Smiles had told her that this might happen one day, but Virginia had never imagined the strength of the emotion, the almost physical blow.

She felt her nipples becoming erect, and something stirring at the very pit of her stomach. Her legs no longer belonged to her and all sound around her went dim.

He was beautiful.

"Tall Girl!"

The peremptory call and the tug at her dress brought Virginia back to reality.

Pocahontas waved her hand at the guards and they led the prisoner back to his hut. Imperiously, the girl motioned to Virginia to follow her back to her own lodge.

All that day, all during her songs of flowers and honey-bees and birds, Virginia's mind stayed with the prisoner. How old was he? Perhaps only a year or two older than she. Was he English? Perhaps he wasn't. Perhaps she was wrong in concluding that he belonged to her first parents' people and so could help her get to Chesapiuc.

She had to see him again, to speak to him, to find out

more. She remembered his eyes, so bright blue, so sharp and clear, as they gazed back at her. She had to do something.

"The stranger will die before your father can execute him," she said to the little girl, interrupting her endless prattling.

"The stranger?" Pocahontas said, her child's mind almost forgetting the morning's momentous event.

"You saw the wounds on his hands," Virginia said. "If they are not treated, he will become very sick and his sickness will spread among us. You must tell the guards to let me see him again so I can treat him with my medicines." She patted the herbal pouch that always hung at her waist.

"Your father will be very proud that you have prevented sickness in his town," Virginia went on. "We will say nothing to anyone until after the stranger is cured."

A precocious child, Pocahontas jumped at the opportunity to make such an adult decision. She led Virginia back to the prisoner immediately, ordering the guards to let her in.

Virginia stepped into the gloom. The man was lying on a bed of rushes. She knelt down beside him and studied his face. It was soft in repose, with a golden beard, short and silky. She wondered if he normally went clean-shaven, like her English father said he had done before he came to Roanoke.

She put out a hand to touch his face, and it was grasped immediately by one of his. He had moved so quickly, like a striking snake, lying there awake.

He peered at her face and seemed to recognize her. She was about to ask him if he understood English when he spoke.

"It is you," he said, and his voice was soft too.

She gasped, for he had indeed spoken English.

At last, at long last, she was meeting an Englishman. He couldn't be from the colony at Roanoke, for she knew the youngest child there had been ten years old when she was born. So he must be from England. Her heart beat fast. She must speak, for at any moment the inquisitive Pocahontas would come bustling in to see what she was doing.

But the words would not come. It had been so long since

she had spoken English. Apart from a few words that Manteo had remembered, she had not heard English for most of her life. What if he did not understand her? What if she did not understand him?

She put her other hand out and he took it, looking questioningly at her. He seemed to know she wanted to say something. She opened her mouth, but no sound came. Her heart was hammering wildly against her ribs. She tried again.

"My name—" she said. It sounded like a croak, but he understood, for his eyes lit up.

"My name—" Again her voice strangled on the words. Then it came out with a rush.

"I am Virginia Dare and I am English!"

It was the words her English parents had taught her to say, and her confused mind had snatched them out of the past.

"My father is Ananias Dare and my mother is Elinor Dare—"

She got no further, for the young man had risen to his feet in one incredibly smooth movement and raised her with him.

"Virginia Dare?" he whispered, his voice incredulous. "Are you Virginia Dare from the Lost Colony at Roanoke?"

"You know me?" Virginia asked, surprised at his apparent recognition.

"Know you? Everyone in England knows of you! We all thought you were dead. What happened? What are you doing here?"

Before she could speak, Pocahontas's voice came through the doorway.

"Tall Girl! Are you finished?"

"In just a moment," Virginia called back. "Wait and I shall be with you."

She looked up at the Englishman.

"I . . ." She faltered. "I captured," she said finally. She had lost her grasp of English. "I raised Indian. Come to look for English from Roanoke at Chesapiuc." His face lit up at the word. "You know Chesapiuc?" she asked.

"I know it," he said. "Will you help me get away? Will you? They will kill me if I stay, they've told me so."

She looked around the lodge, then pointed to the wall by which he had been lying.

"Tonight I come, open wall. You follow, we go away." She had an afterthought.

"You know boat?"

He smiled for the first time, and it transformed his whole face.

"I am a sailor, a navigator. Yes, I know boats."

"You swim?"

She had to find out, for it was a part of her hazy plan, and she knew from Manteo that few Englishmen, even sailors, could swim.

"I swim," he said.

"Sleep now," she commanded. "Tonight I come."

But she did not turn away to leave him, continuing to gaze up at him. To her surprise she saw his eyes fill with tears. She had never seen a man cry before, and the sight gave her a great pang of mingled love and pity.

She reached up, closed his eyelids, and squeezed the unshed tears onto her fingers.

Then she pulled his head down and kissed him, his cheeks, his eyes, his mouth. She was awkward, like a child learning to walk. The gesture was spontaneous, meant to comfort. She had never kissed anyone on the mouth, had never seen it done since she had been taken prisoner at the age of seven. Indians did not know mouth kissing but she had seen her English parents embrace that way.

"Your name. What your name?" she asked.

"John," she repeated. A beautiful name. "I go now, John."

Later, taking Pocahontas for a walk in the woods, Virginia could not stop smiling. There was danger ahead in just a few hours, great danger. But there was also freedom and John Trevelyan.

14

The escape was surprisingly easy, for it was completely unexpected and no precautions had been taken against it. Prisoners of Powhatan simply did not attempt to run away. Their capture and subsequent punishment were inevitable. Virginia knew this, and her upbringing as an Indian told her she could never evade recapture.

But suddenly something else told her she could defy the great king and succeed. Was it Badger's courage and fighting spirit, so dearly remembered, that finally gave her the will to try? Or was it her English blood, rekindled by her meeting with John Trevelyan?

Or was it Trevelyan himself, his eyes, his mouth, his touch . . .

Like all the True People, Pocahontas was a sound sleeper. Virginia had to force herself to stay awake until the whole town retired, with only the guards on duty calling out to each other at regular intervals.

Fearfully, holding her breath, she slipped out of the lodge she shared with the child, gliding silently to the rear of the prisoner's lodge. There she sat for a long while until she had picked out the movements of each guard and fixed the area he patrolled firmly in her mind.

She tugged at one of the mats that had been lowered to the ground to enclose the lodge; it raised easily. So secure was Powhatan of his power that not even the walls of the captive's lodge were pegged down.

Virginia crawled under the mat, lay still for a moment, then whispered:

"John!"

He was beside her immediately, lifting her to a kneeling position, his arms around her, his cheek pressed to hers.

"Come," she whispered, and crawled back into the open.

Sometimes wriggling on their stomachs, sometimes on their hands and knees, they made their way between the guards and into the edge of the forest.

There, Virginia led the way to the river.

"There are men at boats," she told Trevelyan. "We must steal boat and cross river to other side."

"Which way?" he asked. She did not understand.

"North, south? Which way across the river?"

Virginia thought for a long minute. Her English parents had trained her carefully in the points of the compass.

"South," she answered.

"Then the Chesapiuc is to the east," said Trevelyan. "Why do we not simply take the boat all the way to the Chesapiuc?"

"Because tomorrow, dawn tomorrow, king's warriors begin look for us, look all over, all over—" She couldn't find the words. "King have three thousand men, all look for us. We need help. Go to Chickahominy people. They help us."

He gave a low laugh.

"I'm not sure that I understand, my dear," he said. "But you lead and I will follow."

"Yes," she said. "I lead."

They found a small dugout downstream from the guards, carefully pushed it into the water, and set off. Virginia, in the rear, was amazed at the skill and strength of Trevelyan as he dipped his paddle from side to side, varying the depth of his strokes to keep the boat aimed due south.

As they approached the farther shore, Virginia called her instructions.

"When we closer, we swim, let boat go by self to east. Men follow boat."

Trevelyan understood instantly.

"In that case, why don't we take the boat farther to the west, in that direction"—his pointed arm gleamed palely in the starlight—"before we turn it loose. That way, if our followers get suspicious and backtrack, it will take them longer to find where we swam ashore."

They paddled several miles upstream before they decided to leave the dugout. With luck, the current would take the vessel well downstream before it was spotted. Perhaps they would be believed drowned.

She saw Trevelyan ripping off the remains of his shirt and ruff and asked him what he was doing.

"I'll leave this in the boat so they will know it is the one we escaped in and look no further."

How clever he was, she thought.

She pulled her dress over her head and tied it in a bundle with her beaded belt. She felt no shame for her nakedness for he could not see her body in the darkness. She was unaware of how white her skin was, covered as it had always been by her dress.

They slipped into the cold water and together pushed the dugout back toward the mainstream. Then they swam to the shore. Virginia balanced her bundle on her head with one hand and swam smoothly, partly on her side and partly on her back. Trevelyan swam with a great deal of splashing, like a clumsy but enthusiastic child.

He was exhausted when they reached the shore, but he insisted on carrying her bundle until they were inside the trees.

"It is heavy," he said as he handed it back. "You are a wonderful swimmer."

She smiled to herself with pleasure at the simple compliment. The dress *was* heavy, for her supply of copper beads and pearls was stitched to it.

Trevelyan stripped off his breeches, wrung them out, and pulled them on again. Virginia turned her back and slipped the dress over her head.

"Where do we go now?" he asked. She was in charge again.

"South, where Chickahominy live. We go all night, hide in day."

"How far to these Chickahominy?" he asked.

"Perhaps one day. But we cannot go by day. Too dangerous. Go by night. Two nights."

Then she remembered.

"No food. We no have food." She thought that over and started again. "We *not* have food."

Trevelyan laughed.

"I understand you, Virginia. We have no food. Very well, we shall go without food for one day and two nights. I never eat food at night in any case, so that leaves only one day without food. I have gone without food before."

They reached the land of the Chickahominy early on the second day. They were greeted warmly, fed, and allowed to rest before being taken to the chief town on the banks of the Chickahominy River.

The tribe's priests and elders listened to Virginia's explanation that she was from the south, that she had lost her way while on a visit to the Chesapiuc and been captured by Powhatan, for whom they expressed little affection.

But the Englishman intrigued them.

"Is he a human?" one asked her.

"He is a human, but not a Person," she replied.

They accepted this, for they had heard there were people who were not the True People. Where was he from? What was his tribe?

"He is from a tribe that lives far across the great sea beyond the Chesapiuc," she told them. "He was in his canoe when a great wind sent him across the sea to the land of the People."

Did everyone in his land have hair, skin, and eyes the same color?

"They have many different colors, for they are many different tribes who now live together. Some are dark and some are light. Some have eyes like the True People, and some have eyes like the empty sky."

"Do they see better with these eyes?" one of the priests asked suddenly.

Virginia was growing uneasy. She had thought it would be simple to persuade the Chickahominy to escort them to the Chesapiuc. But she had not reckoned with the inquisitiveness of the priests.

"How can anyone know this if they do not possess such eyes to see with?"

The answer brought appreciative nods from some of the

priests and elders. The True People loved a good answer. Virginia almost relaxed, but the next question put her on guard again.

"You also have different eyes. Are you from the same land as these people?"

If Virginia had answered that she was, all might have gone well. But she attempted to pit her wits against the most astute and powerful men in the Chickahominy tribe and disaster followed quickly.

"In my country," she replied, "there are those whose eyes are as mine. But our skin is not the color of this man and we are not of his tribe."

"Then how is it that you speak his language, for the messengers from King Powhatan who came to us about you told us that you had never seen this man until you met at Powhatan's town."

Virginia's mind went blank. What happened? One moment she had been doing so well, impressing these men with her clever answers. And now, catastrophe! The priests had known about their escape even before they had arrived and had not betrayed their knowledge by a single gesture, a single glance.

Trevelyan was watching her closely. He was grateful to this beautiful girl for saving his life. And he could not forget the feel of her soft lips on his, or the outline of her slim, sensuous body when she had stripped off her clothes in the dugout. He wanted no harm to come to her.

"Is something wrong?" he asked.

She shook her head. There was nothing this Englishman, inexperienced in Indian ways, could do. The less he became involved the better.

"Do you claim to be stronger than we are?" a priest was demanding of her. "Would you pit your strength against us? You come here with your lies and expect us to help you? A woman? A woman demands this from the priests of the Chickahominy?"

The man who spoke was outraged; the others nodded vehemently at his words.

"You will both be imprisoned until we decide what to do with you," the priest said. "Guards!"

"I sorry, John," Virginia said haltingly, explaining what had happened. But he only patted her shoulder, gave her a smile, and turned to face the semicircle of priests and elders.

The Honorable John Prendergast Trevelyan, age twenty, was the third son of the Earl of Budleigh in Devon, in England's West Country.

For younger sons of earls there was no inheritance, either title or lands, and often they sought their fortune in military service. Through his friendship with Sir Walter Raleigh, the man who had established the first colonies at Roanoke, the Earl had arranged for his son John to go to sea at the age of sixteen.

He had sailed as an apprentice navigator and then, some two and a half years earlier, at the beginning of the year 1603, he had set sail as a full-fledged navigator for a study of the northern lands of the New World.

One of his ship's tasks was to visit Virginia for sign of the Lost Colony, but the vessel had been wrecked in a violent storm inside Chesapiuc Bay. Trevelyan had been the only survivor to reach shore and had been taken, on a journey that lasted several weeks, to Powhatan's brother and thence to the king himself.

Although he had no rank or property bequeathed to him, Trevelyan had been raised by a wealthy father, had been well schooled, was an expert horseman, swordsman, and, of course, sailor. He had also been well trained in the social graces and it was these that now came to their rescue.

Using Virginia as translator, he told the priests some of his past life, the strange land he had come from. He praised the hospitality he had received at the Chickahominy's hands and thanked them for taking in the weary wanderer far from his own people.

The priests were beginning to nod and smile. This, surely, was someone who knew how to speak in the words of the People.

Finally, he asked forgiveness for not telling the truth, explaining that it was only because they feared to be returned to the vengeful Powhatan. He could see how wrong they had been.

Yes, the woman was of his distant tribe, lost many years before. He was taking her back to their own people.

What was more, they had copper beads to pay for an escort to the lands of the Chesapiuc . . .

He said more—much of which made Virginia furious at the way he disparaged her, but she saw the results of his words on the faces of the priests—and then it was over.

That night, the priests, elders, and chief warriors gave a feast for Trevelyan; Virginia was not invited. The next day they set out in a great dugout with twenty paddlers. Their offer to pay in copper was airily refused and they were given a rousing send-off.

o

It was a long journey, down the twisting Chickahominy River to the wide Powhatan, so named because the town from which the king took his name was on the higher reaches of the river, and then to the Chesapiuc. They hugged the northern shore until they came to the narrows that led into the great bay, then crossed to the southern shore.

Virginia sat subdued during the long hours in the dugout. She and Trevelyan were separated by several of the crew, so they had little opportunity to talk. At night, when they camped on the shore, she remained aloof and, after trying unsuccessfully to draw her out, Trevelyan simply left her alone.

Near the end of their journey, Virginia finally spoke. How far was it to the Chesapian town, she asked. The leader pointed. About half a day's journey by canoe.

"We will go ashore here," she told him.

The Indian looked at Trevelyan, shrugged, and called an order to his men.

The canoe turned smoothly and headed for the shore. When they beached, Trevelyan turned to her.

"Have we reached our destination?" he asked, looking around him and seeing nothing but the forest. Virginia did not answer as she stepped into the shallow water. Instead, she turned to the Indians who were waiting patiently for the Englishman to disembark.

"The stranger wishes a bow and quiver to hunt," she told them. She pulled her small bag of precious copper beads from inside her dress. "I will pay you."

She did not have to bargain. They were eager to exchange. She took her time in choosing and carefully spun the arrows to check that they were straight. She still had her own wrist bracer in one of her pouches.

A minute later, the dugout backed off the beach, and Virginia led the way into the forest. She walked until they came to a stream, laid the bow and quiver on the ground, and sat down with her back against a tree. Trevelyan squatted beside her.

"Virginia," he said softly. "Why are we here? Why did you stop them from taking us to the Chesapian's town?"

She answered without looking up.

"I not want see English."

He was astonished.

"But you have spent years searching for them, and now, when we are almost there, you are giving up?"

She looked at her hands in her lap and said nothing.

"Are you angry with me because I said those things to the Chickahominy priests?"

She almost nodded, then changed her mind and shook her head.

"What are we going to do, if we do not continue looking for the English?"

"You go," she said. "I stay here, hunt."

"But I can't go anywhere without you, Virginia. I can't leave you."

He thought he heard a sob and reached out to put his hand under her chin.

When he turned her face toward him, he saw her eyes were full of tears. He took her gently in his arms and cradled her. She did not resist, and lay there quietly. But when he began to caress her long, sleek hair, she put her arms around his body. He gently stroked her face and her grip tightened; suddenly, she burst into a torrent of tears, sobbing bitterly.

Astonished, he held her until the torrent subsided, until there was only the infrequent hiccup and sob. Finally, she was quiet and the tears slowly dried on her face.

Then the words poured out of her. Her English was broken, her grammar was taken from the Indian language, and she did not pronounce many words correctly, but Trevelyan grasped her meaning, and realized that, despite her life in the wilderness, living with what he had been brought up to regard as godless savages, she had retained a vulnerability that amazed him. He had been seeing the creature of the forest, who could paddle a dugout like a man, swim like a fish, and find her way in darkness through what was to him trackless woods.

Now here was the other side of her, a troubled, confused girl who cried in his arms as though her heart would break.

She told him of her upbringing in the little town of Chammayoac, where she had been a princess, of her training as a medicine woman, of her skills with the bow and her sling.

She told how she had escaped the Opossum and spent two years making her way to Manteo on Croatoan. How, on the way, she had been accepted by the tribes she had passed through because of her knowledge of medicine.

She told of her desertion by Manteo's warriors and subsequent shameful capture by Powhatan.

All her pent-up fears and pain came pouring forth. She was worthless, she said, of no use to anyone. She could not go to the English, they would not want her now.

Once she had been a princess, the daughter of a fearless werowance. She had been brought up to believe that when her Indian father, Badger, was no more, she would rule the tribe as queen. She had been told that her knowledge of medicine came from the greatest of medicine women, the Swallowtail Butterfly. She had expected her life to be filled with respect and accomplishment.

But after the Opossum destroyed her village, her claims of being a princess had met with ridicule. Her beloved

Indian father, Badger, was dismissed as a small tribe's chief of no consequence. Even her knowledge of medicine, which had earned her hospitality among the tribes she had visited on the long journey to Manteo, had been ignored by Powhatan.

She had offered him her great skills as a medicine woman but he had made her a servant to a spoiled child.

And now she had almost cost Trevelyan his life by blundering with the Chickahominy priests.

"I nothing," she said bitterly. "Indian woman nothing unless she be princess, medicine woman . . . priestess maybe. I not princess, not medicine woman; English say I only savage. Not want me."

In her words, however awkwardly expressed, he could hear the conflict between two widely different cultures and how they were tearing her apart. Virginia recognized that her Indian upbringing made acceptance by the English difficult. She had heard her first parents disparage the Indians too often. Her royalty and knowledge of medicine would gain her acceptance, but these had been stripped from her, and now she felt that she was only what her English parents had described with such scorn and hate. A savage. The devil Indian.

Trevelyan spoke slowly so his words could easily be understood by someone lacking a fluent knowledge of English. "I will tell you what my father explained to me when I was a boy.

"Who you are depends on you, not on what others say. You did not lose your knowledge of medicine because Powhatan chose to ignore your skills. You still know everything the Swallowtail taught you.

"You never stopped being Badger's daughter, a princess. Your Indian father is no less a valiant warrior because he belonged to a small tribe. His heroic death at the Opossum village is in no way diminished because fools have tried to lessen its impact.

"Look at me," Trevelyan said. "Who would recognize me at the Court of Queen Elizabeth in these rags, with this scraggly beard? But I am the third son of an earl, nevertheless. In my country, in England, that is not very much, I admit. But no one can take it from me. I am what I am, even in Powhatan's bloody hands."

Virginia listened gravely.

"I shave you," she said. "Your queen know you then."

Trevelyan burst out laughing, Virginia giggling with him. She had understood what he was trying to say, and was grateful for it.

15

Virginia shaved him with her knife, and trimmed his hair with mussel shells. Then she washed his hair and combed it with the little tortoiseshell comb that had been her mother's.

She examined him, and decided he was the most handsome of men. She promised to make him a cloak of pure white doeskin when they reached the English colonists.

She found a turkey feather and twined it in his hair. He plucked flowers and placed them in hers.

She hunted with bow and arrow and sling, and they roasted the squirrels and small birds at the fires she lit.

He was amazed at her dexterity, and praised her lavishly. They bathed in the stream, washing each other, then drying off in the sun.

They held hands and walked in the woods. He told her about England and London. He didn't like London, he said. It was dirty and smelly and had too many people. She scolded him and said it was beautiful: they would live there in a great house when the great ships came to take them back.

They sat by the fire at night, close together, dreaming and planning for the future.

In the darkness, they lay down on a bed of freshly pulled grass and flowers. They held each other silently as their passion grew.

He pressed his lips to hers softly at first, and then with more and more strength. He felt reason deserting him as he slowly drowned in her mouth, responding to her body as it arched upward to meet his.

His pulse was pounding, his heart beat through his chest as though it would burst. He could not get enough of her mouth, so soft and moist, opening hungrily under his. Her arms were around his neck, her fingers dug deeply into his flesh.

As a girl, Virginia had stumbled over lovemaking couples in the woods, and had been trained by She Smiles to think nothing of it. She knew all about the sex act, and how it created babies. She also knew what men's private parts looked like. For the aprons covered only the fronts of men's bodies; when they squatted for meals, nothing was hidden.

Now she watched as Trevelyan slowly got up from her side and began to undress. Without taking his eyes from hers, he pulled off his ragged breeches. She saw his hard masculinity and her hand instinctively reached to touch him, to bring him back to her.

"Not yet," he said softly, leaning down to bring her to her feet. She stood before him, trembling as he undid her belt, then raised the dress over her head and tossed it aside.

He drank in her beauty. Her breasts were exquisite, round and jutting, silky and sensuous. The rosy nipples were rigid.

Her waist was incredibly small, giving her hips an exciting fullness. Her stomach was flat, and where her legs met, the V was dark and lustrous. Her legs were long and strong and slim, the smallness of the knees giving the thighs and calves a deceptive roundness.

He opened his arms and she stepped into them. They stood, the flesh just touching, looking into each other's eyes. He slid his hands up, cupping her breasts. Her body quivered and her eyes half closed. He kneaded one breast gently and she slipped her hands around his waist, her strong fingers biting into his flesh.

His hands went behind her and found her buttocks, pulling her toward him. She raised her mouth to his and felt his organ slip between her legs and press urgently against her. He was big, as She Smiles had said a perfect lover would be. She groaned and clamped her legs together. They stood transfixed for a long moment, their arms around each other, their mouths hungrily together.

Then he lowered her to the ground and lay gently on top of her. She opened her legs and arched her back to allow him to enter.

He hesitated, wanting to make certain she was ready for him, using his hands on her secret places until she felt ready to explode.

She reached down and grasped him. He was huge. Gently, she guided him to her throbbing opening and pushed him into the entrance. There was an obstacle there, her virginity, which she knew had to be pierced. She arched her body higher as he began to move into her, stifling the small scream that rose in her throat at the sudden, sharp pain.

But then she felt a marvelous warmth envelop her body, a tingling that touched every nerve fiber. She could feel him press deeper and deeper into her until he seemed to fill her completely. She began to move with his thrusts in a steady rhythm, their two bodies joined tightly together as one. She curled herself around him, wrapping her legs tightly around his buttocks, thrashing in his arms like a wild thing even as she kept moving with him, moving, moving, her body floating in air, every inch of her drenched in the marvelous, throbbing sensation.

He seemed to be taking her to the heights of ecstasy again and again, pulling back at the last possible moment. Virginia cried out, a hoarse, incoherent sound that rose to a sharp scream. He urged her on and on with his body, his tongue making wild forays into her mouth as his masculinity drove savagely into her still one more time.

Virginia felt as if she could not go on, could not endure another moment of this exquisite, impossible, all-consuming feeling. Then he began again, plunging into her savagely, this time taking her to even greater heights, and then they went the last step together, building to a thundering climax, white-hot in intensity and emotion.

They lay under the tall trees in each other's arms, and she

kissed the marks she had made when she had bitten him in their frenzy of lovemaking. After a while they made love again.

They stayed by the stream for another six days. Virginia was supremely happy, even as a small voice inside her kept insisting that this was not how it should be.

There should be discussions with her parents, there should be presents, then there should be a marriage ceremony performed by the werowance of the town where they lived.

But she had no parents now, and there was no town and no werowance. The marriage ceremony would be in their mating. She felt Trevelyan's hand caress her thigh and moved closer to him.

o

They walked into the Chesapian main town in late afternoon, when the women and children had returned from the fields and as the evening meal was being prepared, with the braves resting after the day's hunting and fishing, repairing their weapons and fishing nets.

They had been in no hurry to reach their destination. Virginia's desire to meet the Roanoke survivors, which had driven her for years, was replaced by another emotion. Her hunger for John Trevelyan.

They were seen before they reached the first lodges and a crowd of children quickly surrounded them, calling greetings and pointing excitedly at Trevelyan.

Virginia saw him suddenly, in the midst of the throng—a small boy with fair hair.

"Look at him, John," she cried. "The English are here!"

She pushed her way through the growing crowd until she came to the boy, who was about four or five years old. He was naked except for a tiny leather apron hanging down in front. His skin was brown, a lighter shade than the children around him, but definitely tanned. But it was his hair that Virginia stared at. And his eyes. They were brown, too, a light, tawny brown, not the jet-black eyes of the Indian.

She knelt down in front of the child and the boy tried to back away. But an older girl behind him, smiling with anticipation, held his shoulders and pushed him forward.

Virginia spoke in English, a language she had only begun to speak again within the last few weeks.

"What you name?"

The boy stared at her. Virginia was puzzled. Perhaps she had not said it right. She felt a hand on her shoulder, looked up, and saw Trevelyan standing behind her. He bent down and whispered something in her ear. She turned back to the boy.

"What *is* your name?" she said, enunciating each word carefully.

The boy continued to stare. Clearly, he understood no English. She asked him the same question in the language of the True People. His answer was immediate.

"Flies-Like-Squirrel," he said.

Trevelyan looked over the heads of the crowd.

"Ask him where his parents are," he told Virginia. She did, but before the boy could answer, other children began pointing to the left. A group of men were standing outside a large lodge, looking in their direction.

"I think they want us over there," Trevelyan said.

Virginia took the boy's hand, taking him with her. As they began to move through the crowd, the children gave way before them, leaving a wide path to the lodge of the werowance. Suddenly the boy tugged on Virginia's hand.

"My name is John Withers," he said.

"You hear?" Virginia exclaimed to Trevelyan. "John, he say John. We home, really home now!"

There were about a dozen men clustered at the door of the lodge. They were all dressed alike, with a simple leather skirt in front. Their hair was shaved on the right side and hung long on the left, and they wore stiff cockscombs on top.

But two of them had fair hair.

Virginia and Trevelyan stopped about a dozen feet away from the men.

The boy squirmed and Virginia let go of his hand. He ran to one of the fair-haired men and stood beside him. The man looked at the strangers uncertainly for a moment, then stepped forward, the boy clinging to his skirt.

"I am William Withers," he said in English. "Have the ships come?"

"I am Virginia Dare," came the answer, and the man's face lit up at the name.

The second fair-haired man came forward.

"I am Thomas Smart," he said. "Are you Virginia Dare from Roanoke? We are from Roanoke, too."

Virginia's heart almost burst within her. The years of searching were truly over. She had found the English.

There was a small commotion at the edge of the crowd and people pulled apart to let a woman through. She was short, brown, and wrinkled, her black hair tied behind her ears like an Indian. But she wore a leather dress that covered her body as Virginia's did hers, and her eyes were blue.

She rushed to Virginia and stared up at her, searching her face. She took in the fringed dress and the longbow and quiver slung over the young woman's shoulder.

"Are you really Virginia Dare?" she asked in a wondering voice. "Little Virginia? I was your nurse, Emma Merrimoth. You went to Croatoan. We thought you had gone to England with the ships and forgotten us."

There was a catch in her voice and Virginia instinctively put out her hands and took the woman's in hers.

"Have you brought the ships? Have you come to take us to England?"

Over the woman's head Virginia could see the two fair-haired men waiting for her answer.

She turned to the woman and looked into the blue eyes. Tired eyes, eyes that had felt despair. Virginia had recognized the woman's name and so knew she could be no more than thirty-six or -seven, but she looked fifty years old, bowed down by disappointment, frustration, and loneliness.

"Ships never come to Croatoan," Virginia said as gently as she could. "I thought they come here; that is why I spent years trying to . . . to find English."

The light died in Emma Merrimoth's face and her head dropped. Virginia took the woman in her arms, holding her tightly. Emma was silent, letting herself be rocked by Virginia like a child. Then she pried herself away. She brusquely wiped away the tears and looked up. Virginia was surprised to see a glint in the blue eyes and hear the brisk voice that now spoke to her.

"Well, that's that. Now, Virginia, it is time you had your old nurse look after you again. First, introduce us to that nice young man with you. Then you had better meet the werowance."

Suddenly, the gloom lifted from the little group of English. There were handshakes and hugs, and the werowance, Fights-Like-Bear, welcomed his new children.

Virginia and Trevelyan were married by Fights-Like-Bear in a ceremony attended by the whole town. Only after the joyous wedding feast did the English survivors attempt to explain how they had reached Chesapiuc. A total of twenty-four persons had left in the pinnace, eleven men, four women, and nine children. Of the children, five had been boys between the ages of twelve and fifteen, and four had been babies of two and younger. Nine of the twenty-four were still alive.

None of the men who had come from Roanoke had survived. One by one they had died of disease and accident. Two of the four women lived. Both had been unmarried servants—Emma Merrimoth, Virginia's nurse, and Jane Mannering, brought to the New World by John and Alice Chapman to look after their daughter, Elizabeth, born on Roanoke.

Of the nine children, seven had survived. Four of the boys from England—William Withers, Thomas Smart, Thomas Humphrey, and John Pratt. Pratt and Humphrey were now both twenty-eight, Smart was thirty and Withers, thirty-one.

Three of the children born on Roanoke were there—John Harvie, born a few days after Virginia, Winifred Powell, and Elizabeth Chapman, both aged sixteen.

But there were more than nine who now claimed to be English.

Virginia discovered to her great delight that the four men had taken Indian wives and had a total of twelve children between them. Jane Mannering, who had been a mere girl on Roanoke and was now aged thirty-five, had married a brave and had two children.

This redoubtable woman and her husband, Arrow-Flies-True, a famed hunter, had also raised three of the English children, Elizabeth Chapman, Winifred Powell, and John Harvie. The two girls were now "spoken for" by young braves, and John Harvie, under the tutelage of his foster father, had already a reputation for his hunting skills.

Emma Merrimoth had remained single by choice. She had refused to accept the permanence of their exile—or abandonment, as some called it—and had never ceased to dream of rescue.

She had kept the spirit of England and Christianity alive by setting up a little "school" in a lodge erected by the men who had survived the first few years.

As a result, the three youngest children had been taught to read English from the tattered Bible—just as Virginia's parents had taught her. They and the four older boys had been given the basics of religion as interpreted by Miss Merrimoth.

Moreover, to Virginia's and Trevelyan's amazement, Emma had taught all the half-English children, too, and had even coached the four Indian wives. Arrow-Flies-True had simply grinned at the suggestion that he learn about Christianity. His gods, he said, were sufficient for a simple man.

But, Emma confided to Virginia, she'd had her misgivings when her "flock," as she called them, had begun to marry into the Chesapian tribe.

"I tried to dissuade them," she said, "at least until the savages had adopted Christianity. But they rejected my counsel, and I fear they may have jeopardized their souls' eternal salvation."

Trevelyan did not fear the loss of his salvation, he told Virginia later. And, he added, if the happiness evident in the mixed marriages was any portent of the afterlife, no one's soul had anything to fear.

Unlike the faded, gray Emma Merrimoth, Jane Mannering was buxom, exuded good health, with a face that was constantly wreathed in smiles. Like Miss Merrimoth and the two sixteen-year-old girls, she wore a buckskin dress. But she had taken to Indian life with gusto. She spoke the language fluently, whereas Emma spoke it badly, and her brood of five obviously adored her. Her husband, Arrow-Flies-True, might have been taciturn had he married anyone else, but in the glow of Jane's love he had grown into a quiet, contented man.

Virginia and Trevelyan were given a lodge to live in and ample food. But Virginia was restless. She knew that the town of Chesapiuc was built on an inlet that led from Chesapiuc Bay, and that between the bay and the Atlantic there were several small freshwater lakes. Virginia wanted to explore them for a very special reason.

She and Trevelyan were given a dugout and paddled into the lake area. The lakes were narrow but spread over several miles. The banks were grassy and covered with flowering bushes, the forest surrounding them filled with pines, gums, bays, tulip trees, walnuts, and oaks.

They left the canoe and walked through the woods until they reached the Atlantic Ocean. There was a beautiful sandy beach that reminded Virginia of Croatoan.

Staring pensively at the wide expanse of ocean, Virginia said, "Small lake hold enough water for thirty people.

"All fish we need is here." She waved her arm at the sea. "We clear forest now for planting in spring. We build lodges around one lake. All English be together. We be very happy."

Trevelyan knew what she had in mind—fulfilling an old yearning for a place with her own people.

"You and I can live here, darling," he said. "But why would the others leave town?"

"Because we make this England, speak own language, follow own religion."

From what he had seen, Trevelyan doubted whether any of the English—except for Miss Merrimoth—retained any great desire for Christianity. Virginia herself had been brought up a heathen and seemed no worse for it. As for John Trevelyan, he was from the English aristocracy and had not the same need for religion as the poor classes.

"If we live here," Virginia said, "we see ship that pass. You can't see English ship from town."

"You want very much to go to England, don't you, Virginia?" Trevelyan said.

"Yes, John. Is all my English parents tell me. It keep me strong during years of search."

Trevelyan looked at her. He loved her fiercely. He wondered how the English, back in England, would find her and how she would react to them. He dreaded the pain reality would bring.

The time had come to tell her about John White. It had been on his mind for a long while but there never seemed to be the right place or the proper time for speaking of it. He had to do it now.

"Your grandfather, John White, *did* return to Roanoke," he said to Virginia. "But the colony had gone. I have to tell you this. I am only sorry that it will cause you pain."

Virginia turned white. "He back?" she said incredulously.

Trevelyan told her about John White's return to England in 1587, and of White's plans to go back to the colonists the following year. Of how war with Spain intervened, and how the mighty Spanish armada had been vanquished by the English. And how, by then, interest in colonizing the New World had faded, and how it was not until three years later that White was able to get a ship and return.

Trevelyan described how White had visited Roanoke, finding it deserted, with only the word "Croatoan" carved at the fort entrance to suggest where the colony might have gone. He had tried to sail to Croatoan but a storm had driven him out to sea, and he returned to England without seeing Manteo and learning of the survivors.

"The English may never come again," Trevelyan said. "You could be watching for a ship in vain."

"But *you* came, John."

He acknowledged that.

"Then other ships come; I wish to be ready for them."

He couldn't bear to crush all her hopes. "I will do my best to persuade the others to settle here," he said.

They walked back along the path through the woods, their arms entwined. She raised her face to be kissed. After a while, he picked her up and carried her under the leafy trees. Their lovemaking, as always, was fierce and passionate.

16

Trevelyan's revelation about John White's return caused great excitement among the English. Like Virginia, they, too, believed that others might come for them again. Thomas Smart even brought up using the pinnace.

Virginia assumed, from what Manteo had told her, that the pinnace had been left at the head of the Currituck Sound, south of where they were now.

"It *was* left there," said Smart. "But when we settled in with the Chesapians, a group took the vessel through the Outer Banks, sailing it north on the open sea and then rounding the point to Chesapiuc.

"They lost some men in bad weather and the pinnace was damaged. Still, they managed to sail it into the bay here, although they never took it to sea again. It's been beached for ten years now and its timbers are ruined. I doubt if she'll sail again."

Trevelyan wanted to see the vessel. The four Englishmen took him and Virginia down the bay to where the pinnace lay, half hidden under the trees.

Trevelyan examined the hulk carefully. Some of the planking was gone, but the oak frame was intact, as was the rudder.

"It can be made seaworthy if we have metal tools,"

Trevelyan said. The Roanoke survivors did have a variety of metal tools, including carpentry ones.

"I can make the planking," Trevelyan told Virginia. "With your glue from deer horn and sinew we can make it watertight. The pinnace will sail again."

William Withers asked the question all of them were thinking.

"Will it sail to England?"

Trevelyan shook his head.

"I would not attempt to sail it across the Atlantic, not even to Bermuda. But it will go to sea, and if a ship is passing by, we shall be able to try and catch it."

The hope of returning to England, which had disappeared from their minds over the years, surfaced again. After much discussion, most of the colonists agreed to move to the lakes and set up an "English" town. Only Thomas Humphrey held out.

A solid, well-muscled man, Humphrey waited until the others were quiet, then stepped forward to speak.

"My wife and I"—he nodded toward the buxom, pleasant-faced woman sitting with their three fair-haired children—"have responsibilities here in Chesapiuc. My wife's parents are old and live with us; they would die without us to shelter and feed them."

"But they can come, too," Virginia said. "They are most welcome." There was a chorus of assent.

"They do not speak English," Humphrey said, "and they are not Christians—they do not understand our religion. I fear they will be lonely without their own people. They are too old for such a change in their lives."

"You must join us!" Miss Merrimoth bounded to her feet. Trevelyan marveled at the little ramrod figure giving orders like a sea captain.

"You owe it to England to return. You owe it to the Christian God of England to tell everyone about this land, so that when they come to colonize and convert the savages they will know the dangers and tribulations.

"If you stay here, you will miss your chance to come back, miss receiving the honors that will surely greet all of us who have survived so many long, arduous years in this heathen land."

She sat down, an expression of quiet righteousness on her face. Tactless and stubborn though she might be, she was certainly English through and through. Despite himself, Trevelyan smiled at Miss Merrimoth's unchanging character and views.

"There is nothing for me in England," Humphrey said quietly. "I have no one to return to. I was an orphan, sent as a servant to the Roanoke colony. I have no profession that would enable me to feed and house my family if I return.

"I came here to start a new life, and I have found it. I have family and friends now, and the honorable profession of hunter and warrior. I am no longer English. I am Indian."

"Very well, Thomas Humphrey," said Emma Merrimoth in her clear, crisp voice. "If you wish to lead the life of a heathen, spurning God and England, then be it on your head. I shall pray for your soul."

Arrow-Flies-True, with an English wife, three adopted English children, and two half-English children, was prepared to accept his wife's urging and join the new tribe, but he had a question. What about priests and healers? A tribe could not function without religion and medicine.

The Chesapiuc priests would always be welcome, Trevelyan assured him before Emma Merrimoth could speak. And Virginia was a trained medicine woman. Arrow-Flies-True was satisfied.

"Who will be your werowance?" Fights-Like-Bear asked. "There is no order of accession in a new tribe, so you must decide among yourselves. If you wish, I shall decide for you."

Having lived among the Indians for many years, the English recognized the importance of a chief for their group. But none of their own had shown any real sign of leadership and so they had no particular person in mind as the "English" werowance. They decided to let Fights-Like-Bear make the selection.

The old man knew Virginia's history by this time, knew of her upbringing as the daughter of a werowance and her training to rule her tribe as queen when her father joined the spirits of his ancestors.

He spoke now, long and eloquently, about making Virginia werowansquaw, queen. Did they not have a queen in England, their much loved Elizabeth? Tall Girl would lead them wisely and bravely, as her father, Badger, had led his tribe.

"In seven days' time we have the feast to make Tall Woman your queen," Fights-Like-Bear said. "It is good. It is agreed?"

It was agreed.

Virginia was finally fulfilling the role Badger had told her she would one day perform, the role she had longed for during all her years of wandering.

The whole of Chesapiuc helped the English dismantle their lodges and set them up again around one of the lakes. The Indians also helped erect a large lodge for Virginia and Trevelyan.

The men cut the straightest poles they could find with their sharpened stone axes. These poles, with one end chipped away to a point, were staked into the ground at intervals in the rectangular shape of the lodge. The poles were built up to the height desired—the taller a lodge, the cooler in summer and the more room for the smoke to disperse in winter.

All lodges were built the same. Along both sides inside were beds, sleeping platforms raised a foot or more above the ground by forked poles, and covered with willow wands. On top of this the rush mats were spread for sleeping, and rolled up again in the morning.

The walls were also covered with mats. By means of cleverly arranged rawhide strings, they could be raised or lowered at the lodge dweller's pleasure, opening up a wall for light or air, covering it for warmth and privacy. Mats were even rolled up above the entrances, and lowered to make the lodge windproof and warm in inclement weather.

Trevelyan fitted new shafts to the rusting ax heads the Roanoke survivors had hoarded, and soon the trees were falling down, providing wood for the fires and dugouts, helping to clear the ground for planting the following year.

The frame of the pinnace was placed on a log raft and towed to the inlet at Chesapiuc town, then along the canallike stream to the freshwater lakes. There it was carried ashore and Trevelyan began his work. It took him a year to get the vessel in shape.

Virginia supervised the planting of the crops and the tanning of the skins. Jane Mannering was in charge of the children, making sure the boys received their daily lessons in archery. Emma Merrimoth saw to it that everyone spoke English some of the time.

In the fall, Virginia discovered she was pregnant. She had waited a long time for this joyous news, holding her breath each month when her menses were due. She and John had spoken often of a child—children, even—happily deciding on a son first, a daughter later. But as time passed and Virginia did not conceive, they had gradually come to avoid the subject.

As a medicine woman, Virginia was familiar with the herbs used to promote pregnancy, and resorted to them regularly. Some time ago, she had also carefully set aside the medicines needed for childbirth—to relieve labor pains, black cherry and lady fern; to speed delivery, partridgeberry and blue cohosh.

But month after month, as she felt the familiar twinge in her belly signaling the start of her menstrual period, the medicines needed for childbirth were pushed farther into the back of the lodge, out of painful sight.

Then, in September, there was no twinge, no pain to precede the flow of blood. In fact, there was no blood at all. Virginia was overjoyed, but said nothing to Trevelyan.

Perhaps it wasn't a child, perhaps she merely skipped her menses this one month. The Swallowtail had taught her that such could easily occur in a woman's life.

So Virginia hugged her secret, waiting half-joyfully, half-fearfully for the following month, sometimes filled with smiles and happiness, sometimes sad and depressed, seemingly for no reason at all. Her odd shifts of mood—troublesome and puzzling to her husband—served to reassure her. She had learned about moods at this time from the Swallowtail and had observed it herself with pregnant women.

In October, when she missed her period for the second time, Virginia knew it had happened. She was with child! She was, gloriously, with Trevelyan's child.

She told him that night, after they had made love under the stars in the woods, with his body still covering hers, warming her in the chill of the fall air.

"Is it true?" he said, his breath catching in his throat from joy and excitement. "Is it really true? Oh, my darling." He kissed her eyelids, her cheeks, her mouth, as his hands entwined themselves deeply in her hair. She opened her mouth under his, arching her back.

"No," he protested, drawing away from her lovemaking for the first time. "We must think of the baby. You must rest now, my love. We need to wait."

He remembered how expectant women in England were pampered and cosseted for the nine months of their pregnancy, and he was determined to do the same for his wife and child. But Virginia only laughed at his concern. "It is not the same here," she said. "The Swallowtail told me that the husband needs to keep the birth channel well greased for the easy descent of the child."

Trevelyan laughed with her, his lips finding Virginia's once more. Their lovemaking was never sweeter than at this sweet and happy time.

By the third month of her pregnancy, Virginia did not feel like making love. She didn't feel like doing much at all, buffeted as she was with constant nausea. Keeping food down was becoming a major challenge.

Miss Merrimoth, who had shown no interest in childbirth before, observed Virginia's pale and sickly face and announced she was taking charge. From this point on, Emma Merrimoth was supervising Virginia's pregnancy.

"Your child is precious, Virginia," she said. "It will be the grandson of an English earl. You must receive the best of attention and not be left to the mercy of primitive medicines and witch doctors."

"Emma," Virginia said sternly, "you must not speak like that about Indians. You owe your very life to them. You know their medicines are good. You need only look around to see how healthy everyone is. From what I have heard," she added, raising her voice for emphasis, "it was the English on Roanoke who brought all the sickness to the New World."

Miss Merrimoth drew herself erect.

"Virginia Dare, how *could* you say such a thing! You know that is not true."

She stalked away, heading straight for Trevelyan to state her case. To Miss Merrimoth's surprise, John Trevelyan agreed with his wife.

"In England," he said, "many children die stillborn or shortly after birth, mostly as a result of poverty or disease. But children here are remarkably healthy. If the Indians weren't always warring with each other, many more babes would reach maturity.

"I think the Indians are rather more efficient in matters of childbirth than we English. And Virginia herself is an accomplished midwife, so why don't we leave this child to her?"

He smiled winningly, and the Englishwoman gave a dutiful, rather bleak smile in return. She was in awe of Trevelyan because he was an earl's son, and she failed to understand why the others did not appear to be equally impressed.

She took what he said more as an injunction than a suggestion, but was still not happy.

"I looked after all the children here," she began, and he looked up quickly in disbelief. She caught the look and amended what she had said. "I looked after their scholarly and religious education. Surely, that is as important as pushing Indian stew down their throats."

Trevelyan was amazed to see the woman's eyes fill with tears.

"Without me, they would have grown up untutored savages. Now, at least, they can speak English as well as that heathen tongue, and they can read, too, after a fashion, thanks to lessons with the Bible. I have done my duty in arranging their easier return to civilized, Christian society. It will be difficult enough as it is, as you well know, John Trevelyan, for them to be accepted at home. You know what our Church thinks of mingling Christian blood with the heathen's. Half-breeds are degenerates."

Trevelyan was fully aware of how the children of his village would be regarded in England. With true English perversity, the Indian wives would be considered quaint but acceptable equals; only the children would be looked upon as tainted.

"Why don't we wait until the child is born?" he suggested. "Then it will need a nanny and a teacher. You could be that, if you would do me the great honor."

Emma Merrimoth nodded yes, but still tried to explain why she had been so determined to step in now.

"I like the other children, you see, and I do not hold it against them that they have savage blood. But your child is different. It will be completely English, the first completely English child born among those who survived the destruction of the Roanoke colony. It is a special child. *An English child!*"

She did not wait for his reply, which was just as well, for he had none. As she left their lodge, he saw her beckoning imperiously to several children, and grinned when they stopped their games and, obviously reluctant, followed her to her lodge for still another lesson from the Bible.

Despite her promise not to interfere, Miss Merrimoth stepped in again just before Virginia's child was due. They had to arrange for the most important men of the tribe to be present at the birth, she said. Jane Mannering was aghast.

"Have you lost your senses?" she demanded. "Men are not allowed at the birthing. This is not a play performed on stage."

"You are confused by Indian childbirth customs," snapped Miss Merrimoth. Jane Mannering's eyes flashed in anger, but she could only manage a haughty "Well!" by way of a response. Miss Merrimoth continued.

"In England, when the queen gives birth, the king's representatives are there to witness it and to report on the condition and sex of his heir."

"But I am *not* the queen of England," Virginia said, trying hard not to smile.

"You are the queen *here*," was the reply.

For months now, Virginia had looked as glorious as any queen in the world. She brewed herself a tea made from the pink flowers of the harback shrub to ease the tiredness and slight choking feeling that accompanied the swelling of her body. An ointment from the milk of purslane, its root mixed with animal fat, helped her sore and tender breasts.

But her skin and eyes glowed of their own accord. Her hair had never been more lustrous, her color never a warmer, rosier pink. Trevelyan thought she positively shone as the months passed and the child within her grew.

And she felt wonderful, bubbling over as she spoke of their return to England with renewed zeal. She asked Trevelyan endless questions about all he had ever seen. How large was London, really? How stately was the queen? What did the ladies wear at court? What did Trevelyan's father and mother look like?

Her labor began one sunny day about noon. Virginia felt the first contractions and asked Trevelyan to fetch the midwife to their lodge.

As a midwife herself, Virginia knew what to expect when her child came. But helping other women in childbirth and feeling the knifelike contractions herself were worlds apart. She longed for her husband, wanted to be held and petted by him, wanted to be reassured that it would be over soon, that the child would make it all worthwhile.

It continued for hours. No medication, no carefully brewed black-cherry tea could ease the hurting, the throbbing pain that filled her body.

Almost in a haze, she heard the midwife exhort her to press down, press harder, harder still; she was not aware of the woman's hands pushing on her distended belly to help the child move. Then Virginia screamed and suddenly, miraculously, the tiny, wet babe slid from her womb.

"It's a man child," the midwife cried and Trevelyan rushed into the lodge. He looked down at the little red face and felt a great tenderness wash over him. He turned to Virginia with wet eyes, his hands brushing at her matted hair, his face split in an enormous smile. Then the midwife urged him outside, for there was more work to do.

When Virginia was comfortable at last, the midwife gave her the child. Virginia held her son carefully, tenderly, as if the tiny miracle might break.

"My husband," she said.

Trevelyan stepped inside. For a moment, he only looked down at Virginia, taking in her glowing beauty, then knelt beside her. She motioned to the midwife to leave, and the old woman, smiling and nodding, backed out of the lodge.

"I have given you a son," she said in a whisper, following the tradition of Indian women in apprising the father of their newborn. Trevelyan gave her the slow smile she loved.

"You have given me a prince," he said, and bent to kiss her shining face.

17

Virginia's son was born on what Trevelyan assumed was the twenty-fifth of May in the year 1606. But it was a guess, for he had lost track of days and weeks. Virginia was now eighteen. They named the boy Richard, after his paternal grandfather, the Earl of Budleigh. He had dark hair and gray eyes.

Trevelyan launched the pinnace at last, finding it waterproof and seaworthy. The iron oarlocks were still in good condition and he had painstakingly carved four oars. He taught the boys to row and steer, letting the children take the pinnace into the lake for use as a moving diving board while he made the mast and yard.

It took months to prepare the skins for the large square sail and sew them together, and by the time it was finished it was too late to take the pinnace out into the open sea, for by then the late fall storms and winds had started.

Virginia had marveled at Trevelyan's singlemindedness in

rebuilding the pinnace. He had spent almost every day for a year working on the boat and its fittings.

Virginia had never been happier. With winter, the game birds came to the lakes by the thousands. She taught Trevelyan how to hunt them with the bow. He made thin wooden javelins, tipped with sharp stones, which he used for spearing fish.

After the evening meal, their lodge was open to all members of the tribe. In the winter evenings, everyone gathered there to tell stories of the New Land and reminisce about the old.

At times, Virginia thought she could stay here for the rest of her life. But contented as she felt, England stayed uppermost in her mind. This place was wonderful, but it was only an interlude until they all returned to England.

o

Arrow-Flies-True was the first to hear the sounds from the direction of the Chesapiuc town. He rushed to a large tree, climbing swiftly to the top. He stared straight ahead for a few minutes, then came quickly down, running to Virginia and Trevelyan's lodge.

Chesapiuc was being attacked. They must all flee from here, Arrow-Flies-True told Virginia and Trevelyan. The fighting he had seen was fierce, with many lodges already in flames.

"It's happening again, John," Virginia said. "We must save ourselves, escape while we can."

The ferocity, and regularity, of the Indian tribes' attacks on one another never ceased to shock Trevelyan. He was used to wars; the countries of Europe were forever battling over sea or land. But the Indian fights seemed so much more personal, always taking place amongst women and children.

Trevelyan knew Virginia would never allow her tribe to suffer what Badger's people had had to undergo after the Opossum attack. From what Arrow-Flies-True had told them, the warring party attacking Chesapiuc town was large. There was no question of the English putting up a fight.

Virginia was already making her calculations.

"The Chesapiuc have one hundred warriors," she said. "The attackers need four times that number for victory. We do not know why they attack. If it is for women only, they will strike and flee. If it is to conquer, they will kill the men, and then old people and some children.

"We must board the pinnace and head to the open sea. It is our only chance."

During her years as queen of the tribe, Virginia had matured remarkably. She had regained her full use of grammatical English with Trevelyan's help, and had used the leadership abilities learned from Badger and Screams-Like-Wildcat. She was an effective and intelligent leader, and her people followed her readily.

Under Virginia's supervision, it took only a half hour to load up the pinnace.

Trevelyan arranged the mats and skins along the bottom and piled the children on them. Then the baskets of food—corn and roots—were placed in rows to protect them. Gourds were filled with drinking water. All the iron utensils were loaded. Not only would they be needed wherever they were going, they would serve as ballast in the open sea.

The men put their weapons aboard and Trevelyan his javelins. They were still loading the vessel when the scouts they had placed at high vantage points shouted that the town of Chesapiuc was ablaze. Virginia ordered everyone into the pinnace.

The women were pulled on board and settled down with the children, Emma Merrimoth holding Virginia's baby. Virginia ordered mats and skins pulled over the youngsters. Someone wanted the little town burned to prevent the attackers from looting, but Virginia pointed out that that would simply let the enemy know a town existed.

Without a backward glance, she told Trevelyan to cast off. He pulled up the stone anchor, shook down the sail, and the pinnace moved off.

They sailed slowly along the lake with a slight following breeze. Then they turned into the canallike stream. Trevelyan had fixed the sail with a series of pulleys so that without any help, he could adjust the sail from where he sat at the rudder. But the tall trees thickly crowding the narrow banks sealed off the wind, and the boat slowed, with hardly enough way from the current to keep the bows pointing downstream.

Trevelyan ordered out the oars, and men and boys pulled together. It was three miles to the inlet. When they passed the first bend and entered the long, almost straight stretch to the inlet and the open sea, the breeze was able to descend to the level of the water and, with a sigh of relief, Trevelyan ordered the oars shipped.

Now, finally, they picked up speed. As they neared the inlet, they could clearly hear the battle. Virginia positioned men on each side, with bows at the ready, and put some of the boys on either side armed with javelins, to repel boarders.

She drew an arrow from her quiver and nocked it, the men quickly following suit. They were ready for battle.

They came into the inlet at a fair clip. As Trevelyan turned north toward the sea, the breeze from the land caught the sail and it billowed out.

All eyes turned to the town now only a few hundred yards away. The lodges had burned swiftly and there was nothing but piles of glowing embers where they had stood. There were bodies everywhere and bands of yelling, rampaging warriors—the conquerors—running hither and there, waving long-haired scalps, booty, and even human heads. It had not been an expedition to steal wives, nor even the conquest of a tribe that had resisted a rival chief's demand for domination. This had been a war of utter extermination.

Trevelyan had seen death before, at sea, on the gallows in England. But he had never seen total destruction like this.

A town of two hundred and fifty people had stood here this morning. Now, it had ceased to exist. The invaders were sure to attack other small towns farther down the inland bays.

From the opposite shore a small flotilla of dugouts was heading toward them, jammed with fiercely painted warriors. Their paddles dipped in unison, the canoes seeming to spring out of the water. Trevelyan knew how fast the brawny paddlers could drive these small, sleek boats.

He saw from under the billowing sail that the mouth of the inlet was now only a few hundred yards away. Once through it and into the open sea, they would be safe. No canoe could keep up with a sailboat for long.

He measured the distance to the nearest dugout. If he turned closer to the shore from where the stream emerged, he could outdistance it easily.

Virginia was shouting at him.

"In front! There's one in front!"

Trevelyan cursed. He had not noticed the dugout ahead. The warriors had shipped their paddles and were fixing arrows to bowstrings.

Trevelyan watched as the pinnace drew closer to the small vessel. If the outgoing current would only swing the canoe around until it was broadside to the pinnace, he could do it. There, it had begun to swing, the paddles no longer keeping it under way and pointed at them.

"Get everybody down!" he yelled to Virginia. She relayed the message and the men and boys huddled at the bottom of the pinnace. "You, too, Virginia." She squatted beside Trevelyan.

The pinnace was wide-beamed with a shallow draught. With luck, what he was about to do would succeed. If luck deserted them, they would all die.

The arrows had started flying. From Trevelyan's vantage point at the stern, he could see their points sticking through the thin leather sail. He realized that the Indians had never before seen a sail and might have been hoping to halt the pinnace by shooting at it.

As the two boats drew closer, he saw the first sign of alarm on the faces of the men in the dugout. When they were but a few feet away, they realized what was going to happen and all of them—there were about a dozen—stood up. It was exactly what Trevelyan wanted them to do.

The pinnace struck the dugout with a loud booming

noise, its bows rising out of the water and over the canoe. The Indians flew over backward into the water.

The pinnace came to a complete halt, its prow sticking out of the water, the dugout firmly wedged underneath it. Trevelyan had hoped the pinnace would ride clean over the canoe, driving it under with its weight. But the dugout was deep and it had not gone over on its side to fill with water.

The Indians from the canoe were swimming back to the dugout and beginning to climb back aboard. In a moment they would be swarming onto the pinnace. Trevelyan glanced behind him and saw to his horror that other canoes were rapidly overhauling them.

Virginia shouted at the men in the pinnace to use their bows; she was already on her feet, bowstring pulled back at full draw. She released the string and the arrow vanished, appearing swiftly in the chest of a brave who had just reached out from the dugout to grab the larger boat.

The men on the pinnace loosed a volley into the warriors swimming around the canoe. Virginia saw sinewy brown arms reach over the prow of the pinnace and shouted, "Javelins!"

The tribe's male children, ranging in age from seven to ten, sprang up from behind baskets of food, javelins in their hands. They had learned how to throw the light spears from Trevelyan. As the first enemy face appeared, one of the children threw his weapon. There was a scream of pain. The Indian brave reared backward, grabbing at the javelin stuck firmly in his left eye.

One of the attackers tried to heave himself out of the water at Virginia's feet. She kicked him in the face, forcing his head back in pain and surprise. Then her bowstring went taut and an arrow flew straight into the man's open mouth.

The brave fell, thrashing, into the water. Trevelyan could see the point of Virginia's arrow protruding almost two feet from the back of his neck.

Others from the dugout were grabbing at the edges of the pinnace, trying to haul themselves aboard. Trevelyan felt his vessel move forward, but it was only due to the wind in the sail and the current pushing both boats. The pinnace was still trapped on top of the dugout.

There was a sudden, loud scream. One of the boys on the pinnace pointed to his right. A fiercely painted warrior was clambering over the side, his eyes fixed on Virginia. She had her back to the man, loosening her arrows into the fray.

In one fluid movement, Trevelyan dropped the rudder and sail ropes and sprang at the Indian. Just as the man rose to his feet, Trevelyan grasped him by the throat, his fingers digging into the neck, his thumb pressing into the Adam's apple.

For an instant the man stared at him, and Trevelyan looked into black eyes shining with hatred. Then he bent down, grabbing the man between the legs. Raising the Indian high above his head, he pitched the brave over the stern into the water.

Suddenly, the pinnace gave a great lurch and surged forward. Trevelyan grabbed his ropes. The dugout had finally capsized and filled with water, allowing the pinnace to push it under and slide over it.

They were free! But there were still other canoes, one just yards behind the pinnace.

Virginia was drawing her bowstring again when the capsized dugout, no longer held under by the pinnace, bobbed to the surface behind them. The pursuing canoe smashed into it. One of the Indians in the dugout, dropping his paddle and stretching his arms to grasp the stern of the pinnace, shot out of his craft at the same time that Virginia released the arrow. It caught him in midair, full in the chest. He splashed into the water, blood spewing from his mouth.

Several of the pursuing dugouts changed direction to avoid the deadly missiles. Trevelyan saw Virginia shoot smoothly and steadily at the pursuers.

Then they were out of range and at the mouth of the inlet.

"Everyone down and hold on," Trevelyan called out. A moment later they hit the waves of the open Chesapiuc Bay. He held on course, due north, until they were clear of the shore and the sea was calmer. Then he looked back.

The dugouts were clustered inside the inlet and, although they were out of range, he could see the destroyers of Chesapiuc town gesticulating angrily with their paddles.

He turned quickly back to the others in his boat, shouting, "We won! We won!"—relieved and thankful over their escape. From under mats and skins piled down the center of the boat, heads began to appear. The women and children were daring to come out from their hiding places. It was truly over.

o

The pinnace continued to sail up the bay while Virginia tended the three men who had been slightly wounded.

Now that they had some time to assess the situation, the tribe discussed the reason for the attack. Virginia felt certain that the warring party had come from Powhatan. No other chief destroyed as ruthlessly—only Powhatan's braves killed everyone in a town they had come to attack. Chesapiuc seemed to have no survivors. They had seen no women and children grouped together while the victorious braves ran through the town. They had seen no one, except the victorious warriors.

There was no sign of Thomas Humphrey, the lone Englishman who had decided to stay behind in Chesapiuc with his Indian family.

In the heat of battle, no one had thought of Humphrey and what might be his fate. But now the memory of the man—one of their own, perished so cruelly when he and his wife and children could so easily have been saved—cast a terrible pall.

Virginia held her son tightly as she thought of Humphrey's three children, two boys and a girl. Dear God, why hadn't they come along? She should have insisted, forced Humphrey to join them somehow.

Finally, Emma Merrimoth spoke:

"We must say a prayer for their souls."

She took the dog-eared Bible from one of the leather purses hanging at her waist and thumbed through it, reading the passage she chose in a loud, clear voice.

"Ecclesiastes, chapter three.

"To every thing there is a season, and time to every purpose under the heaven.

"A time to be born, and a time to die . . ."

Jane Mannering wept aloud. The others whispered the words along with Miss Merrimoth.

"And a time to die . . ."

It was many hours before Virginia finally felt able to turn her mind—and the minds of the others—to what they had to do next: decide where to continue their journey.

Virginia vetoed Croatoan, even though Manteo had made her feel so welcome. She could not forget the way his warriors had abandoned her. Trevelyan agreed that they could not go there. Besides, he pointed out, their small pinnace could not survive the long sail south to Croatoan.

Virginia suggested that they sail north, out of Powhatan's range, trying to find a friendly tribe and settling near them. She was still certain that the English would come again and find them. She spoke long and convincingly of this, at last persuading the others to follow her unwavering belief. It was decided that the pinnace would head north.

They had to land somewhere for the night, however, to find water and meat. So as soon as they passed the great opening, from the bay into the Atlantic, Trevelyan steered to the right shore. They moved slowly, keeping well off the coast in case any hostile canoes set out to intercept them, but they saw nothing. As dusk fell, Trevelyan edged closer, lowered the sail, and they rowed to the shore.

They fed again on crushed corn, and Virginia described what lay on the opposite side from them. The great river on their left was called the Powhatan. On its banks were the towns of Nansemond, Mattanock, Warascoyack, Kiskiak, Quayoughtcohanek, and Paspahegh.

The next river, which they passed that evening, was the Pamunkey, she said, and listed the towns on the shores of that river too.

Only Trevelyan was surprised that she could recall from memory so many towns she had never seen, whose names she had only heard from little Pocahontas.

William Withers, a quiet, intelligent man, saw the perplexed expression on Trevelyan's face and sought to explain.

"In England, there is little need for a good memory," Withers said. "Everything is written down, and need only be researched if memory fails. Even the illiterate can ask for assistance.

"But the True People have no written language. Everything they learn must be stored in their minds, for that kind of knowledge means survival. Even we who were born in England but raised here have acquired this ability. When you realize, John, that your memory is the only book you have to read, you, too, will remember."

They lit no fires that night, and posted guards. Virginia was moody and depressed. Trevelyan knew that the battle at Chesapiuc had brought back terrible memories. She tossed and turned by his side, unable to sleep.

He murmured soft words of comfort, trying to soothe her, but nothing seemed to have an effect. At last he brought her gently to her feet and led her into the forest.

Virginia had been brought up among highly gregarious people; Indians loved doing everything together—hunting, working, playing, eating. But what happened between man and woman was private. Communal living did not include lovemaking.

In the silence of the forest, Trevelyan gathered his wife in his arms, stroking her hair, her back, her arms. She leaned against him silently, returning his soft kisses. He lowered her to the ground, removing both their clothing before he entered her.

Their lovemaking this time was not the ferocious joining of bodies that usually took place. Instead sex was to comfort, to reaffirm their deep feelings for each other, to show love and caring in a physical way.

Afterward, Virginia lay in the circle of her husband's warm body and was finally able to sleep.

At dawn they hunted, taking a fine buck and a score of squirrels. They gathered firewood and put out from the shore before it was full daylight. Trevelyan arranged the cooking platform he had put on board months before and gave the boys their fishing lines. The gourds and clay cooking pots had been filled at a small stream.

They set off up the bay, with enough meat, fish, corn, and water that they did not have to put into shore until the next evening.

On the fourth day a mighty estuary loomed on their left. It was the Patawomeck River, the northernmost boundary of Powhatan's empire, Virginia told them. This river ran west to the lands of the Manahoac tribes of the Siouan peoples, deadly enemies of Powhatan.

In the Siouan territory, Pocahontas had told Virginia there was a ridge of blue mountains with pleasant valleys on the other side.

They were still within sight of Patawomeck—which the English would later call the Potomac—when the storm struck. Trevelyan let the pinnace run before the wind, and they almost flew up the Patawomeck estuary. They were a dozen miles along it before they managed to shelter from what had now become a gale.

The storm lasted three days, during which time they concealed the pinnace in a little creek. By the time it had abated, the group was weary, dejected, tired of the monotonous meals of crushed corn with no fire to cook over.

Should they go back to Chesapiuc Bay and retrace their route north? Or should they continue to follow this great river?

Trevelyan asked about the dangers along the Patawomeck. Virginia named the towns—Wighcocomoco, with a hundred and thirty warriors, which they had already passed on their left; Sekacawon, with thirty; Onawmanient with one hundred; then Patawomeck with one hundred sixty.

"Can you lead us through the Manahoac to the mountains, and perhaps across them?" Trevelyan wanted to know.

Virginia thought for a long while.

"If we sail past the Patawomeck main town, we could

land and start crossing to the mountains, but it will be a long way."

She turned to Trevelyan.

"I wish I could count distances like you do in miles on land and leagues at sea. But I can only count the days it takes to travel on foot. We have thirty-seven persons—nine men and ten women, the rest children, four of them babes in arms. The men cannot bear any goods for they are needed to guard us and hunt. The elder children must carry the babes, for the women will have to carry the baskets. Children not carrying babes will also help with our goods.

"So the going will be slow, for we shall be heavily burdened. I cannot say how long it will take."

She was worried about something else. "If we cross the mountains and the English come, will they still find us?" she asked Trevelyan.

"If they come here to settle, they will colonize and move over ever larger areas. If I know the English, they will not rest until they have conquered all the land they can see. They will cross the mountains."

Virginia was satisfied. She turned back to the others.

"I will lead you over the mountains. It is possible we shall be safe there, for we shall be in the land of our enemy's enemy. But I leave it to you to decide if you will go. I shall not order you."

There was, actually, little choice. The group agreed to go overland, and the next day they set off up the river again.

They passed the town of Patawomeck and continued many miles past. Then they landed and unloaded their goods, spreading the weight equally among the nine women. Virginia carried nothing. Her place was to lead.

She appointed Arrow-Flies-True chief hunter, and William Withers chief warrior. Trevelyan she placed at the head of the column, armed with a metal ax and several spears.

Before they set out, she told Trevelyan she would set fire to the pinnace so that no trace of the tribe would be left behind.

"If you do, Virginia, we must continue until we find a place to settle. There will be no turning back."

"It must be done," Virginia said, ordering the children to pile kindling into the boat. She herself set it alight.

Virginia set the pace, allowing the heavily burdened women to walk only two or three miles a day, with several rest periods.

It took them over a month to reach the foot of the mountains, where they met the Manahoac, who provided food and guides to help the little group on its way. They also cautioned Virginia to wrap protective coverings around everyone's legs to guard against the poisonous snakes in the mountain scrub.

Virginia knew about snakes in the swamplands where she had been raised. She had been taught not to kill a snake, for their children would come and kill her children. So, in the swamps, she had waited until they simply slid out of her path. But on a mountainside one could step on a snake before it had time to move away.

They reached the top of the long mountain range and looked down the other side. They saw a beautiful valley with a blue river that writhed like a snake from one end to the other. Beyond the valley long ranges of mountains loomed blue in the distance.

That night they camped on the mountaintop and marveled at the myriad twinkling lights in the clear sky. The valley was well named. Shenandoah—the Daughter of the Stars.

18

The years went by and the little tribe prospered. The Siouan were friendly and agreed to their moving on a piece of land that stretched from across the river to the summit of a mountain. The first winter would have been bad, for they had time to make only one corn planting after their arrival, but Virginia had carefully saved a good quantity of the pearls they had taken from Chesapiuc Bay, and she bargained with these for more corn.

The following year they planted extensive gardens. The fishing was limited, unlike the great quantities of fish they had been accustomed to take from the saltwater bay, but meat was plentiful.

They built a fine lodge for Emma Merrimoth's schoolhouse. After their lessons there at the Bible, the boys would learn all the warrior skills from Trevelyan and the other men.

Virginia once asked Trevelyan if he would like to try and domesticate animals for constant food supply like they did in England.

"Do we not have enough to eat, my love?" he asked. "Do we not have enough skins to clothe us?"

"You speak like my Indian father Badger did," she said. "The others say you are very wise, John. I say this too. You always know what is right."

Everyone agreed that a heavy snowfall was due; they could smell it in the air. The children thought only of rolling in the soft white blanket, the older boys excited about learning to track game by their spoors.

For the men, the snow meant one last try for venison before the storm made hunting all but impossible. They greased themselves well with bear fat for protection against the cold, donned fur mantles that covered their shoulders, and headed west across the valley to the foothills, where the deer were running thick.

They chose a camping spot in the afternoon, lighting a great fire to roast dried meat from their packs and settling down for an early night. The next morning they were up and on the hunt before dawn. There were seven hunters including Trevelyan, and by noon they had bagged three good-sized bucks and a smaller deer. They dressed the animals immediately to lighten the load, trussing three of them to poles, each to be carried by two men, one behind the other, the poles slung over their shoulders.

Trevelyan threw the smallest deer, weighing about one hundred twenty-five pounds, across his great back with ease. That night, the men roasted fresh venison strips taken from the animal Trevelyan bore.

The next morning, the sky was heavily overcast, the clouds obscuring the hilltops on both sides of the valley. The deer carcasses were frozen solid. The men reckoned that, moving steadily, with only a short break to rest, they would reach their town by early afternoon. But soon after they started back, the first snowflakes began to fall. Within an hour, the snow was several inches deep. And an hour after that, snow reached over their ankles, inching upward to their knees.

As they descended the foothills, they found the snow drifting, and Trevelyan went ahead to break trail. Near the valley floor, he fell back to the rear for a respite, and two other Englishmen—Thomas Smart and John Pratt—took the lead. The snow was over a foot deep now, and although the men's exertions kept the blood pumping through their bodies, it was not enough to prevent numbness creeping into their bare feet. They began to slip and stumble, but still kept on, unwilling to abandon their burdens while there was a chance of getting the venison home.

Then abruptly the snow, which had been a steady though heavy fall, turned into a blizzard. They struggled through the first buffets of wind until it became a gale, as suddenly and as unexpectedly as any Trevelyan had experienced at sea. The biting wind tore the upper levels of snow from the ground, tossing them in every direction. Within minutes, visibility was gone. The men dropped the deer, shouting at each other through the howling wind.

If they had still been in the wooded foothills, their predicament would not have been serious. They would have gone deep into the trees, piled branches around themselves for a wind break, and kept a fire going. With plenty of venison to roast, they could have outlasted any storm.

But now they were halfway across the valley, and it was the same distance in either direction to safety. They decided to go on, untying the ropes that held the deer to the carrying poles, using this to tie themselves together at the waist so none would be lost—or they would all be lost together.

It was then they discovered that Trevelyan had vanished.

They retraced their trail, calling his name, but soon saw that the wind was drifting snow across their footsteps, obliterating them as fast as they were made. They realized that if they were to have any chance of reaching safety they would have to abandon Trevelyan and strike out for the town.

So they set off, bent almost double against the wind, instinct alone guiding them eastward across the valley.

Trevelyan had been caught off balance by the first gusts of the blizzard and spun around. Starting off again, trying to follow the group, he had walked away from them instead. Thinking he was following his friends, he plunged on through the snowdrifts for long minutes, until at last some inner sense told him he was alone. He tried retracing his footsteps, shouting out names and stopping to listen for the replies, but there was only the howling of the wind in his ears.

When he was back to where he thought he had left the trail, he walked deliberately in circles, hoping to come across the others if they had halted or were looking for him. He realized that unless he actually stumbled across them now, he would never find them, and he would never hear them above the shrieking of the wind.

He was on his third ever-widening circle when he stepped into space and plunged into a snowdrift. He landed on his back but the deer, which to his numbed surprise he discovered he was still carrying, broke his fall.

He pushed the snow away from his face and lay for a moment to get his breath, feeling around him and discovering that he had fallen from a rock outcrop. He sat up and had to clamp his hands over his mouth and nose to prevent himself from suffocating on the snow.

The temptation to strike out in a panic was almost overwhelming, but he conquered it, and slowly began to make a space for himself.

Gradually, he was able to get to his knees and clear the snow from the rock face to lean his back up against it. He could hear the blizzard outside, but here, in his little snow cave, it was almost peaceful. It was freezing, but there was no wind.

Little by little he enlarged his cave until he could stretch out on his back and sit up with his legs crossed. He kept widening his refuge until his arms pushed through the drift and a gust of freezing air blew in. He patted the snow back in place, keeping a tiny hole open where the drift met the rock wall.

He dug up the packed snow underneath him and piled it all around. Then he drew his knife and, by feel alone, half cut and half ripped the skin from the frozen carcass beside him. He spread the body, split and ragged though it was, under him, hair up, and immediately felt the difference when his bare legs and feet were protected from the wet, freezing mud underneath.

As his body temperature and breath heated up the little room, Trevelyan felt drowsiness creeping up on him. He knew Indian men could survive in zero temperatures, but he wasn't sure of his own ability. He had to fight off sleep.

He cut a piece of meat from the frozen deer carcass that shared his white tomb, and chewed it slowly. His breath and the heat from his body melted the snow walls just enough to keep them from freezing over, thus giving the cave a thin, but hard, inside wall. It was completely windproof and sealed off from the outside, except for the tiny hole he kept open for air.

It grew warm and, despite himself, Trevelyan slept, but only intermittently. In his waking hours, he wondered what had happened to the other men, if they had reached the village, and when they would be able to come to search for him.

As night wore on, he took out his little pouch of bear grease and spread it thickly on his hands, feet, and other extremities.

The snow caused great excitement in town. Moccasins and leggings were unearthed, children ran about the white covering, women stopped their preparation of an early meal.

From time to time, Virginia walked to the river's edge and stared across the valley, but she was not unduly worried until the blizzard struck. With her child inside the lodge, snuggled up in warm skins next to a small fire, she went to see Arrow-Flies-True and Jane Mannering.

"You have nothing to fear," the chief hunter told her. "As soon as the snow became heavy, they made camp in the woods, and will stay there until the storm is over.

"They are experienced hunters, not young braves. My son is with them and I have no fear for his safety. Do not be concerned about John."

Soothed but still worried, Virginia returned to her lodge, eventually crawling under the heavy winter blankets of buffalo hides. She lay for a long time listening to the howling wind, then fell asleep.

Shouting woke her and she ran outside. The blizzard had not abated; she could see nothing, for snow covered the roofs and sides of all the lodges.

Then the shouts grew nearer and she heard Arrow-Flies-True and William Withers calling to each other.

"They're back! They're back!"

Now Virginia could see figures coming from the river. She sank up to her knees in snow as she ran forward jubilantly, calling, "John! John!"

She could see Arrow-Flies-True, William Withers, and others dragging members of the hunting party from the rushing, bloated waters. Virginia knelt by the nearest hunter, collapsed on the ground, and felt his face. The eyebrows and hair were coated with ice. The man was almost frozen stiff.

It was not Trevelyan, and with a cry she moved to the next. By this time women were pouring from the lodges to claim their men. Virginia reached the last hunter and stopped. There were only six men. Her husband was not there.

She grabbed Withers, who was helping to carry one of the frozen men, and shook his naked arm.

"Trevelyan is not here," she yelled into his face. "Where is my husband?"

"Let us get them inside and we shall find out," he shouted back.

A few minutes later, all six men were in their lodges. Indians knew how to fight off cold and frostbite by rubbing snow over the hands, feet, and face, although this time there was no real fear of frostbite. The hunters were well covered with bear grease and had collapsed more from exhaustion than the cold.

John Pratt was the first to recover sufficiently to talk. "He vanished," Pratt told Virginia and those around him. "He was walking behind us when the blizzard struck, and he just vanished. We went back for him but our tracks were disappearing as fast as we made them. We had no alternative but to give him up for lost."

There was a terrible dead feeling in Virginia as the other men spoke, each telling how they tried to find Trevelyan but were forced to give him up. Her brain was numb, trying to escape into black forgetfulness as it had done when she was first captured by the Indians as a child.

Then the sickness rose in her and she rushed outside. Her husband was dead. That was what they all told her. But she could not accept it.

She looked around their lodge. Everywhere, in the pale light of the little fire, she saw signs of Trevelyan. No, she could not accept life without him, could not sit idly by and dumbly mourn his passing.

She went to Emma Merrimoth's lodge. "I am going to find John," she told the older woman. "Will you look after the child while I am gone?"

"You will die out there, Virginia," Miss Merrimoth protested. "In this blizzard, you will—"

But Virginia cut her off.

"He is my life, Emma. I cannot live without him."

She covered herself thickly, from head to toe, with bear grease, then wrapped her body with skins, the fur side out. She put on a hat made from red-fox skin that covered her ears and fastened under her chin. She carried her moccasins and thick leggings and a pair of snowshoes made from birch bark.

She knelt and kissed her sleeping child, embraced Miss Merrimoth, then slipped out of the town.

When she crossed the river and put on her moccasins, leggings, and snowshoes, Virginia could hardly believe the fury of the storm. How could John, born to the comfort of a great house, survive in such weather? She trembled at the thought that he could not.

Raised as an Indian, Virginia's sense of direction was acute. She put her back to the river and started due west, the snowshoes gliding smoothly over the surface of the deep snow.

She stumbled over the bodies of the three deer around dawn; Trevelyan must be somewhere near here, she reasoned. She hid her face in her fur coverings until the ice on her eyebrows and eyelashes melted, then she began traveling in ever-widening circles, calling his name.

Trevelyan could scarcely believe how snug and warm he felt in his little snow cave, and he pushed his hand out through his air hole to make sure he was not simply suffocating on his own expelled breath.

The fresh air that poured in dried the slight film of sweat that had gathered on his forehead and he put his face closer to the hole, wondering if he was becoming feverish. Certainly, he was hallucinating. He distinctly heard a voice calling his name.

He listened. There it was again. "John! John!" If his companions had reached safety, they would remain there until the storm died before they came looking for him. If they had not reached safety, then they were dead. But the voice came again, nearer this time. He pinched himself and knew from the pain he was awake.

Again the voice. It was Virginia!

With a cry he thrust himself into the snow wall, threshing his arms until he broke free. He stood up, suddenly deafened by the screech of the wind. He looked around desperately but could see nothing through the swirling flakes.

"Virginia," he yelled at the top of his lungs. "Virginia!"

And suddenly she was in his arms. He dragged her backward into his refuge, tore off her snowshoes, and laid her down while he repaired the broken wall. When the storm was once again locked outside, they were finally able to speak.

"Why didn't you stay with the child? Even if I die, the child will need you."

"They told me you had died," she said. "And I cannot live without you."

On the third day, the storm abated and the skies turned blue once more. That afternoon, the rescue party, led by Arrow-Flies-True, found them. They had cleared a patch in the deep snow and Virginia had coaxed a fire into life. They were eating roasted venison when they heard Arrow-Flies-True calling their names.

For months afterward, their close brush with death subdued both Virginia and Trevelyan, making them oddly morose even with each other. It wasn't until spring that Virginia's customary vivaciousness returned and Trevelyan's banting good humor was heard again. But never a day passed that they did not fall silent at the memory of those terrible icy days, only to smile deeply into each other's eyes in loving relief.

With spring came the creamy white flowers of the bloodroot, bursting like stars through the late snow blanket. Trillium blossoms changed from white to pink, and blue violets, azaleas, anemones, joined the parade of flowers, adding their brilliant splashes of color.

In the spring Virginia gave birth to a daughter, a beautiful, golden-haired, blue-eyed creature with her father's slow smile. They called her Elinor, after Virginia's English mother.

During the five years they lived in the valley of the Shenandoah, five other children were born—to Elizabeth Chapman and Winifred Powell, to John Harvie and his doe-eyed wife, and to the wives of Thomas Humphrey and Thomas Smart—swelling the tribe to forty-three persons. Several of the sons and daughters of those married in Chesapiuc were now old enough to be asking for marriages.

As there were no blood relationships among this first generation of native-born, plans were made for weddings when they became of age.

19

They heard it in 1612. The English had come to the Chesapiuc!

It was a garbled tale from a Siouan hunting band that had crossed the mountain into their valley. Strange men with great canoes with white wings had entered the Chesapiuc, sailed up the Powhatan River, and settled their tribe on its banks, warring with the Powhatan empire.

The strangers were described as having generous amounts of hair on their faces, some hair being without color. And their eyes were strange, too, some the color of earth, or smoke from a lodge fire, or even like the empty sky.

"It must be the English!" Virginia exclaimed. "They have come for us. We must go and meet them immediately."

She wanted to strip their lodges and start out as soon as they could, but Trevelyan thought otherwise.

"If they are settled on the Powhatan River, it could be dangerous to try to get there. We must find out more about this. If it is really true, then only one or two of us should go to meet them, leaving the others here in safety."

Trevelyan's advice prevailed. It was agreed that Arrow-Flies-True and William Withers would cross the mountain ridge to find out more about the strangers from the Manahoac on the eastern side.

They were away almost two weeks, returning in great excitement. It was true! Europeans were settled on the Powhatan. And they had been there for four winters.

Trevelyan worked out the time on the inside of a piece of bark with a burnt stick. The foreigners must have arrived in 1607, the same year Virginia and her little tribe had escaped. If Powhatan had not come, they would have been saved long ago.

There was no time to waste. Virginia and Trevelyan must leave immediately for the English.

Arrow-Flies-True, John Pratt, and Little Bear, the husband of Elizabeth Chapman, would accompany them to the headwaters of the Chickahominy. Then Virginia and Trevelyan would continue by themselves, trusting to the friendship established by Trevelyan with the Chickahominy priests on their meeting years before.

The farewells were subdued. Trevelyan solemnly presented his small son with his spears and gave him the hand ax that he used for delicate woodworking. He hugged both children, the golden-haired girl registering her dismay through loud howls when he handed her to Miss Merrimoth.

They reached the Chickahominy River within a week, stopping only to be greeted and fed by the Manahoac tribes they passed through. The Chickahominy priests did indeed remember Trevelyan, providing him with additional information on the Europeans.

Trevelyan was subdued when he joined Virginia in the lodge they had been given to spend the night.

"It is the English who have landed, there is no doubt. But the priests told me that there has been nothing but war and trouble since they came.

"They say the English plant few crops but expect to be given food by the Indians. They believe this is because the English have no women with them to tend the fields. They do not understand that in England it is the men who work in the fields, and do not hunt wild animals like the Indians. They say the English have brought diseases with them, and before each ship brings new settlers, the ones from the previous ships have died from starvation or disease, as well as the arrows of Powhatan's warriors."

Virginia was silent. This was what Manteo had told her about the Roanoke colony. But it could not be true. The English could not be like that. One or two, perhaps . . .

They left their dugout at the confluence of the Chickahominy and the Powhatan, which Trevelyan had been told the English now called the James River.

The English had their main settlement a few miles down the river on an island from which they had ousted the Paspahegh tribe. They called this place Jamestown.

As they neared the white men's village, Virginia and Trevelyan crept silently through the woods. For they were also in Powhatan-controlled territory, and to be captured now, on the point of rescue, would be a catastrophe.

Virginia walked ahead of Trevelyan. Suddenly, she raised her hand and listened. Someone was approaching. She signaled to Trevelyan and they slipped behind a tree.

It was minutes before Trevelyan, his ears never so attuned to the woodland as Virginia's, heard it. Someone, more than one person, was walking carelessly; the branches were snapping back after being pushed aside. No Indian would make that much noise. Then they heard the voices, loud, raised in what Trevelyan thought was a whining complaint.

English!

Trevelyan took Virginia's hand and they stepped into the open.

Just coming into view in a gap between the trees were six men. Virginia and Trevelyan gasped at their appearance.

They were quite small in stature, shorter than Virginia, and dressed alike. They wore the cuirass, a breastplate and backplate of dull armor, buckled over the shoulders and down the sides. This was worn over a sleeveless, yellowish leather coat that reached to the upper thighs. Their arms were covered by their sleeved leather jerkins worn underneath their coats.

They wore metal headgear. Four of them wore the burgonet, which covered the neck and sides of the face. It had a peak in front, like the stiff hair of an Indian priest, and a ridged cockscomb. The others wore the morion, a high-crowned helmet with a brim all around.

Their legs were covered with high leather boots over canions, breeches with stockings attached to make one garment.

Their hair was short under the helmets, and they all had pointed beards and mustaches.

Thin-bladed swords hung at their waists; some of them had pistols stuck into waistbands. All six carried muskets.

Despite their fighting raiment, they did not radiate manliness. Instead, to Trevelyan and Virginia they looked shabby. Their clothing was scuffed and worn, their breeches and hose faded and torn. Under all the heavy leather and woolen clothing and armor, they were sweating heavily, and even from twenty feet away, Virginia and Trevelyan could smell the acrid stench of unwashed bodies.

Spotting the young couple as they walked forward to meet them, the men, as though pulled on strings by a puppeteer, raised their muskets in unison.

"Halt!"

The cry had come from several throats. Trevelyan and Virginia stopped.

"We are English. My name is John Trevelyan, and this is my wife, Virginia."

The men slowly lowered their guns and looked at one another.

"John who?" a black-bearded man asked.

"Trevelyan. Son of the Earl of Budleigh, in Devon."

The men were smiling now, and Virginia's heart lifted.

"Son of an earl, are we?" said another, a red-faced little man, and the rest burst out laughing.

Virginia and Trevelyan looked at each other in dismay. What was happening? A third man spoke.

"An earl and his countess, eh? That's a good one. Just look at yourselves. You look more like a pair of rascally Indians to me!"

The armed men from Jamestown scrutinized the giant, clean-shaven man with golden hair down to his shoulders. He wore only a two-piece leather apron that hung down back and front from his waist. In English eyes, he was naked. He carried a wooden spear and at his waist was a primitive stone ax.

The woman was beautiful. "In an Indian way," one of them said later, "if you like that kind." Her hair was long, black, and shiny. She wore what appeared to be a single garment, one long, narrow strip of tanned hide with a circle cut in the center and slipped over the head in the manner of a priest's chasuble.

It did not meet at the sides, and was only held in place by a belt of colored oyster-shell and stone beads.

It was heavily fringed along all the edges, but they could still catch a glimpse of long leg and the flesh where the firm breasts began to blossom.

The woman's skin was as brown as a berry. She was carrying a longbow in her hand and they could see a quiver full of arrows protruding over her shoulder. They had no doubt she was Indian.

"Look, she's got gray eyes!" one of the English said.

"A byblow from some Spaniard or Frenchy stopped off his ship for a quick visit to the draggle-tail lodge, I'll wager!"

They all burst out laughing again.

"An 'is lordship there looks like 'e done the same thing!"

"Like mother, like daughter, I say!"

Their accents were so strange that Virginia understood few of the actual words, but she knew she and Trevelyan were being laughed at. She looked at her husband and saw that he had gone white.

"Oh, look, 'e's angry. Mustn't upset the countess, must we!"

They were almost falling down with laughter.

Trevelyan stepped forward, his face twisted in fury.

"Stop this at once!" he shouted.

The men stopped laughing and straightened up.

"I am the son of the Earl of Budleigh, and my wife is Virginia Dare, from the Lost Colony at Roanoke!"

"How did you arrive here?" the black-bearded man asked.

"I was shipwrecked in Chesapiuc Bay seven years ago. We came to Jamestown as soon as we heard the English had returned."

"The English returned five years ago," the man snarled. The laughter was gone. "Why did it take you five years to condescend to call on us? Perhaps you were too busy with your tail-wagging?" He looked pointedly at Virginia.

Trevelyan started forward again, and the muzzles of six guns rose together. The black-bearded one, who was evidently the leader, walked up to Trevelyan, placed the muzzle of his gun directly under his chin, and deftly removed the ax, which he tossed casually into the bushes. Then he took the spear and threw that away too.

"Who is in charge in Jamestown? I demand you take me to him!" Trevelyan shouted.

"You demand?" The black-bearded man had stepped back and was now regarding the unarmed Trevelyan with something approaching hate.

"I'll tell you who you are. You are a deserter from Jamestown! You ran away to join the heathen and now that you're tired of them—or they of you—you come crawling back with this tale of being an earl's son and this your English wife.

"The penalty for deserting to the heathen is death, an' well you know it!"

He motioned to the others and several of them cautiously approached Trevelyan, two stepping behind him and thrusting their muskets in his back.

"Move! Back to the fort!"

Trevelyan was pushed forward. At least they were being taken to the English fort, where they would see someone in authority and have the matter cleared up instantly.

Trevelyan reached for Virginia's hand, both to reassure her and to bring her along with him, but the leader stepped forward again, his gun trained on the young woman.

"Not before she throws down her weapons," he said.

Trevelyan nodded to his wife.

"Do as he says."

Silently, she handed over the bow and slipped the quiver off her back. The man threw them under the trees, then spoke to the group surrounding Trevelyan.

"You take him back to the fort. I have some business to attend to here."

Knowing grins spread over the soldiers' faces. Trevelyan knew instantly something was terribly wrong, and lunged for the black-bearded man. A musket came crashing down on his head and he crumbled to the ground. Virginia screamed.

They kicked him to a standing position again, and this

time the muzzles of two guns were pushed into his back. He was shoved toward the fort.

"I'd just as soon kill you, mate," said one of the Englishmen. "Move, I tell you." Trevelyan stumbled ahead.

Behind him, the other men had thrown Virginia to the ground, and spreadeagled her. One man was pinning her arms down while two others held her legs. Her dress was thrown up over her waist, the dark triangle of hair stark against the white flesh.

The black-bearded man was fumbling at his breeches. He stepped between Virginia's outstretched legs and knelt down, his organ extending hugely in front of him.

Struggling desperately, Virginia managed to free one leg and struck out blindly. The black-bearded man screamed as her wild kick found its mark. His open palm came crashing down on the side of her face.

Trevelyan whirled around, throwing up his arms and brushing the two guns aside. They went off with a simultaneous explosion as he drove his clenched fists into the faces of his captors.

Trevelyan caught a brief glimpse of the black-bearded man's distended penis, then he was kicking the man with his foot, hardened by years of treading the forest floor. The man squealed in agony as the foot caught him square in the belly. He flew backward, crashing into another Englishman.

The men had released Virginia and leaped to their comrades' aid.

"Run! Run!" Trevelyan shouted to his wife. "Run! I will follow you."

Virginia scrambled to her feet and in a flash was among the trees. Trevelyan turned to go after her but something smashed into the back of his head and this time he dropped to the ground, unconscious.

The man who felled him with the butt of his musket kicked him savagely several times.

"The woman got away," he said, "but we'll hang this one."

20

Virginia ran, dodging in and out of the trees, until she could run no longer and had to stop to catch her breath. She turned and looked behind her. There was no one following. She listened carefully, but the forest was silent.

She shuddered with revulsion at the memory of the man unbuttoning his breeches, his red penis about to plunge into her, the heavy breathing of the men holding her down, the nauseating smell of their bodies. Oh, how had this terrible thing happened?

And where was her husband?

There was no sound anywhere. Panic gripped her.

She crept from tree to tree, reluctant to return to the spot where the English had seized them. She could still hear the gunshots reverberating in her ears. Trevelyan had told her about guns, but she had never dreamed they would make such a tremendous noise.

She had to find Trevelyan. Silently, she slipped through the forest, stopping constantly to listen to sounds warning of danger, until she came to the place where they had been attacked.

There was no one there. She watched for a long time lest the men were waiting in ambush for her. But when she saw the animals creeping out of hiding places they had found at the first sound of muskets, she knew absolutely there was no human about.

She moved to the spot where her weapons had been thrown. They were still there. She looked for Trevelyan's spear and ax and found them too. Then she started to examine the ground for signs of what had taken place. Someone had been dragged here, she could see. They had captured her husband!

She followed the trail for some distance until the man who was being dragged was made to walk on his own. She was hoping desperately that it might be one of the English, wounded in the fight with her husband. But the man had bare feet. It had to be John.

At the water's edge, she selected a tall tree for her watching post. Jamestown was said to be on an island, but she could see no island from her vantage point atop the tree.

She followed the river for a mile or so, then climbed again. This time she saw smoke a few miles away. She went closer still and was rewarded by the movement of men, tiny figures moving along the waterfront—and ships.

"The great ships with white wings." There were three of them moored close to the shore, and several small craft were moving slowly around them.

The men who had taken her husband prisoner had spoken of a fort. Virginia knew what that was. A fortified place with great guns. Could she enter such a place? Could she find John?

She stayed in the forest that night, eating from her small store of crushed corn. Dawn found her on the trail that led to the fort. She had decided that she would not go directly to the English village; she would first see who came along the trail leading to it. Surely, some of the English would help her, righting the great wrongs their countrymen had committed the previous day.

At midmorning, she heard a group approaching. Armed with her bow and quiver, Trevelyan's spear and ax on the ground beside her, Virginia watched as the men approached. They were the same six she and Trevelyan had encountered the day before!

She cringed in her hiding place as the men ambled past, talking loudly in their peculiar accents. She let them go a little way, then stepped onto the trail to follow them. She hated them, but they were her only link with her husband.

The trail wound through the woods, and she kept well back lest the men turn and see her. But when she turned a bend, there, a dozen feet away, was one of them. He was just off the trail, squatting down behind a tree. The others had gone on ahead.

Virginia nocked an arrow as she stepped back quickly

into the trees, gliding silently to where the Englishman squatted. He was just about to rise when she confronted him, her bow at full draw, the arrow pointing at his throat. From the side of her eye she saw his musket propped against the tree.

It was the rat-faced man whose remarks had first sparked Trevelyan's anger. Her nose wrinkled in distaste at the smell that rose from him, but she fought down her nausea. There was fear in his small brown eyes, and Virginia was glad.

"Where is my husband?" she demanded.

He glanced quickly at his musket, realizing it was out of reach. Then he glanced in the direction of where his comrades had gone, but they were now out of earshot.

He made to rise, and she said one word—"No!"—and he stayed where he was.

"Where is my husband?"

"They sent him to England!"

She couldn't believe it. They couldn't have. They took him only yesterday.

"You lie. When did they send him to England?"

"By ship. On the morning tide."

"I saw the ships this morning. There were three."

He said nothing and she stepped closer. He spoke hastily.

"He leaves this evening." Something told her he was telling the truth. A great void seemed to open inside her. Her husband. John. Gone to England. How could she live without him?

"Why did they send him away?"

"To see if it's true that he's an earl's son."

She had difficulty understanding the way he accented his words and asked him to repeat himself.

"They don't believe he's nobility, but they don't want to take the risk. Maybe his father's got influence in England, see? So they send him there to see if his story's true. Otherwise they'd have hanged him on the spot."

"Why should they hang him? What has he done to you?" Her voice was agonized and the man noticed it. His glance returned to the musket.

"For deserting the fort. For living with an Indian woman."

"I'm not an Indian. I am English!"

The man smirked. She did not know what to do. She had to go somewhere and think it out. She had just lowered her head in perplexity, trying to figure out her next step, when she heard the click. Her lack of familiarity with firearms made her unaware of the sound's true meaning—a musket being cocked. So she looked up and faced the man instead of diving behind a tree.

She felt the blow on her shoulder at the same time as the tremendous noise of the explosion burst upon her ears. She was thrown backward with enormous force.

Through a haze she saw a man running toward her, a wicked-looking dagger over his head, poised to plunge it into her breast.

She brought up the spear in her right hand, thrusting it at him. It struck the metal breastplate and slid upward, the momentum of his advance pushing the weapon against his chin.

He fell back with an oath, and charged again. Virginia realized the Englishman was going to kill her. She grabbed the spear with both hands—her left shoulder being numb from the bullet now—and drove it with all her force into his face. The slender stone-pointed tip struck the soldier's upper lip and went up his nostril. The man gave a terrified scream and tried to leap backward. But the spear held and he danced in agony, transfixed. She tugged hard and the spear came out, the man tumbling to his knees, screeching hideously.

Virginia gazed at him, horrified. She had killed an Englishman! What would happen to her now? What would happen to her husband when they found out?

She picked up the bow where it had fallen and noticed for the first time that blood was running down her left arm. She remembered now. She had been shot. The others would be coming. They must have heard the musket and the screams.

She turned and ran through the trees, not noticing that she had left Trevelyan's stone ax behind. She had not gone far when she heard shouts, as the other English came upon their dying comrade.

"There she goes! After her!"

The yell rang through the woods. Virginia dropped the spear; fear and instinct merged into one as her hand pulled an arrow from the quiver behind her. It was a smooth action, the result of years and years of practice. She nocked it and drew back the bowstring in one move, aware that her shoulder had begun to hurt. Terribly.

A man appeared about twenty feet away, saw her, and leveled his musket. She released the arrow, striking him squarely in the chest. The man staggered back, such was the force of the blow, but quickly regained his balance and raised his weapon once more.

But Virginia's second arrow was already on its way, and it hit him flush in the face.

She turned to run. There was a terrible explosion and something smacked into the tree next to which she had been standing. The next arrow was nocked before she located the man who had shot at her.

Knowing he had no time to reload, the soldier had drawn his sword and was rushing toward Virginia. It was the black-bearded man who had tried to rape her.

The shock stayed her hand. Her eyes went beneath his breastplate and she felt as though she could see the preat penis extended at her again.

She lowered her aim and the arrow whacked through his leather jerkin where she had estimated his genitals would be. The shock registered in his eyes, but he did not fall. He kept coming at her with short, jerky steps, finally stopping a few feet away, the sword in his right hand still extended.

Virginia snatched the sword from his nerveless fingers. She drew it back like a spear and saw his eyes follow her movements as though mesmerized. He knew what she was going to do but could do nothing to prevent it.

She plunged the sword into his throat!

A brown figure darted from behind a tree, a shining metal ax in his hand. He stood over the dying Englishman, watching him crumple to the ground.

The Indian, wearing no warpaint, studied Virginia in one

sweeping glance. He saw the blood running down her arm, saw the eyes beginning to glaze over.

"How many more of them?" he asked.

"Three," she said. "Three dead, and three alive. They have guns."

The Indian walked quickly to where the dead Englishman lay, the arrow protruding obscenely from between his legs.

The Indian waved his arm and half a dozen braves slid silently out of the trees, following the first man in the direction of the Europeans.

Virginia stretched out a hand to the tree trunk next to her, steadying herself. From a long distance, she heard screams as the Indians attacked, then the sound of a shot. She slid to the ground, unable to stand any longer.

When the Indians returned, she roused herself sufficiently to tell them who she was and explain that the English had captured her husband.

The Indians said they had killed two Englishmen, but that one had escaped back toward the fort. They had collected the scalps of the three Virginia had killed; she was a mighty warrior, they said, and they would take her to their king, Opekankano of the Pamunkey.

Virginia knew that Opekankano was the brother of the Emperor Powhatan. She tried to tell her rescuers not to take her to him, but she slipped into unconsciousness and they bore her away.

Trevelyan was in Jamestown prison, chained by leg irons to the floor. The room stank horribly; looking around in the dim light, he saw that no provisions had been made for tending to the needs of nature, and that the previous occupants had simply defecated wherever their chains would allow them.

That night, Trevelyan was visited by Sir Thomas Gates, Jamestown's governor. Oblivious to the foul odor, Gates patiently heard out Trevelyan's story.

"I shall send you to England instead of putting you on trial here," he said when Trevelyan finished. "It seems to me you are telling the truth about your birth. If the authorities find that your father is the earl and you were indeed shipwrecked, I am sure you will come to no harm."

"But what about my wife, Virginia? I have told the truth about her too."

Gates sighed. "I would advise you not to persist in that story in England. First, the person you say will assist you, Sir Walter Raleigh, currently resides in the Tower of London and has been there since the year 1603, convicted of high treason."

Trevelyan was thunderstruck.

"The queen put Sir Walter in the Tower?"

"Queen? Oh no, King James. King James the Sixth of Scotland and First of England. Queen Elizabeth died in March 1603.

"Also, the survivors of the Roanoke Colony were known to have lived with the Chesapiuc Indians at the time you state. However, Powhatan himself told one of the former governors of Jamestown, Captain John Smith, that his warriors had attacked the colony and wiped it out completely."

Gates refused to listen to Trevelyan's further protestations and rose to go.

"Take my advice. Say no more about an Indian wife. There are laws against miscegenation in this colony.

"Should you think of returning here, I should have to prosecute you under them. Consider yourself fortunate that I believe you did not desert to the heathen voluntarily, that your father truly is the Earl of Budleigh, and that I am firmly convinced you are deranged and not responsible for your actions."

Trevelyan was taken to the ship bound for England on the afternoon of the following day. He asked his escort if a tall Indian woman had been seen around the fort. Taking Sir Thomas Gates's advice, Trevelyan was careful not to call her his wife.

"How did you know about her?" his guard asked. "We just heard ourselves. She ambushed a patrol and killed five men. It seems she had some braves to help her."

Trevelyan felt a surge of elation.

"What happened to the woman?" he asked as casually as his churning emotions would let him.

"They shot her. She's dead."

It took a dozen men to subdue him. Trevelyan had to be beaten unconscious before they could carry him on board. When he came to, he was in irons below deck and the ship was well at sea.

21

The small three-masted ship, with its high fore and stern castles for officers and crew, was taking a cargo of timber to England. The hold was packed with barrel staves, wainscoting, and planks, the deck between the two castles piled high with long poles for ships' masts. The need for wood, used for England's growing fleet, was outstripping supply in the mother country; timber was a valuable export from the virgin forests of the New World.

Trevelyan was crammed into a narrow space between piles of bound barrel staves, his chained wrists fastened to a deck beam above his head.

Three days after they left Jamestown, the sailor who brought Trevelyan's meals added a message to the food.

"Cap'n says if ye gives yer word not to escape, ye can come up on deck."

Trevelyan didn't ask where he might escape, being three days from the nearest land, but gladly gave his word. Thereafter, he spent his days on deck, sleeping in the hold at night. They kept the chain on his wrists, however; the captain had no authority to remove that.

Trevelyan sat throughout the day staring across the ocean. His heart was a cold, dead thing. Virginia dead—he couldn't believe it. Only a few days before, when they walked the last few miles to Jamestown, she had been filled with so much happiness. She was meeting the English at last.

The English . . . What would happen to their children, his strapping boy and beautiful daughter, now that their mother was so cruelly dead?

Once this damned ship reached England, Trevelyan was determined to contact his father immediately and clear his name. Then, although his mentor Sir Walter Raleigh might be in the Tower and an unfriendly king on the throne, he would manage to have the story of the Lost Colony's survival told. His father's friends would help.

And he would procure a warrant for the arrest of Virginia's murderers—for the arrest of the governor, Sir Thomas Gates, himself, for the soldiers were surely carrying out his brutal orders.

Failing that, Trevelyan swore to raise a company of soldiers to rescue his children and the others from Virginia's tribe, taking them back to London and parading them for all to see. He'd be damned if there weren't warrants for Virginia's killers then.

They were ten days out of Jamestown when the hurricane struck. The northern edge of the gale caught them, throwing them off course.

On the second day of the storm, the captain announced he was making a run for Bermuda, the tiny group of islands lying five hundred miles from the Virginia coast.

By this time Trevelyan had been moved from the hold so the hatch on the decks could be battened down. Installed in the forecastle with the crew, he spoke of the folly of trying to reach Bermuda in a storm.

As a seasoned sailor, Trevelyan knew that the Bermuda islands were surrounded by coral reefs, forming a major hazard to ships. Wouldn't it be difficult to try for shelter there, he asked. The ship was spooming now, running before the wind and the sea.

The crew shrugged him off. They told him that three years earlier, in 1609, the *Sea Venture* had been wrecked in a hurricane on the Bermuda reefs. All the one hundred fifty on board, along with most of their provisions, were safely ferried to shore from the reef. With salvaged timbers from the wreck and cedars growing on the island, they built two new ships, the *Deliverance* and *Patience*, and nine months later continued on their way, landing safely at Jamestown.

If this ship were wrecked, the crew was sure their captain could emulate the triumph of the *Sea Venture*. While admiring their faith, Trevelyan wanted to reach England the fastest way. The quicker he got home, the quicker he could return for his children and revenge.

The next day the storm seemed to abate somewhat, and the crew was ordered to put on more sail. Then the cargo shifted. Trevelyan felt the rumble as the wood slid forward. Almost instantly, still running madly before the wind, the ship began to pile-drive, plunging her bow down violently into the troughs of the heavy seas.

Someone was sent below to unchain him and Trevelyan scrambled out on the deck immediately. What had been a vessel racing under control a few minutes ago was now a ship pitching almost at a standstill, plunging in and out of the great waves.

He looked up at the cry of "Land ho!" and saw sailors high on the yards, having just hoisted more sail and awaiting the order to take them in again. Trevelyan could feel the vessel trembling, the masts creaking, as the sails tried to pull forward a ship that simply would not raise its bowsprit and do their bidding.

But the captain was too late in giving his order. With an explosion like thunder, the mainmast splintered almost at deck level and slowly fell.

Trevelyan watched, awestruck and helpless, as the mast slipped a few feet at a time, caught for a second or two by rigging and ropes, then slipped again as the sails tore apart with pistollike cracks.

The mast smashed across the poop deck with a mighty roar of splintering wood. He saw the crew flying from the yards, some landing nimbly on their feet, some thumping heavily on the deck, others disappearing into the boiling sea.

Trevelyan's first thought was to find an ax and cut the mast free from its jagged umbilical cord some two feet above the deck.

Then he felt, rather than saw, that its weight on the rear castle had balanced the boat by pushing down the stern and allowing the bow to rise. The vessel began to make way again under the remaining sail.

It was almost a miracle. Trevelyan wondered if the luck of the *Sea Venture* would be theirs, as the crew believed.

The captain had extricated himself from the sails that had billowed over him, and took over the wheel. As the ship picked up speed, Trevelyan made his way aft, crawling over the deck cargo of mast poles, the clanking of his wrist chain signaling his passage.

He found several men sheltering on the quarterdeck below the poop, and asked them what land had been sighted.

" 'Tis Bermuda," one of them said. "An' if the cap'n can find an entrance through the reef, we'll be ashore within the hour."

Trevelyan stayed with them, praying that the captain could indeed pick his way through the deadly coral. But it was not to be.

The crashing of the sea on the reef carried over the whistling wind, and Trevelyan realized they were too close. The captain must have seen an opening, for he tried to bring the ship to face it. But when the vessel came partly into the wind, it veered sideways and the cargo shifted again. The downed mast began to slide overboard; as it went, the ship listed until she went over on her beam ends, away from the wind.

The mast cleared the poop and quarterdeck and slithered into the sea, but the cargo shift was too great to allow the ship to right herself. The waves pounded her until the bow came into the wind and she struck the reef stern on.

Trevelyan followed his companions in a mad scramble over the poop deck. It had been swept clear. The wheel had gone with the mast, and the captain and helmsman had vanished.

Below them the sea churned over the exposed coral reef. There was only death in that direction. They scrambled down to the deck and crawled over the mast poles to the bow. Looking over, they saw the channel the captain had tried to pass through.

"The mast poles," Trevelyan shouted. "Cut them loose and get them overboard and we can use them as rafts."

Again they made their way back to the deck, one sailor

crawling into the forecastle for an ax. Now that the ship was stuck firmly and was stable despite the seas lashing her, more men began to appear.

Trevelyan took hold of the ax and expertly cut the bindings free. When a pole was cut loose, the crew, acting in unison, heaved it into the sea.

As Trevelyan slashed at the ropes with mighty strokes, the others watched the progress of the poles in the water. At last there was a shout:

"They're through the channel!"

When the next pole went over, a couple of seamen jumped after it. Pole after pole, man after man, until only Trevelyan and two others were left.

"Let's get several over at once this time," Trevelyan shouted, "then we go together."

The men gave their assent and he wielded the ax desperately, hacking at the slippery ropes.

He freed four and threw down the ax. The three of them pulled and heaved, and the poles went over one by one. As the third pole left the deck, one of the sailors jumped after it. With a quick look at Trevelyan, the other followed.

Trevelyan stepped to the edge, looked down, and saw the men's heads bobbing in the seething water as they tried to grab the poles.

He picked his moment and leaped in, holding his arms apart so that the chain between his wrists was taut. He landed next to a pole with one arm across it. He reached under the pole, grasping with each hand the chain near the opposite wrist. Thus anchored, he kicked his powerful legs to keep the pole pointed in the direction of land, and allowed the surging sea to push and pull him through the channel.

When he crawled ashore, he saw no other survivors. Painfully dragging his battered and bruised body from the beach and into the trees, he found no respite from the raging wind, and crossed the narrow island to the opposite shore. There, in the undergrowth, he fell into an exhausted sleep.

When he awoke the next morning, it was as though there had never been a hurricane. He looked up at a beautiful clear blue sky, then his eyes slowly lowered to the horizon. There, right in front of him, anchored in a sparkling blue bay, was a ship.

He rose to his feet with a cry and started forward, only to be thrown to the ground. He rolled over and started to get up again when he saw that he was surrounded by men.

They wore the oddest costumes he had ever seen, some dressed like gentlemen, others like paupers. Some wore leather boots above their knees, others were barefoot. They wore cocked hats with fluttering plumes, and colored handkerchiefs wrapped around shaven heads, or went bareheaded. They wore earrings and pearl necklaces.

And around every waist was a broad belt with a sword, a knife, and a pistol.

They asked who he was and what he was doing on the island, looking pointedly at the chain dangling from his wrists.

He told them of the shipwreck and how he had made it to shore. He said the English governor of Virginia had put the chain on him.

Then they asked him his trade. When he said he was a ship's navigator, they took him immediately on board the long, sleek vessel. He knew who these men were and what their ship was, and expected the worst.

But the captain said he had lost his navigator in a recent battle at sea, and Trevelyan would do as his replacement immediately.

They removed his chains and gave him fresh clothes. Having no alternative, John Trevelyan thus became a pirate.

The ball had missed the bone but had gouged a deep groove in the flesh of Virginia's shoulder; she had collapsed from loss of blood. The Indians carried her overland to a village where her wound was tended. Then women were recruited to bear her to the Pamunkey River on a bed made of poles and reeds, after which she was placed in a dugout and taken west. There she was tended for some weeks in the town of Cinquoateck by its medicine women and priests.

When Virginia was able to walk, she was taken upstream to a great bend in the river where Opekankano had his seat at the town of Menapacant. She rested for several days before he called her to an audience.

Several hours before she went to see Opekankano, women came to bathe Virginia in rose-petal-scented water, and to wash and comb her luxurious hair. They touched up her lips with berry juice to compensate for the pallor caused by her illness. Then they presented her with a dress of white doeskin, shaped like her own, with long white fringes, and decorated in red and black with figures of birds and flowers.

It was a gift from Opekankano, she was told.

Her meeting with the king of the Pamunkey was in considerable contrast to her reception years earlier by Powhatan.

Virginia was welcomed in Opekankano's lodge by fine speeches, even was passed the ceremonial pipe to puff. Only after a suitable time had elapsed would the king question her, gently but shrewdly. But first he told her what he knew.

"My warriors told me that you fought six of the English, who were armed with the sticks that kill and swords of white metal, and that you killed three of them with arrow and spear. You are indeed a great warrior.

"I know that you escaped from King Powhatan, my brother, and took with you the English prisoner. I know that this Englishman is your husband, and that the soldiers on the island the white men call Jamestown captured him and sent him to England."

"It is all true," she said quietly.

"How do you regard the English who did this to you?"

"I think that among the English there are evil men."

Opekankano appeared to be satisfied with her answer.

Virginia closed her eyes and thought of her husband. There was a terrible ache inside her. She could no longer remember a time when he was not by her side, encouraging her, soothing her, loving her. What would she do without him?

Opekankano was one of Powhatan's younger brothers, a man around sixty at this time. He was immensely tall, as tall as Trevelyan, slim and well proportioned. He gave an impression of shrewdness rather than raw power. Nevertheless, his Pamunkey tribe was the largest tribe in the Powhatan empire, with some twelve hundred members, of whom three hundred were warriors.

In the days following their first meeting, he spoke to Virginia often about the English colony at Jamestown, repeating much of what Manteo had told her about the colony at Roanoke.

First the barter of beads and trinkets for food, then demands, and finally raids and confiscation.

"What they cannot carry away, they destroy," Opekankano said. He looked at Virginia carefully before he went on.

"Three winters ago, there was no food at the fort. We thought the English would all die and then we would be left in peace. They were too stupid and too weak to hunt for the water birds that come in winter, or to fish.

"There were three hundred English at Jamestown before winter came, but only sixty by the following summer. We heard that their chiefs ate meat every day, although not giving any to their braves.

"When they killed one of my spies, we heard that the English ate *him*!

"Then they began to eat their own dead, boiling and stewing the flesh with roots and herbs.

"One of them could not wait until his wife died. He killed the woman and ate her; for this, they killed him. But they continued to eat others who died of starvation."

Virginia was horrified. Until now she had not believed Manteo. When she had asked Trevelyan about reports of cannibalism among the English, he had said he himself had never witnessed such a thing and felt Englishmen would be sickened by it. She had wanted to think this was so, and had eagerly accepted the explanation as further proof that the stories of cannibalism were untrue.

The English—so generous with their accusations of cannibalism among the Indians, so guilty of it themselves!

Opekankano continued: "In the spring, ships came to Jamestown, loading the English survivors on board and preparing to sail away. The People rejoiced, for it seemed at last that we would be rid of these cannibals, their vile diseases and bloodthirsty ways.

"But before the ships reached the Chesapiuc, there came other vessels bearing a great lord from England. He made them all return to the fort. They have been here ever since.

"You are married to an Englishman. You can help us deal with them. Bring your tribe to the land of the Pamunkey and I shall give you fields for crops, woods to hunt in, and rivers to fish. In return for your help, my spies will report on every stranger in the fort with golden hair."

It was agreed. The king would send a sizable band of warriors with Virginia to escort her tribe to its new living grounds.

A few days later, Virginia set off for the valley of the Shenandoah. When she had gone, Opekankano consulted with his priests and elders.

"She will be able to tell us many things about the English—what it is that brings them to our land, how it is that they do not wish to live simply like the True People but must garner everything they see or touch and send it back to their distant country.

"And how we can defeat them!"

But Opekankano knew he would have to be careful with his new ally. She was clever. Not once in their discussions had she given away, by so much as a flicker of an eyelid, that she was one of the hated English herself.

22

The years passed without Trevelyan. Virginia was re-learning long-forgotten prayers from Miss Merrimoth.

Often, she would kneel in the forest, praying first to the Christian God and then to the *manito* of the True People to return her love. But the years passed without John.

The pain of living without him never left her. Not a day passed that Virginia did not fear for his well-being, did not ache with worry for the way he was being treated. She prayed for his safe return to England, prayed that the ship carrying him avoid storms and all other calamities.

If there had been a way to follow him, she would have done so immediately, regardless of the danger. But she knew now she could not approach the English in Jamestown for help, and that she had no choice but to wait for her husband's safe return.

Every few months she visited Opekankano to learn the latest news about the English. They were keeping to the Powhatan River, which they called the James, he told her. They dared not settle near the Pamunkey tribe, although they were establishing other settlements, all of them on stolen Indian land. They had begun growing great quantities of tobacco, not for ceremonial smoking, but to send back to England.

Opekankano asked Virginia why they did this, and she attempted to explain the idea of commerce that Trevelyan had talked about. When she said that the tobacco was being exchanged for other goods, the Indian chief understood. But he couldn't grasp why the Europeans exchanged tobacco for goods they did not need—clothing and footwear—for there were ample animal skins for clothes, and the People did not need moccasins except in the snow.

Virginia explained that this was the way the English lived; nothing would change them.

"Then they will make *us* change," said Opekankano. "And what if we do not wish to alter our ways?"

"I do not know," Virginia said.

He told her of an Englishman named Thomas Dale, called the marshal of Virginia, a brutal, ambitious person who ran roughshod over the country, destroying villages, killing the People, although his cruelty was not restricted to Indians.

Many of the English were deserting rather than suffer his

brutality. When they were caught, they were hanged, burned to death, shot, impaled on the stake, and broken on the wheel—their bodies crushed into a ball by metal clamps.

Sir Thomas Gates, the governor of Jamestown, learned of the loss of Trevelyan's ship months after it happened. It took additional months for messengers to reach England and return with the news that the prisoner was not among the survivors.

Gates thought long on the matter. He could send a letter to London asking that the Earl of Budleigh be informed of his son's death. But what if the earl were a powerful man, a friend of the king? Would there be an inquiry as to why the son had been shipped out in chains? Was the earl a more powerful man than he, the governor?

John Trevelyan had been lost to his father for many years in any case. Why resurrect him and perhaps get Gates in trouble?

Sir Thomas Gates went through the colony's records, found the page describing the Trevelyan incident, tore it from the book, and held it to the candle on his desk.

A year after Trevelyan had been sent to England, Pocahontas was kidnapped while visiting a small Indian village. She was taken to Jamestown and a message was sent to her father, King Powhatan, demanding, for her return, several Englishmen held by the werowance along with a great store of guns, swords, and metal tools.

Opekankano asked Virginia if the English would harm Pocahontas. She said they would not dare. Powhatan refused the English demands. A year later, Pocahontas became a Christian and married a planter named John Rolfe, the man most responsible for establishing the tobacco trade with England, a business for which the English needed more and more land belonging to the Indian.

Virginia said they must have drugged Pocahontas to

make her marry a white man. She could clearly remember the headstrong, willful little girl, and her endless, querulous demands.

"Tell me a story, Tall Girl," Pocahontas would say almost from the moment she opened her eyes. "Tell me about those flowers," pointing toward the sassafras growing outside her lodge, the yellow flowers giving off a highly aromatic scent.

Nothing could have dissuaded the child from a story about just those yellow blossoms. And so Virginia could not believe the colonists were able to convince her to marry an Englishman, one of her father's most hated enemies. She had to be drugged. And why had Powhatan himself permitted the marriage?

Opekankano said his brother believed the union would bring peace between the English and Indian, and the True People needed peace to grow their crops and raise their children. There had been too many killings, Powhatan said, and too few braves left alive for further wars. Biding his time, Powhatan decided peace was needed for boys to grow into manhood, become warriors, and fight again.

Virginia remembered that Badger had said the same thing many years earlier, although her Indian father's need for warriors did not include savage conquest.

So there was relative peace, but more settlers arrived at the colony than there were Indian boys who grew to be warriors.

The Chickahominy priests, fearing that the new friendship between the English and Powhatan could turn out to be an alliance detrimental to them, approached the whites and made their own treaty of friendship. It began to look as though the savagery of the English had brought them success. Only Opekankano continued to openly voice his hatred of the invaders.

Virginia learned that Sir Thomas Dale, the man responsible for the loss of so many Indian lives, had sent a messenger to Powhatan asking the king for another of his daughters for Dale himself. Powhatan angrily refused, and never spoke to an Englishman again.

In 1616, Pocahontas gave birth to a son, Thomas, and the child sailed with his mother and John Rolfe on a visit to

England later in the year. With them went Sir Thomas Dale, hated by Indian and Englishman alike.

They were gone before Virginia learned of their departure, taking with them a dozen Indian relatives and agents as well as spies of both Powhatan and Opekankano.

"Why was I not informed?" Virginia demanded from Opekankano. "I could have searched for my husband."

Her ally's dismissal of Virginia's needs and interests greatly angered her.

Virginia was determined to make Opekankano recognize her own status and power.

"I wanted to go with Pocahontas. You had no right not to inform me of the journey to England."

Opekankano tried to soothe her.

"You do not know the English as I do. If you and your tribe were to be discovered by them, you would all be put to death.

"For do not the English in your tribe have Indian wives and husbands? This is forbidden by the whites on pain of death. Do you wish to be responsible for the deaths of all in your tribe?"

"But Pocahontas—" Virginia protested angrily.

"But Pocahontas became a Christian and was married with the approval of the English chiefs. You and your tribe practice the ways of the True People, not Christian ways.

"Englishmen who have come to us for food or to escape their chiefs' brutality have told me that for a Christian to live with one of the True People as man and wife is the same as a marriage with one of the beasts of the forest. The English consider us animals; to mate with us is a crime punishable by death.

"I have told Pocahontas about your husband, and she will try to find him for you," he added gently.

She had to be content with that.

But Pocahontas never came back to the land of the True People. In March 1617, as she was about to return, she died. The unfriendly climate of England had already claimed several of the Indians who had accompanied her.

Trying to make amends for not consulting her about Pocahontas's voyage, Opekankano now made a great show of discussing the Indian woman's death with Virginia. Did she think the English poisoned Pocahontas? Poisoning was a favorite Indian way of disposing of an enemy.

Virginia did not believe this had happened.

"It would have been in the best interest of the English to keep Pocahontas alive," she said. "That would have maintained the peace under which they continue to steal the land of the People."

Pocahontas's death meant Virginia received no word about her husband, gone now for five years. She had learned to live with her grief, but she had not gotten used to it.

She missed him still, each day. Missed his love, his wise words of counsel, missed his body. At night, in her sleep, she would sometimes reach out to touch him, dreaming that they were about to walk slowly, lovingly, into the woods. But when her hand found only emptiness, she would awaken with a start, realizing with a terrible ache that she was alone.

She had told herself repeatedly that there was only a small chance Pocahontas would bring back news of Trevelyan. But now that even this slim possibility was gone, Virginia shed bitter tears.

Powhatan, too, was reported to be greatly saddened by the loss of his favorite child. He had long since moved from the town where Virginia had been kept captive, a place he considered too close to the English. Now, he changed his residence constantly among the Pamunkey.

After Pocahontas's death, relations between the colonists and Powhatan's empire began to deteriorate. The peace with the Chickahominy tribe had already collapsed.

Soon after the hated Sir Thomas Dale left for England, the new governor, George Yeardley, and his soldiers attacked the Chickahominy and slaughtered dozens of them. The Chickahominy promptly went to Opekankano, whom they preferred to Powhatan, and made an alliance to fight their now common enemy.

Virginia realized war was almost inevitable. In the days of relative peace still left, she wanted to look over the English settlements, and learn what she could about them. She was taken in a dugout past the plantations.

She could see the small thatched-roof houses on the shore, each cluster of them enclosed by a thick palisade of sharpened stakes—to keep out the Indians, she was told.

For the first time in her life she saw the "domesticated" creatures she had heard so much about from her English parents and from Trevelyan. She saw cattle—and marveled at their size; also, sheep, goats, and poultry. She knew that hair taken from some animals was made into clothing, and that the milk from others was drunk. She had been fascinated to discover that hens could be made to lay eggs on command by the English, who ate them.

The animal she saw in greatest numbers was what the English called swine or hogs. Even from a distance, she could hear their hideous squealing. She was told they had an unpleasant smell.

She saw few horses, the beast her husband spoke so often about. These creatures seemed more strange than beautiful to her, looking like an elk with thick legs but no antlers, and a long hairy tail.

Each time her braves paddled past a plantation situated near the riverfront, huge dogs ran out, snarling at them. Virginia cringed. She had seen Indian dogs in many of the towns she had visited, but they were small creatures that howled continuously and stole food. They were afraid to attack people.

"These dogs are called mastiffs," one of the paddlers told her. "They are for guarding the towns, just like our dogs, but they are also taught to attack any of the True People who approach the English houses. They are very fierce; their teeth are sharp and they can tear flesh like knives."

Virginia was especially surprised by the way the English dressed. The men all wore thick breeches to the knee, the lower part of the leg being covered in heavy stockings of different colors. The feet were shod with heavy leather shoes or boots. On their upper bodies, Englishmen wore shirts and leather jerkins.

The few women she saw were clad from neck to ankle in layers of what also seemed to be heavy clothing.

The trip was made in sultry weather, and Virginia felt a sudden pity for people who wore such raiment in a hot, humid climate. Her English parents had dressed this way themselves, putting young Virginia in the same sort of unsuitable clothing.

The English brought England with them to the land of the True People. They would never change their ways to suit the climate, the land, or the People.

After so many years in the New World, hadn't Miss Merrimoth suddenly announced that she wanted a four-poster bed with a canopy?

"There is a lack of civilization here," she told Virginia and Jane Mannering. "We must not forget how we will live once we return home."

Virginia was intrigued. What was a four-poster bed?

Miss Merrimoth and Jane tried to explain, but Virginia had no conception of sleeping on anything but the raised platform of the Indian lodges or, as she and Trevelyan had preferred, on the bare floor.

William Withers, a deft carpenter, spent hours making a tiny model, complete with canopy, to show Virginia what Emma Merrimoth had in mind. But Virginia failed to see what was so desirable about a bed, even as Jane Mannering's eyes lit up in recognition and Miss Merrimoth positively glowed.

"Exactly," she said. Without taking her eyes off the flimsy model, made from twigs and hide, she asked, "Will you make a real one for me?"

"And what will you do with a bed, Emma?" Jane Mannering asked, mischief dancing in her eyes. "Is it marriage you're considering at last, with one of our handsome braves?"

"I wish the bed because it will bring a touch of English civilization to my life," said Miss Merrimoth without an answering smile.

She had never slept in a four-poster bed herself, but she had worked as a lady's maid in a great house in London before she accompanied the Dares, and she had seen the handsome, heavy, carved beds of her employers.

She could never afford such a bed in England, she thought, but here in the wilderness, with no one to sneer at a working-class wench with ideas above her station, she could sleep like the English gentry.

And so the great bed sat, in all its magnificence, in a corner of Miss Merrimoth's lodge. Every night when Emma Merrimoth climbed into it, she smiled.

Jane Mannering had confided that Arrow-Flies-True had agreed to put a bed in their lodge too.

As Opekankano had said: "In the end, they will make *us* change to their ways. And what if we do not wish to alter our life?"

Virginia had had no answer then, but she thought she knew now what would happen. The English would finally force the True People from the land.

In 1618, King Powhatan died. Despotic though he was, he had maintained relative peace within his own empire. He had also tried to keep peace with the avaricious Europeans, hoping that their ineptitude and diseases would finally vanquish them. But the English still occupied the land of the People, still unable to live off the land as the Indians did. Now, they brought the things they needed from across the great sea—their strange clothes, strange animals, trinkets to exchange for the furs they sent back across the sea to purchase more things, like guns, which they used to clear the Indians from their ancestral lands.

Although most colonists died from their own diseases, their numbers were continually replenished by new arrivals.

It seemed that nothing could stop them.

Powhatan died a discouraged and disillusioned man. He had designated one of his brothers, Opitchapan, as his heir, but there was a brief struggle for the throne nevertheless. The powerful Opekankano emerged as the new king of the Powhatan, and Opekankano had no intention of allowing the invader to stay, no desire for peace or coexistence.

At the time Opekankano ascended to Powhatan's throne, there were six hundred English along the James River. A total of eighteen hundred had arrived in Virginia in the eleven years since the colony was first settled, but two-thirds of the settlers had died from disease, starvation, Indian arrows, and their own inability to survive in a strange land.

Opekankano could never understand the strangers' method of trading. Virginia was unable to enlighten him, for she also had no conception of what "money" was.

The Indians' idea of trade was barter. They exchanged fur and food directly for trinkets, axes, and the like. In the year before Powhatan died, the English shipped twenty tons of cured tobacco to England for cash. With these profits, they bought indentured servants to clear the land, plant, harvest, and cure more tobacco for more cash and profits. It was a vicious cycle the Indians could not break for they did not understand its operation.

As more English arrived—a high percentage of whom were indentured servants who, in return for their passage, would work literally as slaves in the fields for up to seven years—Opekankano began his raids.

Up to that point, mainly men had arrived. However, in 1619, a boatload of women came. They were to be sold—to pay the price of their passage—as wives. Soon English children would be born on the land of the People, adding to the endless numbers arriving from over the sea.

The mortality rate among the colonists continued to be horrendous. But still they continued to come, and gradually the number of immigrants began to outnumber those who died.

Virginia's own tribe was growing steadily. The diseases of the English had not spread among the original survivors, many of whom were grandparents by this time.

Virginia was now thirty-four years old. Her son, Richard, was almost sixteen, her daughter, Elinor, was thirteen. She had not seen or heard of her husband in almost ten years.

Richard was growing into a skilled hunter. Watching her son come to her lodge carrying a deer across his broad shoulders brought a lump to Virginia's throat. Sweat glistened on the young man's tall body, covered by a fine layer of dust from the underbrush that he had carried his burden through. He always left the deer at the door of his mother's lodge, then went off to the river, still carrying his bow and quiver, to bathe.

Although Virginia supervised the skinning of the animal's hide and the cleaning of its meat, she herself cooked the deer liver that evening, exactly as she had learned it from She Smiles, with wild onions, succulent roots, and spicy herbs.

Apart from some tasty strips of meat to be soaked overnight and roasted the next day, the deer was handed over to the communal cooking pots to be shared by the whole tribe. When there was plenty of game, cooking and eating were communal tasks and pleasures.

Richard was as brown as any of the True People. Only Elinor remained a painful reminder of Trevelyan, with her blazing blue eyes and hair like the morning sun.

Watching her children made Virginia feel as if her husband was still at her side. Weren't their children part of both of them, born of their love as her body and John's joined to bring forth their son and daughter? How she longed for her husband to see Richard and Elinor, how she yearned for more children to give to her beloved John.

Caring for Richard and Elinor kept Virginia from the depths of loneliness. When Trevelyan was first taken, they were all that stood between her and madness. If it hadn't been for her children, she might have even killed herself. She had thought of it, although with shame and disgust.

Her children needed her; how could they grow up without either parent? They *needed* her—her mother's love.

At times, she had to take on the role of father as well, teaching Richard the bow and arrow, using her own superb skills to turn him into a skilled hunter.

Oh, John, she thought, her heart bursting with his memory, how your children would love you. How they would love to hear your rich laugh, love to listen to your stories of the sea and fighting and swordsmanship. How joyous Elinor would feel to have your strong arms around her, how proud Richard would be to watch your skillful hands at work.

She blinked her eyes to keep back the tears. Richard and Elinor must not see her weep.

23

In the spring of 1624, a Dutch merchant ship, returning to Holland from Central America, was caught in a fierce storm and blown off course. It limped into a South American port to effect repairs. Several of the crew had been lost in the storm, and the captain asked the Spanish governor if he could recommend any replacements. It was not an unreasonable request, as often in the Atlantic ports of South America shipwrecked sailors of various nationalities were to be found.

The governor took the captain to the town jail, where he found three men, one English and two French. The men had washed ashore two years before, claiming their ship had gone down in a storm. But the governor suspected them to be deserters from a pirate vessel, and they were thrown into jail until their story could be verified.

Meanwhile, they were taken out each day to work at various jobs in the fort and the town. They were always in irons, the governor said, in case they tried to escape.

Suspecting that the pirate story was simply an excuse to procure cheap labor, the captain asked to see the prisoners. The three were gaunt, bearded, and filthy. The Dutch captain addressed them in English, a language he knew fairly well, asking them first if they were really pirates.

The Englishman, huge, with a shaggy golden mane and beard, answered angrily.

"If we were, we most certainly are not now!"

The captain, amused by the reply, saw the sardonic grins on the faces of the two Frenchmen.

"Are you good sailors?"

This time, one of the Frenchmen replied.

"We are the best, m'sieur. Where do you go?"

The Dutchman explained that he would take them on as

deckhands, sailing to Amsterdam. The three were on their feet, instantly ready to sign on.

There was a small delay as the Spanish governor haggled over the price of their release, to pay for their "board and lodging" for two years. But the Dutchman was no fool; he offered the governor a handful of silver, suggesting he take it or leave it. The Spaniard took it.

On board, the three were given clothes from the slop chest, and allowed a decent bath and shave. When asked their names, the blond English hesitated for a moment, then said, "William Withers."

When the ship called at the Azores, in the middle of the Atlantic, the Englishman deserted, sending as his replacement another Englishman, who had jumped ship earlier and now wanted to return home. The Dutch captain shrugged. As long as he had his full crew, the devil take the damned blond giant.

English ships sailing to the New World often stopped at the Azores for supplies. The Englishman who had left the Dutch vessel appeared on the gangway of the first one he saw.

Learning that the boat's destination was Jamestown, the man asked for passage, signing an indenture form under which he promised to serve as a servant for seven years in the colony in return for his passage. The Englishman signed quickly. He had no intention of keeping his promise. He signed his name Thomas Smart.

As the ship sailed west across the ocean, John Trevelyan paced the deck impatiently. He was going home.

Opekankano told Virginia his plans for finally exterminating the English.

"You intend to kill them all? Women and children too?" Virginia was aghast. She hated the colonists, but wholesale murder was not part of her plan for dealing with them.

They were sitting in the council chamber of the king's lodge. Opekankano was surrounded by priests and elders; Virginia was flanked by William Withers and Arrow-Flies-True, who were now her tribe's elders.

"We have no alternative," said the king. "When the English first came, they said they had simply lost their way and did not intend to stay. But they stayed. When we told them to leave, they took our land by force. And then they brought more of their kind. When they were hungry, they took our food. When we tried to stop them, they killed us. So we made peace with them, and then they took even more land.

"My brother, Powhatan, tried the peaceful way. The English do not understand peace. So now we shall do it *my* way. And my way is war!"

The priests and elders shouted their agreement.

"Have you told this to all the werowances?" Virginia asked.

"Many of them have been told. Others will be as the time grows nearer. I tell you now because I need your advice. I want to know the best time to attack, the best time to surprise these devils."

"But even if you kill them all, more English will come to the land of the People," Virginia argued. "You cannot stop it by killing those who are here now."

"My priests tell me that when the next ships come and find all the English dead, and all their lodges and animals destroyed, they will leave this land forever."

Virginia knew this could not be true. She had heard Trevelyan speak often of the Englishman's hunger for conquest. They would never give up. But she knew she could not move Opekankano by arguing one of the king's cherished beliefs. She decided to try another tack.

"If no more ships come, my husband will never return. I cannot bear that. You cannot ask me to give him up forever."

Opekankano was silent for a long moment. Then he looked up at her.

"Your husband will never return, Tall Woman."

Something in the way he said it made her catch her breath.

"What do you mean?" she said, stunned.

This time there was no hesitation.

"Your husband is dead. It pains me greatly to tell you

this. He died while you were lying ill in this town, soon after they had taken him away."

Virginia looked from Opekankano to her two elders.

"Dead? How can he be dead? You never told me before. Pocahontas was going to look for him in England; it was agreed. That was five years after he was taken prisoner. Now you say he has been dead all this time. He cannot be dead. He cannot be!"

"I am truly sorry, Tall Woman," Opekankano said. "I only learned of it a short time ago. One of my spies heard that the ship carrying your husband to England was sunk after it struck great rocks around an island called Bermuda." He looked at Virginia with genuine sympathy, fully aware of her great pain.

Her face crumpled. She bowed her head but they could clearly hear the ragged sobs. They waited silently until she controlled her breathing and looked up again. Her cheeks were wet with tears.

"You are like my daughter, Tall Woman," Opekankano said. "I do not wish to see the pain of your heart. I told you this because it is bad to hold onto false hope. Let us vanquish the English together. You can repay them for your husband's death by fighting with me."

They sat silently while Virginia thought of the long years she had waited for John's return. What would she have done if she had known immediately that her husband was dead? She would have gone to the fort to avenge him. And they would have killed her. Her children would have had no mother to raise them, her tribe no queen to give them purpose and cohesiveness.

But, oh, she would make them pay now, even if it cost her her life. Her children had grown, the tribe was happy. Only John, her dearly beloved John, was dead.

She looked at the king.

"The English have many days when they pray to their Christian God. You must choose a day when they stay away from work, when they relax in their homes, and give welcome to any who pass by, for the Christian God says they must be generous to passing strangers. As they bask in the light of their own goodness, then you must strike!"

Opekankano's eyes were glowing.

"It shall be so," he said.

"They killed my husband," she said. "My tribe is small and my warriors are few, but they will follow where I go. Before you attack, send me word and we shall take our place alongside your warriors."

Opekankano nodded. Virginia spoke again.

"When I was first brought here, your warriors carried the scalps of the three Englishmen I killed in the woods. I know that you have kept them.

"I wish to have them now. They will be hung in my lodge."

o

When she returned to her tribe, Virginia told them what had happened to John Trevelyan. Then she went to her lodge, covered her face in soot from the fire, and sang the death dirge for a loved one. For three days she lamented, while her children squatted beside her, joining in her sorrow.

Emma Merrimoth lay down on her bed, refusing food or water, when she heard the news. For over thirty years, since they fled from Roanoke, she had lived for the day when she could return to her beloved England. For the last ten, she had waited for Trevelyan to return and take them away.

But this would never happen now. She had nothing left to live for. Within the week, Emma Merrimoth was dead.

Virginia gave her what she thought was a Christian burial. She read random pieces from the tattered Bible that Emma had so treasured. Then she placed the holy book in the grave with the old Englishwoman. The tribe had no further need of the Christian God.

After Emma's grave was covered, Virginia painted her face black and red, rattling gourds filled with small stones and speaking the sacred words taught her by Screams-Like-Wildcat, the priest she knew as a child. She asked the God of the True People to send Emma Merrimoth to the Other World where she would be forever happy.

She called her children to her and spoke to them in the Indian tongue. She explained how, with the help of Miss Merrimoth, they had been raised as English and Christian. But now the English had killed their father.

"For twenty winters I have tried to find the people my first parents told me about, kind people who would take us to the great city of London where we would live in peace.

"But I no longer wish to go to England. I will return to the True People. You shall return to the People with me, and together we will avenge the death of your father."

Although neither Richard nor Elinor could remember seeing Trevelyan, he remained richly alive in their hearts. Virginia had spoken constantly of their father, reminding the children what he would have wanted or liked, telling them of his great exploits: how he talked the Chickahominy priests into releasing Virginia and himself; how he built a ship and sailed their tribe to safety; how he survived a blizzard by burying himself in a snow cave.

His death was as real to them as if he had always lived in their lodge. For ten years, along with their mother, they had waited for his return. Always, they had thought of how it would be when Trevelyan came back, how they would live then, how much happier and fuller their lives would be.

There was no question that they would make their father's enemies pay. There was no doubt of their following Virginia where she led—away from the English, becoming a Person with her.

As she had correctly predicted to Opekankano, Virginia's tribe also followed her lead. Her braves agreed to fight alongside the Indian king's warriors.

24

Trevelyan returned to Jamestown on Monday, March 11, 1622. He was paraded in the square with the other indentured servants, to be examined like livestock before their new masters purchased their papers from the ship's captain. Essentially, they were being sold into slavery.

Although not a religious man, Trevelyan knew his Old Testament. He knew how the "seven years" of indenture had been arrived at.

In Chapter 15 of the Book of Deuteronomy was the following:

"And if thy brother, an Hebrew man or an Hebrew woman, be sold unto thee, and serve thee six years, then in the seventh year thou shalt let him go free from thee."

The English had interpreted the "seventh" year rather freely. Their slaves were made to serve that too.

Trevelyan was bought with several others for a plantation on the north bank of the James. He was delighted. It was nearer "home."

They went up the James by jolly boat and Trevelyan was astonished at the many settlements along both banks. The situation had changed considerably since he had been shipped out in irons ten years earlier.

He was taken to a plantation called Berkeley Hundred, founded two years before by men from Gloucester, in the west of England. Berkeley had over eight thousand acres.

Because of his height and obvious strength, Trevelyan was put to work felling trees for new tobacco and farm land. As he toiled, he tried to work out the lay of the land from memory. He reckoned that if he walked due north, he would cross the upper reaches of the Chickahominy, which he could then follow west to its source, continuing to the mountains that sheltered the Shenandoah.

But first he had to figure out how to steal enough food to

last him until he was well out of English influence. And he had to find out the truth behind the strange friendliness of the Indians, who came and went freely around the plantations. Would they be sent after him when he made his escape? He could never hope to outdistance an Indian tracker.

He ate in the large hall that also served as an assembly room and place of worship. The indentured servants were fed differently from the freedmen. They ate a thick gruel made from Indian corn, while the other, more privileged residents ate meat and eggs and drank milk. But Trevelyan did not complain. He would not be there long enough to weaken on such a diet.

On the first Sunday, he wandered off after breakfast to check out his escape route. That turned out to be a grave mistake. He should have gone to church.

They went after him with dogs, chaining him in a small hut that was used for punishing the indentured servants. It was only then that he learned about his new master—Captain George Thorpe, one of Berkeley's original "adventurers," or investors, a religious zealot with fanatical beliefs.

The punishment for not attending church could mean as much as two years added to the indenture period, or even a year in irons, and Thorpe believed in punishment for sins.

Trevelyan was told of a place called Henrico, on the south shore of the James, opposite Berkeley. Thorpe spent much time there, converting Indians to Christianity. Trevelyan had noticed that Indians at Berkeley Hundred often ate with the English, and were always served meat, not the servants' gruel.

Thorpe came to see the prisoner the next day. He was a thin, graying man with glittering, feverish eyes. He lectured Trevelyan on the iniquities of ignoring the Lord. Trevelyan, whose chain was stapled to the wall, wisely hung his head as though in shame.

Then Thorpe pronounced sentence. It happened so suddenly that Trevelyan was caught off guard.

"I am sentenced to *what*?" he asked incredulously.

"To one year in leg irons and to be kept in this room of

punishment at night for the whole period and bolted to the wall," Thorpe repeated.

He turned and walked away. If he had remained, Trevelyan would have killed him with his bare hands. He had suffered two years in irons in South America. He could not believe Captain Thorpe, an Englishman, would do such a thing to one of his own people for such a minor infraction.

So nothing had changed since he had met those six English criminals outside Jamestown ten years ago. Or rather, something *had* changed. Now even the officers and gentlemen were behaving like scoundrels.

Trevelyan was taken out in leg irons to continue felling trees. As the irons were made of two flattened hoops of metal linked in the middle, he could walk in them, and close or open his legs to a certain extent, but he could not run. And therefore he could not escape.

Another indentured servant was ordered to guard him. Adam Brown was obviously intent on ingratiating himself with his masters, for he led Trevelyan out to the woods like a beast of burden, with a rope halter around his neck.

During a rare moment of rest, as Trevelyan's thoughts turned bitterly to Shenandoah and his children, Brown came up behind him with a whip, slashing him brutally on the head and back. Trevelyan whirled around, knocking his tormentor to the ground.

As punishment for this "savage attack," Trevelyan was tied to a wall and lashed.

That night, Trevelyan nursed his pain and anger. He knew he would never survive a year in this place. He would never live to see his son and daughter, never live to avenge Virginia's death. He had vowed to make them pay; he had to escape, if only for that. For the next few days he tried to ignore Brown's taunting and bullying, but that only goaded the little man to even greater cruelty.

As the week neared its end, Trevelyan swore to escape before dawn the following day, Good Friday. He would not be required to work then. Breakfast would be later than normal and he would not be missed until some time after dawn.

He had watched carefully while they fixed the staple each

night to his leg irons. He saw that if he could pull the iron peg out of the wooden wall, he could slip off the padlock and be free.

He spent hours during the previous night trying to loosen the peg, but to no avail. It had to be done tonight.

Trevelyan was strong. His years at sea and in the Virginia forests had hardened his muscles, though his time in a Spanish prison had sapped some of his former great strength.

But he was desperate now. He tugged and twisted. He put the soles of his feet against the wall, grasped the irons, and threw himself backward time and again. The night was half over before he felt the first movement of the bolt. He renewed his efforts, working himself into a frenzy to keep himself going.

Then the bolt squeaked. He kept twisting and finally it turned. He felt that if he stopped now, he would never get it loose. He kept tugging, twisting, turning, and suddenly he was flat on his back—the bolt was out!

He slipped out the padlock, turning his attention to the next problem.

He could not remove the leg irons. He would need a hammer and a chisel to break the clamp. But he could still walk away if he could muffle the sound of the irons as he moved.

They had given him a woolen blanket and he tore this into wide strips, using his teeth and bare hands. He wrapped the pieces as tightly as he could around the iron joints, then walked around the hut. The bandages were ungainly, but effective. The irons made no sound. The hut door was not locked—they did not expect him to escape while shackled to the wall—but it was pitch dark outside. He would have to find his way to the gate and let himself out. In the darkness, he could stumble over something and awaken the dogs. He would have to wait until first light.

He sat in the open doorway, staring at the east. He had almost fallen asleep when he saw it. A tiny glimmer. Daylight.

He waited until he could discern the woods half a mile

away, then the fields in between, and finally the faint outline of the fence.

He walked carefully to the fence, stepping around piles of cut lumber, until he reached the gate. A few minutes later, he was on his way.

When he got to the trees, he turned north. It was still dark, and he had gone at least a mile before the horizon began to take on a pink hue. Dawn was coming. He broke into a short-gaited trot, which was all the irons would allow him to do, slipping in and out of the trees. He found many clearings in these woods and was able to hurry through them. He was concentrating so much on getting away that he did not stop and listen for any pursuit. He figured he had at least another half hour before they came to release him for breakfast.

He knew there were no settlements between Berkeley and the Chickahominy. He felt that if he could reach that river he would be safe. But it was a long way.

He had stopped to rest when he heard it. The baying of a hound. One of the mastiffs was close behind.

He started running again, but he knew it was too late. The animal was fast approaching and he had nothing with which to defend himself. He came to a large clearing and stopped in the center. He turned to face the beast.

The mastiff, snarling and slavering, ran into the clearing. Adam Brown was hanging on to its leash. The servant had discovered Trevelyan had gone and had come after him. He was alone, obviously intent on the glory as well as the reward for returning a runaway indentured servant.

Trevelyan saw that Brown was unfastening the metal chain leash from the dog's collar. He was not going to return Trevelyan. He was going to let the beast kill him!

Trevelyan went into a crouch, preparing to grapple with the huge animal as it sprang at him. The dog leaped forward just as half a dozen arrows appeared in its side. It somersaulted to the ground.

Brown's face turned ashen. He stared at the dog, then at his intended victim. Trevelyan realized that Indians had shot the arrows, but he could see no one in the still murky dawn light.

He charged and Brown turned to flee. He got two steps when he tripped and fell. Trevelyan was on him in a flash.

He grabbed the skinny little man by the throat with one hand and hoisted him high in the air. Then he turned to the nearest tree. Brown saw what he was doing and gave a high-pitched scream. Trevelyan threw him at the tree with all his might.

There was a crack as the man's head hit the trunk and then he fell to the ground in a crumpled heap.

Trevelyan's arms dropped to his side. He was exhausted. He had done all he could to escape. He could run no more.

Suddenly, there were people at the edge of the clearing, Indians, in full war paint, staring at him silently. They were in a circle about him. What were they doing here? Who were they? They had killed the dog and saved his life, but what would they do next?

One of the Indians stepped forward. He had a stone ax in his hand.

He walked up to Trevelyan and drew back the ax, swinging it down, aiming for Trevelyan's head. But Trevelyan had fought for his life too many times in his eight years on a pirate ship; a blow aimed like that would never catch him while he was awake.

He caught the Indian's wrist and held it, looking right into the man's eyes. They were gray!

"No," said Trevelyan, as though in a dream. "No."

He relaxed his grip and the Indian wrenched his arm free, raising the tomahawk again. But before he could bring it down, a voice cried out, "Wait!"

In a daze, Trevelyan looked around. The voice had spoken in English. He was sure of it.

A figure ran forward, a tall figure, nearly as tall as the Indian with the ax. It was a woman. She wore a fringed dress, her face was painted half red and half black. She pushed the Indian to one side and stared at Trevelyan.

"No, it cannot be. You are dead. I do not believe it."

She was speaking in English.

Trevelyan's head was reeling. He should know this woman, but he didn't. The only Indian woman he knew who spoke like that had died many years before.

"Virginia," he whispered hoarsely. "They told me you were killed when they captured me at Jamestown."

The Indian with the gray eyes had lowered his ax.

"Virginia?" Trevelyan said again, although he knew it was not her, for his wife was dead. He was dreaming. Perhaps he had dreamed about the mastiff being killed by the arrows. Perhaps the mastiff had killed him and he was dead, and that was how he could see dead people.

The woman walked closer; he could see the circle of Indians was drawing nearer as well, carefully and silently.

The woman dropped the bow she was carrying. She stood, staring. Then she screamed.

"John! It's you, John!"

And she was in his arms, crying hysterically, touching his face, kissing him. He was back. She had him again. He was not dead. Her dearly beloved was with her once more.

And then they all gathered around him, William Withers, Arrow-Flies-True, Thomas Smart, Thomas Humphrey, John Pratt. And younger ones he did not know, for they had been boys when he left.

Keeping one arm about Virginia's waist, Trevelyan pointed at the Indian with the ax. As the light in the clearing grew stronger, he could see it was a young man, slim and muscular, but young. Trevelyan pointed mutely at him. Virginia turned her tear-stained face up to her husband.

"Richard. It's your son, Richard!"

All along the James River Indians sauntered casually into the plantations that Good Friday morning. They were invited to breakfast. The English were relaxed. There was no work that day. The guns stood in the corners or hung over the fireplaces. On one plantation, Berkeley Hundred, an indentured servant had escaped, and there was talk of sending word to the owner, Captain Roger Thorpe, who was at his beloved Henrico, converting the savages.

It was almost noon when the massacre began. Three hundred forty-seven English died before one Indian, who had converted to Christianity, warned an Englishman; in turn, this colonist got word to Jamestown. When a band of

Indians arrived on that island, the population was waiting with loaded muskets.

Some people managed to escape the slaughter at Berkeley Hundred, but Roger Thorpe died at Henrico, and the Berkeley settlement never fully recovered.

Despite the ferocity of the attack, two-thirds of the English colonists survived. Opekankano lost his last great battle.

Virginia's tribe did not join in the massacre. When they found John Trevelyan, gratitude and relief replaced much of the bitterness and blood lust. All they wanted to do was return home.

Among the English in the tribe, not fighting other Englishmen came as a welcome relief. They had listened to Virginia and agreed to do battle alongside Opekankano's braves, spurred on by belief in Trevelyan's death. But it had not been an easy decision for most of them.

Yes, they had learned to dislike the colonists—even hate the English for what they had done; killing fellow Englishmen was something else.

Trevelyan's return freed many in the tribe of guilt and divided loyalties.

That night, Virginia and Trevelyan walked into the woods. In the starlight she slipped her dress over her head and watched him remove his English clothes. At first, they merely stood holding each other, for it had been so long they were almost strangers. Then their hands began to move over each other and it was as if he had never left.

Afterward, Virginia spoke of what was troubling her.

"I no longer wish to go to England. I was born English, but I know I am not English any more. I cannot belong to a people who behave as cruelly as the English. I was wrong to believe they were my people."

"Before I knew you were alive," Trevelyan said, "all I dreamed of was revenge, making them pay for what they had done. My hatred kept me alive—that, and the thought of reclaiming my children.

"Now that we are all together again, I only want peace.

But I can't forget. I don't want to see England or the English. I did not want to go to Jamestown ten years ago. I was afraid of what might happen to us—to you, especially. But you wanted so much to be with the English. It was your dream. I went for your sake. I only wanted you to be happy.

"It is far, far better for us here, Virginia. We can live happily, watching our children and our children's children grow."

"Let us return to the Shenandoah," she said, "to the place where life was so good."

"And when the English come there?"

"We shall go south and let them pass."

"It is good," he said, speaking in the language of the People.

Virginia watched the tribe begin its long trek back to the mountains in the west. Her husband was in the lead, dressed in a fringed leather skirt, his ax at his belt and his spear in his hand. Next to him was their daughter, close by was their son.

Virginia had renamed the young man Little Deer and their daughter Owl, as Badger and She Smiles's children had been called. She would have to find an Indian name for her husband, a powerful name for a mighty warrior.

She rubbed her hands across her stomach. She knew there was a new child there. If it was a girl, she would call her Chipmunk. Virginia had only thirty-four winters. There was time for more sons and daughters.

Tall Woman walked proudly after her tribe.

Epilogue

The English took their revenge for the massacre of 1622. They killed and burned unceasingly. Twenty-two years later, Opekankano himself was killed by the colonists as he made a last attempt to drive the hated foreigner off his land.

By the middle of the seventeenth century, the Tidewater Indians of Virginia had virtually vanished. Today there is a Pamunkey Indian reservation in King William County, in the state of Virginia. It is eight hundred acres in size and has thirty members, who are Christian Baptists.

Toward the end of the nineteenth century, there were reports of gray-eyed Indians using Elizabethan English living in North Carolina. Their current whereabouts are not known.

ABOUT THE AUTHOR

Born and raised in Scotland, HARRY SCOTT GIBBONS studied agriculture at Aberdeen University in Scotland and economics in Denmark. He served in Britain's Royal Air Force, and for many years worked as a foreign and war correspondent in the Middle East. It was his experience while covering the Yemen War, watching a Russian-equipped Egyptian army attack barefooted Yemen tribesmen, that gave him some insight into the plight of the early American Indians.

Mr. Gibbons's previous books include *The Conspirators: The Story of the Yemen War* and *Peace Without Honour: The Cyprus Civil War*. He has also written spy novels.

Now you can have an up-to-date listing of Bantam's hundreds of titles plus take advantage of our unique and exciting bonus book offer. A special offer which gives you the opportunity to purchase a Bantam book for only 50¢. Here's how!

By ordering any five books at the regular price per order, you can also choose any other single book listed (up to a $4.95 value) for just 50¢. Some restrictions do apply, but for further details why not send for Bantam's listing of titles today!

Just send us your name and address plus 50¢ to defray the postage and handling costs.

BANTAM BOOKS, INC.
Dept. FC, 414 East Golf Road, Des Plaines, Ill 60016

Mr./Mrs./Miss/Ms. ____________________
(please print)

Address ____________________

City__________ State__________ Zip__________

FC—3/84